THE
MILKMAN
A FREE WORLD NOVEL

Michael J. Martineck

EDGE SCIENCE FICTION AND FANTASY PUBLISHING
AN IMPRINT OF HADES PUBLICATIONS, INC.

CALGARY

The Milkman: A Free World Novel
Copyright © 2014 by Michael J. Martineck

Edge Science Fiction and Fantasy Publishing
An Imprint of Hades Publications Inc.
P.O. Box 1714, Calgary, Alberta, T2P 2L7, Canada

In-house editing by Anita Hades
Interior design by Janice Blaine
Cover Illustration by Jack Kasprzak

ISBN: 978-1-77053-060-7

EDGE Science Fiction and Fantasy Publishing and Hades Publications, Inc.
acknowledges the ongoing support of the Alberta Foundation for the Arts and
the Canada Council for the Arts for our publishing programme.

Library and Archives Canada Cataloguing in Publication

Martineck, Michael J., 1965-, author
    The milkman : a free world novel / Michael J. Martineck.

Issued in print and electronic formats.
ISBN: 978-1-77053-060-7
(e-book ISBN: 978-1-77053-061-4)
    I. Title.

PS3613.A7863M56 2014   813'.6   C2013-905018-3   C2013-905019-1

FIRST EDITION
(I-20140124)
Printed in Canada
www.edgewebsite.com

DEDICATION

"What does that mean?" I asked. "Look it up," my father answered. Which I did, in one of the countless dictionaries placed not so strategically about the house. My father taught me to throw a spiral and swing a golf club, but teaching me to play with words— that I still do. This stab at it is for him.

CHAPTER ONE

TO EDWIN MCCALLUM every act of insubordination was a work of art. Charcoal sketch thefts. Abstract expressionist assaults. A smuggling operation could have all the intricacies of an oil landscape. Despite this, he considered very few policy transgressions to be masterpieces. No one put the time in. Most insubordination spawned from opportunity, passion or a bottoming out of IQ. But this one. This fresco. He saw something more.

The girl could have been his daughter, had his life unfolded into a different shape, if he'd creased and bent this side instead or that, leaving him in another space, not on the street, in the cold, staring at a face turned and pressed to concrete, beautiful if you imagined it asleep, if you ignored the puddle of cold blood and the jagged hack marks in her flesh.

McCallum threaded his fingers and thrust out his arms, bending his wrists back, stretching, stimulating blood flow. He had no extra pounds and used his various muscles frequently and hard. When the cold started poking around, he felt reminders of every indiscretion, lack of good judgment and bad luck his bones had suffered over the years. His face had found some of the creeks and rumples he noticed on other men his age. Only some. His walnut hair showed maybe two strokes of grey. For the most part, he only noticed the middleness of his age in his joints, and on nights like this one.

"Geri Vasquez," the uniformed operative reported. Brick red pants and cap. Black leather everything else. *One of mine*, McCallum thought. "24, lived up on West Ferry Street, grade 15 Marketing Field Researcher."

"Grade 15." McCallum snorted. Was there a grade higher? Newborn? "Anything off her cuff?"

1

"Waiting for the advocate." The uniform op couldn't be too much older than the victim, but he seemed to have his buckle polished, as his old boss used to say. McCallum liked him.

"This an India Group pub?" McCallum pointed a thumb at the large, frosty picture windows.

"Yes sir," another uniform op answered. Black pants and jacket. An India Group patrolperson. Not one of his. She stood close to the pub door, helping to keep a safe perimeter around the body.

"Anyone come out?" McCallum asked.

"No sir," she answered.

"You go in?"

"Waiting for an inspector."

"Really?" McCallum looked into the windows. Faces filled every inch to about the eight-foot line. People used bar stools to get over the first row of viewers and look into the insubordination scene. He hated the lookey-loo part of human nature. This poor girl had been pretty, with nice clothes, a decent hair cut; she would not have wanted them all to see her this way. Still, the ghouls served a momentary purpose. Everyone in the pub knew a dead girl lay outside. Someone inside waiting for her would have stormed out by now.

"She died at the door?" McCallum asked himself. "Why's an Ambyr girl trying to get into an IG place without a buddy?"

"Don't know, sir," the female op answered. "Maybe fleeing her assailant?"

"Lots of maybes," he mumbled.

An India Group detective would be here any second. McCallum wondered who was on tonight. The lazy one, the well-dressed one, or that guy who lost a hand disarming a small explosive a few years back. He was pleasant enough, quiet, but never—

—he never expected to see her.

❦ · ❦

Sylvia Cho didn't care for the choice of restaurant. It was the kind used to woo people— clients, actors, investors, whomever. Sylvia didn't like to be wooed, schmoosed, ass-kissed or sucked up to. At least... most of the time. She believed in merit. She judged people and projects on their value and expected the same. No one should ever need to be sold on something. She also understood that here, in Hollywood, in this belief, she was quite alone.

Adorned in miles of bamboo and white cotton, lit with millions of tiny candles, the place had appeal. She didn't deny that, it just reminded her of a great looking guy who knew it. The kind that aimed his smile, prying a rise out of you. The town was full of them, many trying to get this very spot, at the top of two small stairs, peering out for a well-juiced producer.

She didn't feel out of place. She kept herself fit, her obsidian hair current and paid attention to fashion. Sylvia had chosen a pencil skirt and sheer top for this meeting. She knew the effects of tight clothing. She also knew her way around a restaurant. She had found herself in most of the Los Angels catchment's finer places, at one time or another. That was, after all, how things were done. She hadn't had a meeting in an office or conference room in nine years, since that impossible year after college, when she thought she'd have to club someone in the head to get any attention. Club several people, actually. One murder didn't turn heads.

Gavin Stoll sat in the center of the room, smiling. Black suit, white silk T-shirt, over a near-perfect body. He was the unnatural offspring of a cheetah and a penguin. He gave Sylvia a quick flick of the hand. Sylvia smiled, using her forceful, professional grin. The mask, she called it. The face that fooled all the boys, and some of the girls. Gavin stood as she crossed the room.

Good God, she thought. *What the fuck was he going to want?*

"So happy to see you," he said like he meant it. Maybe he did. She didn't know him any better than he knew her. "Tobacco Road was a blast. Loved, loved, loved it."

Thank God for the mask. She doubted this guy saw, saw, saw her last film.

"Thank you," she replied. "It's done better than I expected."

"You're too modest. Refreshing, but useless. Revel in your success."

"I'll try my best."

"So how does it feel?" They both sat.

"Stunning." She didn't like to lie if she didn't have to.

Gavin laughed. "I knew the movie tested well, but it hadn't prepared me for... the explosion. With no disrespect, I don't think anyone foresaw your peculiar demographic draw. You've had more females 18 to 34 down your picture than any other documentary in decades, while holding on to the boys. Hybrid demos, sister. Those frost the cake, eh?"

"Mmmm cake." Sylvia said.

"You've come to the right place."

The waiter stood next to the table. Sylvia hadn't seen him approach. Creepy.

"I'd like the St. George," Gavin said. "And hope you don't make any mistakes back there." He locked eyes with the waiter and waggled his head.

"Excellent choice, sir." The waiter gave a conspiratorial smirk and padded away.

"I hope you don't mind that I ordered for us." Gavin leaned over the table and dropped his voice to loud whisper. "They have a St. Germain pinot noir here, accidently delivered by an IG truck. It's exquisite. I'll cry when they run out."

"Perhaps there'll be another accident."

"I can only pray. IG has so many choice vineyards, I've been tempted to jump ship."

Sylvia laughed politely. She didn't want to encourage Gavin's pretentions. When it came to wine, she wasn't a hair-splitter. She could tell the difference between good, bad and awesome. Further subdivisions held little interest to her. Comparing vineyards outside the company held even less. The taste of forbidden fruit? There were probably two India Group people dining right now, pining for Ambyr wine in hushed voices.

"What's the deal?" Sylvia said.

"A movie. Funding is locked up."

"Already?" *Without a director?* she decided not to say out loud. "Who's attached?"

"No one," Gavin said. "I'm hoping you want to come aboard."

There is a formula in Hollywood. Good director, good cast, good script. You can only afford to take a chance on one. Everyone knows this rule. Nobody puts up money without two absolutes. The fact that Gavin didn't have a director or cast, but plenty of money, didn't all mesh. This scene wasn't working.

"This must be one Hell of a script."

"There's no script."

Check please, she yelled in her head.

❦ · ❦

Emory Leveski drove his blue Mazda sedan. Somehow. He couldn't see the black and blue night, the spots of light from other cars, street lights, sconces over house numbers and ground-level lanterns releasing the last of their solar charge from the day. His body remembered how to keep the car in the lane and the peddle at the right angle and when to turn left and right. His conscious mind had no part of it. It refused to process any new information. That last chunk, with the stabbing and shrieking and collapsing body... that plugged up the pipelines. He was lucky he remembered how to breathe.

Chapter Two

"OPERATIVE MCCALLUM," she said as a simple statement of fact. No question, no surprise, no rise in volume to get his attention.

"Operative McCallum," he said back, trying to match the flatness of her tone.

"Effchek, now. Again."

"Back to your maiden name. That's tough to do."

"I know people," she said. "What we got?"

Her uniformed operative gave her the rundown. McCallum watched. Rosalie Effchek. Now. Great. He knelt down next to the dead girl. Blond, in great shape, save the six deep lacerations in her back, clear through her coat. A weird coat. McCallum couldn't recall ever seeing one like it before. Orange fabric, covered in a kind of transparent jelly. The blood oozed off it, like rain on wax.

"She was cute." Rosalie squatted down next to McCallum.

"Congratulations on the promotion," he said.

"Thanks. I guess. Nights like tonight…"

"I know."

McCallum stood. He watched the egg back up, a mobile forensics lab. Looking more like a breadloaf, and officially called a Mobile Evidence Processing Unit, he had no idea how it got its nickname. Didn't make any sense. So much about this job failed to make sense.

The egg had an advertisement on the side, a photo of a cigarette smoldering on a dead man's mouth. Tobacco Road. A movie he'd never see. He hadn't seen a movie since…

"You going inside?" McCallum glanced in the direction of the pub.

"Yeah," Rosalie. "I'll check out the feeds."

6

McCallum's uniformed operative brought him a small, clear bag with a woman's cuff inside. Thick. Brushed aluminum with thin strips of pale bamboo embedded at set intervals.

"The egg heads cleared it," the op said. "And the advocate."

McCallum took the bag and held it up for a second, in the glow of the egg's rear work lights. The bracelet looked caught, like a fish. Dead outside its natural habitat, which was a young woman's wrist. Cuffs were such personal things, beyond the obvious, McCallum had learned. The type of cuff a person chose, the number and depth of its scratches, did the owner lock it around his or her wrist or something else? He knew a sculptor who kept his bracelet around his ankle so it wouldn't mar his media. He had to sit down cross-legged every time he wanted to make a call. The tiny details said big things. This bracelet had been on the shelf two months ago. Flawless. A smart design, went with everything, a bit too expensive for grade 15, but not so expensive that it was a gift from a well-off other. Fresh, new, ready to advance. Flawless. No signs of a fight. Somebody stabbed this girl from behind without any kind of build up she knew about. McCallum wanted to toss the bag into the egg and walk away. He slipped the cuff out of the bag, tapped it awake, called Help.

"Ambyr Communications," he heard in his ear.

"Police over-ride. Authorization—" He gave his code.

The top of the bracelet changed from dull silver to something like rice-paper. Geri Vasquez's life appeared, organized into little bubbles of data. She had 60 friends, eight of whom she called regularly, none of whom had been selected tonight. No messages for the last two hours. No one asking Geri where she was, why she was late, how the date was going. Prior of six tonight, she exchanged between 10 and twenty messages an hour. Then nothing. Odd. McCallum tapped the name Geri called the most. "Katrina."

A buzz in his ear, then "Gee?" A young woman's voice, crystal clear, popping with energy.

"I'm afraid not."

Katrina's voice lowered, tensed and nastied up. "Who is this?"

"Detective McCallum. Ambyr Systems Security. Sorry to alarm you."

"What are you… where's Geri?"

McCallum had heard the confusion before. No one called from someone else's cuff. Unless…

"Katrina, what was Geri doing tonight?"

"Where's Geri?"

"I need your help. Can you help me, Katrina?"

"Yeah. I'm rattling here. Is she OK? Is something wrong?"

"Something's wrong. I won't lie to you," McCallum said slowly and softly. "Can you tell me what Geri was doing tonight?"

"Work," Katrina said. "She was working tonight. A pie night. No idea what that means."

"That's alright."

"Is she alright? Why are you on her cuff? Can I talk to her? She can't be in trouble. She was working."

"I will have to get back to you." He clicked off. He couldn't listen to her descent into pleading. He couldn't tell the girl her friend was dead before telling the parents.

Official messages were easy to find on Geri's bracelet. She had them separated by color and shape. Aqua squares for work-related memos. None related to tonight.

"What were you up to, honey?" McCallum said.

"No feeds," Effchek shouted from the door of the pub.

"What?" McCallum turned, scrunching up his face. He must have misheard.

"No feeds," Rosalie shouted again. "Either end. The manager says they're malfunctioning."

Damn them all to Hell, McCallum shouted in his head. The uniform operative didn't need to hear his frustrations. Not yet, anyway. He'd have to see how long he was going to keep all this steam in his kettle. With no video images of the act, that might not be too long.

❦ · ❦

Sylvia stared at Gavin Stoll's mouth. The tiny curl in the corners, the 'I know something you don't' grin both irked and intrigued her. She didn't get into the movie business because she was incurious; she could get past a grin she wanted to slap away.

"The Milkman," Gavin said.

"What the fuck are you talking about." She decided coy time had elapsed.

"The Milkman. In the Lake Erie region."

"Is this a title? A working title, I hope."

"There's a guy somewhere in the Niagara Falls catchment who tests milk and posts his findings."

Sylvia's lips scrunched hard to the right, all on their own. This didn't make a whole lot of sense. "The company lets some guy product test and post results?"

"Yeah," Gavin said. "He outs dairy farms that hold milk too long or contain too much feces or whatever."

"And the company lets him."

Gavin leaned forward, full smile glaring. "The company can't find him."

"No way." She didn't give the answer any thought. Her mind jumped ahead, tracking the vigilante down, interviewing supporters and dairy farmers, wide pastoral shots, cut to tight dark ones of some ghost-geek in a barn, with bales of electronics, fooling the company, a Robin Hood of milk.

The waiter returned with a bottle swaddled in a napkin. He made a show of secretly giving Gavin a glimpse of the label. They exchanged grins and the waiter uncorked and brought the neck to the top of Sylvia's glass. Her hand sliced over the opening, peach-color knuckles like a tiny but impassable mountain range.

"None for me, thanks," Sylvia said.

Gavin said, "Really? You don't know what you're missing."

"Sorry." She wanted to get on with the conversation. It took the waiter five hours to pour a drop into Gavin's glass, watch him swish it and smell it and taste it and pronounce it perfect. *The Milkman*, she wanted to snap. Is he real? Can we sniff around better than Ambyr Systems detectives? Is this doable? Because if it is...

"Interested?" Gavin asked.

"What are we talking?" She knew how to be crisp. Don't ever let them see your tongue hanging out. Hold the drool. Besides, it sounded too good to be true.

"A quick documentary. Couple of talkers, a little corporate shit, how this bastard can't be trusted. That type of thing. Of course, you ... you, Sylvia Cho ... you can hide the pill in the peanut butter. You could slip the real message in under the corporate one without their lifting an eyebrow."

She could. She knew she could. Let Public Affair's coifed, tailored models talk while the whole time she gets to tell the world about some wacko who is actually beating the system. Amazing. It didn't even matter if the guy existed. Just the chance to prance the idea around was golden. This could be a masterpiece— redemption for all the propaganda she had to film. Art. Meaning. A difference.

"Who has sign off?" She asked.

"That's the best part. I bundled. Lots of private savings and surplus. Corporate has little to say."

"Little's not nothing."

"Such is the world," Gavin said. "Such is the world you can change."

That was a bit strong, but the sentiment was right. She loved the Milkman. Three minutes in and she was in love.

"What do you need from me?"

Gavin glanced at the empty wine glass, then up to her.

"An abortion. Then you'll be clear to work."

❧ · ❧

Emory Leveski sat at his kitchen table, in the dark. He wanted a glass of water. Warm. Body temperature. Nothing too cold. He just wasn't sure he could handle a glass. He still shook. Maybe if he concentrated. Maybe if he used both hands, like a little kid. Yeah, that gave him another idea. Emory stood, went to the cupboard and took out a plastic sippy cup, with a lid and a stopper, hiding a tiny membrane. The cup had cartoony butterflies and frogs and bent green cattails on it. He got the lid off, water in and the lid back on without too much spillage. He sat back down to suck on the little spout.

The water felt so good in his mouth. He could feel cell walls cheering the rush of liquid, imagined them opening their gates and welcoming water like a hero returning from battle. Dry spots cracking and surrendering across his palate and down his throat. *This is better*, he thought. *The sippy cup makes me drink more slowly*. You had to work at it, suck... like that girl, wheezing in her last breath.

The tremors returned. He set the cup down and pressed his palms to the table. No matter what he tried thinking about — sex, long division, picturing the most perfect brook rolling over speckled, polished stone — his mind replayed the same scene. That girl, the jelly coat, the stab, the stab, the stab.

Crazy. He had to get control. Emory was a compact person. He understood that. That didn't mean fragile. He could do better than this. What about those Lamaze techniques? Those classes weren't that long ago. Breath in through the mouth, out through the nose? No.

"What are you doing?" Lillian's voice, from his right. He turned and looked at her, arms folded across her chest. A T-shirt and long, flannel pajama-pants. She looked so cute in her short, new-mom hair.

"I don't know," he answered.

"It's creepy." She turned on the kitchen light and strolled to the refrigerator. "How did things go?"

"I don't honestly… I saw a girl get murdered."

"What? You're kidding me."

"No," Emory said. "Right where I was going. Right at my meeting spot. I was still in the car and…"

Lillian plunged into the chair next to him.

He said, "God, it was awful."

"Did you… what did you do?"

"Nothing. I couldn't. It was like… like when you're running up a beach, in the water, you know? You can't move half as fast as you want. It was like that. By the time I figured out what was happening, it was the past. I'm so freakin' slow."

"Oh, sweetie," Lillian said. "Are you all right?"

"I don't know. I mean, nothing happened to me. Nothing physical."

"Did you get a good look at the killer? Did you tell the ops? Did they give you any trouble?"

"None," Emory said. "I didn't stay."

Lillian reached over and took his hands. She tried to press the shaking out of them. "It's OK. I'm sure they'll do what they do."

"No, it's not OK. I wanted to help, but then, I kept thinking… I wanted to stay and tell the ops everything, but, in the back of my head, I kept thinking, 'Shit, Emory. You're insubordinate yourself.'"

"You are not insubordinate. Not that kind."

"Yeah, see what you just did? Not that kind."

"What you do is not murder. It's the antithesis."

"To the company?"

Lillian gave his hands another squeeze. "There are policies and there are policies."

"I agree," Emory said. "But what if someone else understood that too? What if they decided to mix things up? No… together."

"Calm down," Lillian said. "I'll make you some tea or something."

"No. Listen. What if this wasn't a wrong place, wrong time thing? What if this wasn't a coincidence? What if somebody out there decided the best way to get the Milkman was framing him for a murder?"

CHAPTER THREE

"THIS PLACE GOT liquor approval?" McCallum said. "Seriously. The IG give it out like candy or did you all dispense with the charade altogether?"

"Hey." Effchek put up her palm. "Don't make it like that. One busted camera is negligence. Two busted cameras and a murder?"

McCallum pressed his lips together. Rosalie was right. She was always right, though he'd figured that out too late.

"Who's next door?" McCallum shouted to the Ambyr Systems Security operative in uniform.

"A Kong place, sir."

McCallum bowed his head. The only other cameras that might have collected footage of this girl's murder belonged to a BCCA/ Hong Kong Holdings business. As the girl didn't work for them or fall on their doorstep, the company had no stake in the matter. They'd never release any feed. Another dead end. Each one raised the cost of the investigation.

"You want to come in?" Effchek poked a thumb at the entrance to the pub. "It's a stupid kind of cold out."

He thought about it. Going inside, with her, grabbing a beer, warming up. They could hunch over the oak, shoulder to shoulder. Talk about asshole insubordinates and asshole bosses and every-thing in between. She'd have to lean in to listen to him, put her lips against his ear to talk back. And all the while the clock would be ticking. His timesheet filling itself in.

"Thanks," he said. "I've gotta check in at the egg. Make some calls."

"You know where to find me."

❦ · ❦

Sylvia stood outside the restaurant, by the valet's stand. She told the kid to hold off getting her car for a moment. She needed to dash off a few messages.

To her friend Shirley, at Moshi Pictures, she sent, "Gavin Stoll. Who is he connected to? How can he raise a million dollars minimum?"

To her friend Han the film editor, "Gavin Stoll. My file says you worked with him. Need to play fuck or duck. Can't say my trust-o-meter ticked too high."

To her best friend ever Marshall St. Claire she recorded and sent, "Face-to-face soon. Private as possible."

"Your car, Miss?" the boy asked.

Such a pretty face, she thought. They all have such pretty faces out here. He looked so official in his short jacket with the stripes on the sleeves. Which helped, as she would've put his age at about 15.

"How old are you?" she asked.

"17, miss." His eyes darted right and back. His left nostril flared, but not his right one.

"Really. If I tell you I'm a big movie director and I need your file because I've got a part that's perfect for you, your bio's going to say 17?"

His upper lip rippled. "Eventually."

Sylvia grinned. "I'll tip you for the answer alone. How old are you really?"

"15."

"You get your homework done?"

"I work on it between ups."

"Ups?"

"People with cars to park or get."

Another boy walked up behind them carrying a car chip. He dropped into on the valet stand. It landed next to 20 or so others. He couldn't have been a year or two older than the other boy, or any cuter. Such a full chin.

"Are you transitioning into feature work, if you don't mind my asking."

The valet knew exactly who she was, Sylvia realized. He must have run her face and found her bio.

"You're not interested in documentaries," she said.

"Oh no, it's just—"

"I know, but you'd be surprised how many actors I actually hire. Is that why you work here? To troll for movie people."

He nodded. "Series work, too. We're not picky."

"That's good. Keep your doors open. You can get my car now."

Sylvia tapped her cuff.

※ · ※

Emory knew something was wrong before the night began. Part of him said to avoid the meeting. He didn't think he'd see a girl get stabbed to death, but he sensed wrongness. A thing. He didn't have any word for it. He certainly never claimed to feel vibes or premonitions. Emory was about systems. Processes working in order, as planned, to their utmost efficiency.

Paper amounted to none of those things. When he saw the note, pinned under the windshield wiper of his car, trapped like damsel from an old movie, his nerves lit up. Just a little. A tingle. Because it was so odd. In his 32 years, he'd never seen someone use paper that way.

Of course, he'd never known anyone like John Raston before. They met just before John retired. John knew everything. His actual job for the 50 most productive years of his life — testing artificial compounds for absorbency qualities — applied little pressure to oceans of knowledge John sucked up. How to wire lights, unclog a drain, finance a house, get rid of mice — quickly or humanely, your choice — John had answers for everything.

Until he ran out. His husband of 35 years died five months after he retired. He had no children. He had, he told Emory, run out of answers.

Emory had one. He told John his idea. His big, dangerous, important idea that would probably only work because someone like John existed for Emory to meet. John Raston felt as if he'd been born again.

In the year since Emory started The Milkman, John had never sent him a note on paper. The man loved secrecy, he preached caution every step they'd taken, but he sent electronic messages just like everyone else. Cryptic, yes, but text-based, cuff-to-cuff messages.

The short, hand-written note meant, by form alone, that there was trouble. The fact that John failed to respond to Emory's last message made the night more sinister. Emory understood the risks his hobby entailed. The company could screw him to the wall for The Milkman. This murkiness, though, none of this fit.

Lillian slept. Elizabeth slept. Emory sent another message: John, how are you? How's the Jeep coming?

Midnight messages were common for them. The company would not notice anything odd. John and Emory did not have a set code; codes could be broken. Instead, they relied on context. Any old noun could stand in for the ones that mattered. In this case, 'Jeep' represented testing milk John purchased around the area. He monitored dairies from the region surrounding the city of Niagara Falls, measuring contaminants, bacteria and radiation counts. Emory posted these on an anonymous board, along with results sent in by other volunteers. The fact that John really was in the middle of restoring an old military-grade general purpose vehicle made the obfuscation work. John knew Emory didn't much care about the truck. He cared about the milk, so it all made sense—

—more sense than a handwritten note saying to meet him in the parking lot of an India Group bar, anyway.

Emory's cuff made warm pulses. He touched his wall screen so he could read it in large format. He had a message from John, which gave him a wave of relief. This would all make sense very soon. John would give him answers like he always did, since he was a fresh out of school, dazed by the world, amazed at what they didn't teach you in college. He tapped the note.

The screen filled with video of Niagara Falls. Not the city, the actual water fall, huge and horseshoe shaped. A mammoth fork stabbed down from the sky, poking it like the Falls were a piece of cake. He couldn't concentrate. Emory couldn't get past the fucking, God damned stupid ass video. What the Hell was that? The paper note, that was queer. This?

Emory slapped the screen off. He stood. He raked both hands through his hair. He had to work in the morning and would never get to sleep again. Ever, he figured.

A fork in Niagara Falls.

CHAPTER FOUR

MCCALLUM PANNED THE area, standing in place, turning a full 360-degrees. He didn't see any more video installations. Cameras monitoring the streets were supposed to make this job easy. They watched everything, all the time. When they worked. Tonight, it was back to the old days. The time before McCallum was born, much less an op. He'd have to piece together whatever happened to that poor girl from a bunch of nothing. Fibers and fingerprints and fine ideas. All of which took time and money.

McCallum opened the back door of the egg and climbed in.

"Evening, Donny," McCallum said to the field tech. "I'm open to good news."

"I'd like to give you some." Donny sat folded onto a stool. The kind of sitting only the very young and very thin can achieve. He pulled down his monocle.

"But?" McCallum asked.

"Give me a budget."

McCallum knew what he meant. All the cursory evidence was as clear. Stab wounds were not subtle. Patrons going into the pub gave them a time of death within minutes. For Donny to give him anything else, McCallum needed to give Donny a line of credit.

He tapped his bracelet. "Peggy?"

"Go," the woman's voice sounded in his ear.

"Who's in Econ tonight?"

"Clement."

Wayne Clement. McCallum had worked with him before and found him fair and straightforward— the two highest compliments he could ever bestow on an economist.

"Send me over," he said.

16

"Later." Dead sound followed the dispatcher's voice. McCallum knew his audio monitor was active, but not by any discernable noise.

"Hi ya." McCallum recognized Clement's voice.

"Good evening, Wayne."

"You pull the Vasquez case?"

"Yes indeed," McCallum answered. "Very young, very attractive. Long career ahead of her."

"Selling me already. There must be trouble."

"You run any numbers?"

"I'm modeling a lifetime earning potential now. She was in marketing, which is always tricky. Sometimes those people are cash cows. Other times, they suck the company's teat."

"She's got 'talent' stamped on her forehead."

"Her immediate supervisor thought so. Human Assets wasn't so sure."

McCallum straightened up. "They note anything?"

"Sorry," Clement said. "Nothing so overt. An HA manager named Whelen requested she make a lateral move three times."

"Maybe some old dog got his tail up."

"Three different positions, it looks like, so no. No horny coot looking for a special assistant. Don't know what it's about."

McCallum felt another clue fall away, like petals plucked from a daisy. He will solve this? He'll solve it not. He will solve this? He'll solve it not.

"Bottom-line me, Wayne."

"I'm lookin ... at ... two-thirty."

"What?"

"230,000 dollars."

"She's brand spanking—"

"That's all we can really hope to recover."

McCallum's stomach turned a notch. He could get a second opinion. They were rarely any better. Just requesting another analysis would come off Geri Vasquez's case budget. The meter started running when the call came in. The uniform op, himself, the egg and the tech. Wayne's thirty minutes of attention, deciding how much a young girl's life was worth, probably cost her a couple hundred bucks.

He finished up with the Economics Department, checked in with his duty captain and gave Donny his budget. They could afford some basic forensic tests. Accent on basic. McCallum hoped the killer proved sloppy.

The chill of the night multiplied. You could step outside and not feel it. Stand outside and it drew the energy out of you a little, then a little more, then as much as the icy claws could grab. He had to make his call now. He couldn't stand out here any longer. And he didn't feel right making it from any other place than the scene of the insubordination.

Like dropping a bomb, McCallum thought. Two middle-aged, middle-management parents, sleeping through the middle of the night, in their middleclass home. He had to wake them, speak the worst news they'd ever hear into their groggy heads and know all the time that it was all for nothing. No amount of jumping, dressing, crying and racing through the city would bring their little girl back to life. If there was one thing McCallum hated about security work (and there wasn't, there were 24 things he hated about security work) but if he had to simmer and scrape and boil the others off, it would leave 'reaction'. The killers and thieves always got to go first. He got to go second and the next move was always crap like this. Calling people at midnight.

He wanted to drive over to the Vasquez house. He didn't know if delivering the news in person ever helped the loved ones. Probably not. Nothing could. It frequently helped him, though. The more you knew about the victim, the better your chance of finding their murderer. This home held no suspicious husband, sketchy boyfriend or roommate with a 30-gig file of prior policy breaks. What he could learn from mom and dad would be minimal. Not worth the cost. In the end, he didn't think he could afford anything more than a call.

By midnight, McCallum knew he couldn't procrastinate any longer. He rolled the cuff around his wrist, feeling the cold ceramic slide across the bone. He once chased a suspected rapist down a manhole, into the City of Buffalo sewers. Shit and freezing water, salty from the chemicals they put on the roads to keep ice from taking hold. No light. No sound after his splash settled down. The suspect had a 12-inch hunting knife, McCallum a flashlight. Right now, he wished he could do that again. That was better than this.

He pressed a thumb to his bracelet. "Call Richard Vasquez," he said. Three rings. McCallum didn't want him to answer, but they always did. Late night calls, the cuff would spell 'ASS' on the screen. They always opened a line, already scared.

"Hello," the man's voice sounded like putty.

"Mr. Vasquez, I have some news about your daughter..."

❦ · ❦

Sylvia Cho threw up in the toilet. A routine now; a cliché. She didn't care for it. There was nothing beautiful, motherly or fulfilling about hurling your guts out and gagging. Fulfilling. Ha. Fullemptying. That's what pregnancy had been so far. Fullemptying. And she knew the worst was yet to come. The swelling, the aches, the weird appetites, the lack of appetites, the stomach burn, oh, and the dying. You couldn't forget that. One in 800 women died in child-birth. OK, that wasn't true of the Pacific Coast Region, per se. Still. This affliction could kill her.

Along with her career. Turning down a job wasn't an issue. People did it all the time. Turning down this job — a fully funded, social piece — would be painful. Turning it down because she was in a family way, that would get her name deleted from a lot of lists. There were always new kids coming up, always old geezers looking for one last chance, the middle, by nature, meant pressure. Going back to corporate videos? Passable. She'd still function. Would those offers dry up? How far would a baby knock her from the table? All the way back to "How to find the fire extinguisher on your floor" videos? Could she ever? Again?

Sylvia sat on the floor, back against the potty. The cold tile stung her bare legs and she liked it. The sensation took away from the tiny carousel spinning in her entrails.

The Aptitude Placement Office told her to become a landscape architect. At 18, she had no clue that was anything, let alone a career. She liked flowers, she scored well in math and the tests had, she realized years later, identified her creative strengths. "Movie Director" wasn't on the list. There were only a handful of those in the world. Why get a kid's hopes up? Point them towards an attainable skill the company could use. Let this chick learn how to place viable foliage. That's a job.

Sylvia glanced up at the flowerbox in her bathroom window. Tuberous begonias. Fat, watery, wide and red, she still liked flowers. She had learned how to take care of them, along with image acquisition, editing, lighting and sound design, scripting and all the other skills she had to suck up on her own time.

"And your *actual* training?" the manager of programming said. She'd never forget it. She could — and did far too frequently — play the scene back in her head with brutal clarity. She'd given him her first short film for his festival. He watched all 10 minutes, without twitching, shuffling or confirming in any way that he was still alive. Then he asked what else she did. Actually. As if she were bereft of moving picture skill.

He had been the first and far from the last, to insult her ability. She kept a list of people who didn't return messages, ignored her, or the worst of all offenders: the ones who look over, past or around you while you're trying to talk. She didn't want to keep a list. She just couldn't forget all the men and women who told her she couldn't make films. Those who gave Sylvia an honest, 'we're not interested' to her face didn't make her list. She didn't know why she wasn't to everyone's taste, but she accepted the fact. As long as you acknowledged her. Fair enough.

Not so fair were the people who bought or financed movies based on nepotism, bribery or stupidity. She remembered them. They all, in their own little way, made her better.

The first professional video project she was offered was a short format piece touting a micro car. The marketing manager wanted a director who fit the demographic for the product. Urban woman, early twenties, Ambyr professional grade 15 through 13. The manager had seen her film project at a festival and liked the edge it held. Sylvia had just started at an industrial complex near Pittsburg, as an apprentice grounds keeper. The marketing manager asked her new boss for her hours. He declined. Sylvia spent the next four months drawing, digging and dragging foliage, stabbing the ground with a spade, pretending it was her boss's gut, snapping roots and twigs as if they were his spine— until her transfer request came through.

One day she sat to check her mail and viewed a micro car commercial— girls shopping and clubbing and cruising boys. She cried.

Sylvia cried again, sitting in her bathroom, staring at the begonias, bright against the frosted glass. The strangest things made her cry lately. That proposal about real-life pirates. Two little girls holding hands in the mall. The empty milk jug.

The closer you are to the bottom of the pyramid, the more people there are telling you what to do. And what you may not do. Success, for Sylvia, was never about money or even power, in its raw form. She'd climbed to the point where only a handful of men and woman could move her around like a gnome in a garden. On her plateau you could move yourself around, by your own design.

She could climb back down, right?

No, she couldn't. She couldn't jump, either.

And she'd make damn sure she didn't get pushed.

᠊᠊᠊ ᠊᠊᠊ ⳾ · ⳾

Emory worked. More or less. They needed his input on specs for a new pressure monitoring system. What would be the impact on productivity? The eternal question. Perhaps the only question. Everything you learned in school — economics, ergonomics, physics, mechanics, any other 'ic' the academics got around to creating — flowed to the sea of productivity.

Today, he couldn't do it. No matter how hard he tried, he couldn't read the analysis. All the numbers and acronyms jumbled in his head and faded to the image of Niagara Falls with a giant fork. At least that image of the girl getting knifed to death moved back a step.

The Milkman was never supposed to interfere with his job. He made that deal with Lilly, and with himself. It was a hobby. His version of golf or building radio controlled airplanes. As long as it stayed in the basement, everything would be A-O-K. And if it didn't? Emory never contemplated the consequences. He knew he should have. He had software for dynamic tooling, capable of modeling possible outcomes from his extracurricular activities. He never bothered to run the tests. Why ask a question to which you don't want the answer? He needed to maintain his conviction that the Milkman would have no impact on *his* productivity.

It was all about impact on productivity.

OK. Slurry processing from the batch plant—

"Emory."

Emory looked up. Jack Everette tipped his upper body through the office door. His boss.

"I'm working on it," Emory said. "You can't rush greatness."

"Conference room."

"I'm not ready."

"Don't imagine you ever would be for this." Jack leaned back out and waited.

Emory stood and stepped into the hallway. Jack motioned for him to move along. Ahead of him. Odd. Did he forget a meeting? Did some emergency bloom, under his nose, without him knowing? Or, should he be more paranoid. They walked to the conference room. One man sat at the table. Simple blue suit, no tie. Trench coat over the back of a chair. He'd planted his elbows on the table and held his head up with his thumbs. His brown hair couldn't have been a five millimeters anywhere on his head. The cut didn't prune all the gray and did nothing to hide the wrinkles sprouting from his eyes. New wrinkles, Emory thought. New gray.

"I've got it," the man said past Emory. "Thanks."

"No problem, sir." Jack closed the door behind Emory.

Jack said 'sir' to a guy younger than him. This guy didn't get up, shake hands, grin and comment about the weather. He performed none of the usual business rituals.

Oh no.

"Emory Leveski?" the man asked.

"Yes."

"Detective Eddie McCallum. Ambyr Systems Security."

Oh no. Oh no. Oh no.

"What can I do you for you, sir." He suddenly knew how Jack felt. This guy pulled the 'sir' out of you.

"First, you can take a seat."

Emory crossed and sat on the other side of the bamboo conference table. The op watched him walk, looking him up and down without concern for social norms. Emory's mouth dried. His guts tightened. Again. This time they felt like they bulged between fingers of a mammoth internal fist.

"Can you tell me where you were last night, Mr. Leveski?"

Don't lie, Emory said to himself. *Much. He knows some things. Not all things.*

"Time," he said as it occurred to him. "I mean, what time? I was a couple of places, until I was home in bed. So, is there a time you are concerned about?"

McCallum watched him. Emory thought the man had tiny MRI machines for eyes, piercing and probing. He wanted to talk. Gab away. Mention Lilly and the baby and all the nice things in his life. He forced his lips closed, like a diaphragm in pressure regulator.

"Around 8:15," McCallum said.

"8:15. Mmmm." Emory couldn't think up a lie that wouldn't make things worse. He couldn't spill the truth, either. That would expose his secret life. And John Raston's. And possibly the other volunteers who risked their careers to feed him data. Security could pinpoint his car any time in the past. That must be why they were here now.

"That's probably around the time I was in a parking lot."

"Any parking lot in particular?"

"I couldn't say," Emory said. "I just pulled in to get off the road."

"Why is that?"

Couldn't say a call. They'd have his records. Couldn't say a drink. That bar wasn't an Ambyr place. The cars were all makes from another company. He didn't know which. He couldn't delay any longer, either.

"I was supposed to meet a friend. But we couldn't decide on a place. A place that was equidistant. And I didn't want to drive in the wrong direction any longer."

McCallum's face crinkled in disbelief. Emory sensed the technique. The expression on the op's face had been carefully chosen. A tool. A signaling device to prod Emory into further action.

"I'm a…" Emory stammered. Fuck. "I'm a systems specialist. I can't stand waste. Even in my personal life."

"So you just pulled into a random parking lot and…" McCallum trailed off, waiting for Emory to finish the thought.

"Call," Emory blurted. Fuckety fuck. "I waited for my buddy to call."

"Your buddy's name?" McCallum flicked his sleeve back. The cloth would not have interfered with the cuff's recording abilities. Emory understood the theatrics. Understanding it made the show no less effective.

"John Raston," he had to say. He couldn't help it. He had no other choice. His brother, his sister, his friends Carl or Scott, anyone he could think of couldn't fake their way through a call from ASS ten minutes from now. Not from this guy, who looked like he had seen everything there was to see and was slightly pissed off that you hadn't.

"Address?"

"Not sure. Long Meadow's the street. Up in Wheatfield."

"Great." McCallum continued to look at Emory. Mouth closed. Emory decided to do the same. He'd ride out this silence. He would.

"See anything?" McCallum asked.

"In the parking lot?"

"Yes."

"No," Emory said. "Should I have?"

McCallum shrugged his shoulders.

"What's this about? Did I do something wrong? Pulling into another company's parking lot? I didn't think that was against policy."

"No, Mr. Leveski. Not at all. I'd hoped you'd seen something out of the ordinary."

"I don't know what you mean."

"Thank you for your time." McCallum stood. He poked his cuff and snatched up his coat. "I'll tell your supervisor you were cooperative."

Emory sat alone in the conference room, relief passing through him like a fever. Warmth, followed by slight shaking. He sat for… he didn't know how long. His boss let him sit. Security business trumped making sponges.

CHAPTER FIVE

THE LITTLE BEAN-LIKE creature floated in its fluid-filled capsule, eyes wide, too curious to blink. Hands splayed and rubbery. Legs cocked, ready to leap. This tiny thing wanted to see it all and do it all just as soon as he or she could breath air on its own. Sylvia watched it on the big screen. The microphone the technician ran across her belly took in sound waves. A computer took those and modeled the creature and the capsule. Then the model rendered on a large monitor hung over the table, so she — so any mom laying here in wait, prickling with anticipation, desperate for news, barely breathing because so much of her brain's capacity had been diverted to the 4.2 million questions at hand — could see, for the first time, the being living inside her.

"Do you want to know?" the technician asked.

"What?" Sylvia asked back. The question stunned her. Know what? She wanted to know everything. Was the baby healthy? A brain? Lungs? Could they foretell complications? Like... she didn't know. She didn't even know what she was supposed to be obsessing about. She needed to know that to start. What were the questions. She had no preparation. No storyboards, no script, no notes. She had no idea about anything at all and didn't deserve to be here.

"The sex," the technician answered. "Boy or girl."

"I... a..." Sylvia loved and hated surprises. She liked to have everything in her life working with precision, on schedule, but it was nice to have a little excitement? How boring it would be to expect every turn.

"You can tell?" Sylvia asked. "For certain?"

"I've never been wrong." The tech smiled.

"Thanks, Janice." Doctor Caldwell entered the room. The technician turned. Sylvia saw 'Janice Vogel' on her nametag. "I need a moment with Ms. Cho."

Surprise. Sylvia could see it on the young woman's face. Not on the doctor's. She had beautiful skin, all creased and furrowed, like a bag of coffee beans. It seemed like such a shame. Janice left. The Doctor glanced at a computer monitor Sylvia couldn't see.

"Ms. Cho—"

"Please. I'm half-naked. Call me Sylvia."

"Sylvia, it says here that Human Assets has scheduled you for a procedure."

"Yes."

"Are you ready? Do you have any questions?"

"Ha. That again. I've got more questions than you can handle."

"Try me."

Sylvia sat up. She looked at the doctor more carefully. Thin, strong, just enough make-up to be pretty without over-powering. Oh she hated women who looked like they were going to an awards dinner everyday. Becoming a doctor took dedication from early on. Companies didn't invest that much time and money into people who weren't rocks. And people didn't put up with the constant grinding and polishing of a med school who didn't want it. Really want it. For whatever reason. Prestige, money, or — and this one Sylvia always wondered about — or to help others. This Doctor Caldwell, Sylvia had no facts on her. Just what she could take in, right now, with her eyes and ears. What did this character give off? Compassion? Not exactly. Authority? A little bit. Professionalism? Was that a thing? A thing that mattered right now?

Screw it, Sylvia said to herself. *She looks like me.*

"This procedure," Sylvia started. "Do they ever not take?"

Surprise. This time she saw it. She smiled, seeing the doctor's face flatten and smooth, her eyebrows stretching the stern wrinkles flat.

"What do you mean?"

"The abortion. Does it ever go wrong?"

"No." The doctor shook her head. "This is pretty cut and dry."

"What if there were twins? And you didn't notice the second one?"

"I've never heard of that happening."

"Maybe this could be the first time? No one could blame you for just a one-in-a-million mistake?"

Doctor Caldwell's expression changed again. The outside corners of her eyes tipped down. Her mouth drooped to match. Sylvia's eyes filled. Another surprise. Her body knew before the rest of her. The moment slid towards finality. That little creature in its little capsule destined for nothing.

"I can't," Sylvia croaked.

"It's your job. It's both our jobs. I'm so sorry."

"What if—"

"There will be other chances."

"What if they never know?"

"You can't keep this kind of thing a secret."

Two little falls of water streamed down the center of each of Sylvia's cheeks. She could no longer see the doctor; she couldn't read her face. All she could do was point her eyes at the woman.

"I can. I work magic everyday. Making dreams into reality. Making the outlandish plausible. Misdirection and special effects."

Doctor Caldwell shook her head. "This is no movie."

"No," Sylvia said. "But it works the same way. Misdirection and special effects. This is a little more important than a movie, don't you think?"

❦ · ❦

McCallum said, "Who doesn't answer a call from the ops?" to no one in particular.

"I don't. It just means more work." Wayne Clement entered the squad room, a field of 12 flat, featureless workstations, with McCallum the only operative currently in residence.

McCallum laughed. He didn't know the economist had a sense of humor. He didn't know the man well at all. Tall, trim, red turtleneck and khaki pants, McCallum put Clement in his mid-fifties, at 190 pounds. Wedding ring. Tightly trimmed black hair. He had the look of a grade 8 or lower, but McCallum knew he was a 10 and would be for life. Which meant he either truly screwed up at some point in his past or he liked police work. McCallum sympathized with both situations.

"Counselor," McCallum said.

"Detective," Clement replied. He sat down in the nearest chair and locked his hands behind his head.

"You stretching your legs or am I a destination?"

"Little bit of both. I like to get out of my cubby hole, otherwise I can go a whole day without seeing another soul provided I time my trips to the restroom right."

"Sounds nice."

Clement chuckled. "Some days. Not everyday. Look, I found some outstanding debts on that Vasquez girl. Clothes, of course. Her student loans. It's just not as much as I'd hoped. She was pretty frugal for her age. The company likes to carry paper on people."

"Yeah." McCallum nodded. "I swear, if you're debt free they'll sneak in and sabotage your fridge or something."

"You ever get a call like that?"

"Worst part of my job." McCallum made a half-smile. "Debt Services is always asking me to tear up an overcoat or put a wrench in a furnace because a guy finally zeroed out his last loan."

"I knew it." Clement returned the half smile. "Look, Ambyr doesn't throw good money after bad. There's not a lot of debt load to pin on the perpetrator. This investigation is not coming off as a wise investment. If you add in legal services, we've got about 87 thousand for the girl's investigation."

"What's the floor this quarter?"

"The company's not too interested in anything under 15 thousand."

"So I can spend about 72 thousand on the case?"

"And you've already spent about 10."

McCallum stared, his eyes focusing on nothing. Simple larceny — an asshole swipes a monitor from an apartment-runs about five grand. A grand larceny — an asshole steels 10 monitors off an assembly line to trade under the table. That might cost you ten, once you track everything and everybody down. Capital cases? Forensic evidence and their associated experts, witnesses and their lost time due to interviews, data searches, records and time spent sitting and thinking— murders averaged 100 Gs in op and advocate time. This was not turning out to be a good math day.

"What's this conversation costing me?"

"This one's on the house," Clement said. "I feel… I wanted to find more."

"I appreciate it."

"People who are in the shower or dead." Clement rose.

McCallum looked puzzled.

"You asked who didn't answer calls from the ops."

"You're right." McCallum's mind drifted back to the case. Clement strolled away. McCallum tumbled things around in his mind. A shower? Not too many people took a shower for more than an hour. Dead? Just his luck. Where was this joker? Up in cow country?

He poked his cuff. "Call John Raston."

He didn't have the budget for two hours of driving.

❦ · ❦

Every morning about seven o'clock
There's a hundred tarriers a workin at the rock
The boss comes along and he says, "Keep still
And come down heavy on the cast iron drill."

Emory sat at the high counter running along the window. He faced out onto the city street, holding the wide coffee mug high and watching the steam dance to the song. *Drill ye Tarriers Drill*. A song one could only hear live, in places the company didn't much care about— precisely why Emory had picked the spot.

"You don't like to meet," the woman next to him said. He just heard her over the guitar and voice. They didn't look at each other.

"There may be complications," Emory said forward. "I wanted you to know."

"What's going on?"

"I can't say. I mean, I really can't. I don't have enough data."

"Did the company do something?"

"No," Emory said. "Perhaps. J—" Emory stopped himself. *No names*, John had told him many times. *Don't use names*. "Our friend has gone missing."

"Gone missing?" the woman said. "What does that mean?"

"He's not responding to any attempt to contact him."

"Have you told the others?"

"You are the first." Emory sipped his coffee.

Now our new foreman was Jim McCann
By golly, he was a blinkin' man
Last week a premature blast went off
And a mile in the sky went big Jim Goff.

"I don't care," the woman said.

"It may not be safe." Emory tried to be forceful through a hushed voice.

"You know why I do this."

"I just…"

And when next payday came around
Jim Goff a dollar short was found
When asked the reason came this reply
"You were docked for the time you were up in the sky."

CHAPTER SIX

A ROUND MAN, Sylvia thought. A terribly round man. He wasn't fat, so much as a series of round shapes strung together, as if his creator had started with those balloons they use to make animals. The only hair on his head, aside from his eyebrows, crossed his face in a short, peppery beard. His profile said 39 years old. An age she knew nothing about.

"Sigh," she said.

The man titled his head, not understanding.

"Don't take this personally, Mr. Samjahnee, but I usually choose my own cinematographer."

"It is rather personal," he replied. "I'm very accomplished."

"I'm sure you are. It's not you."

"It is me. I'm good, I'm here, and the producers want me."

"It's about control. These are my choices, my decisions, the producers want me, too, and one of the things 'me' does is select a cinematographer."

"Alright, how about this. How about you give yourself the chance to select me. Look at my reel."

He sat on the end of the beige chair in the beige office they'd loaned her. No distinctive color had made its way into the room. None. All shades of sand. She laughed at first, until she started to like it. The overt plainness. The work it took to drive all personality from the space gave it a personality. As the office had no regular occupant, the room was its own. It didn't belong to the person behind the desk. Sylvia decided that was delightful. So delightful, that her mood remained elevated despite Gavin inflicting Mr. Samjahnee on her.

"Sure," she said. "Show me what you've got."

31

Samjahnee set his left arm down on the desk, allowing his bracelet to make contact with the rubbery beige transfer pad.

"Do you prefer sex with men or women?" Sylvia asked.

Samjahnee found Sylvia's eyes. She presumed they searched for some twinkle or playfulness that they would not find. After a moment, he pulled his head back an inch, understanding how this was going to have to go.

"Women," Samjahnee answered. He tapped his bracelet.

"Your profile says 'single'. When's the last time you had sex?" Sylvia watched the bamboo-framed monitor on her desk, waiting for his reel to appear.

Samjahnee looked off to the left, then back to Sylvia, eyelids low. "About two weeks ago."

"Girlfriend?"

"Hobbyist."

"Here in L.A.?"

"Vancouver. Vancouver catchment, technically."

A tiny illustration of an old, steel movie reel appeared on her monitor, with 'Samjahnee' typed across it. "Here it is. Let's spool it up." She poked the reel, then poked the word 'run' when it appeared.

"I was shooting a 'big foot' movie," Samjahnee said. "Some gorgeous scenery up there."

"Especially in fall. CGI will never replace that kind of effect."

"I got some height a few times, did a couple of low fly-ins."

"Fun." She poked 'pause' at the bottom of her monitor. "Are you religious?"

Samjahnee drew in a full chest of breath. He looked for a moment like he would decline to answer, then exhaled, answering. "Raised Hindi, but non-practicing."

"What do you most hate about yourself?"

"The smell of my feet."

"What do you love about yourself?"

"I don't know. My... durability."

Sylvia looked up at him. She made a hmpf face — tips of her lips pointed down, chin puffing into a little pillow — and nodded once. She pressed her finger onto the 'play' button and sat back.

Her computer screen became a thick, black and green jungle. Huge boulders, long sword-shaped stalks, the camera's point-of-view moved quickly, darting left and right and left again, scurrying at ground level. Grass, she realized. We are tiny, running across a lawn. Towards a sandal. Pink. A woman's foot. We climb a tanned, toned leg toward the dark cave of her white shorts. The camera sails backwards and the young, blond woman screams, slapping her thigh.

"Was it tough lighting the lawn?"

"LEDS," Samjahnee said. "Micro lighting. I used two-dozen positions. I made the diffusers myself, out of Scotch tape."

The view swooped over sand dunes, which became ocean waves, then waves of prairie grass. The view dimmed into a sunset.

"Your external stuff is good. Is that why Gavin likes you? He thinks we'll be soaring over green pastures and red barns?"

"I don't know why Gavin likes me. I've never met him."

"Do you have any other connections to the project?"

"Not that I'm aware of."

"You've been a grade twelve for 14 years," Sylvia said. "Is it because you can't keep a secret or because you keep too many?"

"Both," Samjahnee said. "But at the wrong times."

Sylvia watched the monitor again. An attractive couple smiling over a candle-lit dinner. Candlelight created a number of challenges, the ever-changing levels, lots of indirection. She never used it in her work, for just that reason. Indirection. She couldn't bark at a candle. She couldn't coax a flame to flicker a little more to the left. She thought the same of Samjahnee. He had a fire in him and she couldn't place the source. Directing was all about picking your battles, though. At least this guy knew the difference between light and shadow.

☜ · ☞

Emory received no further messages from John Raston. Other amateur investigators sent in their reports on schedule. Milk from the St. Catharines, Buffalo and Rochester catchments came in clean. No dangerous levels of bacteria or other contaminants. If John saw something in his test that made him even more paranoid than usual, it didn't appear to be epidemic. Emory took the reports and added them to the Milkman site. His finger wavered over the 'enter' key. Pressing it would publish the findings for the world to see.

The moment always came with a ping of apprehension. His site was not sanctioned by the company. He had no idea how they felt about it. First, there was the danger of using the collective 'they'. Ambyr had roughly three billion employees across the globe. He didn't imagine even the grade ones ever found complete consensus. Still, reporting on a defective product, publicly, outside of approved corporate channels, stood in violation of company policy. If some high tower executive from the milk industry called the sponge factory, his life could become much more difficult. He'd seen people dropped a grade. Or four. Sent from a cushy marketing position to sweeping floors on executive whim.

He'd also seen worse. Olin Cassavetti. A line worker Emory met in his first weeks at the sponge plant. Olin had one of those jobs Emory knew, in his gut, that he'd never be able to do for long. He operated an extruder, rolling out ream after ream of sponge on its way to the cutter. In three four-hour shifts, day after day, Olin watched the flat cake slide across dull stainless steel. Brilliant yellows, oranges, pinks and greens. He attended to imperfections, rumples, a shift in yaw— anything interfering with artificial sponge perfection.

Emory neither liked nor disliked Olin. The fifty-five year-old man had a dispassionate affect. All Emory really knew was that his numbers were good. Backups on the sheetcake feed were statistically nonexistent. Slowdowns were rare.

On a Saturday in May, Olin laid down across the silvery sluice. Bright blue sheets of sponge, eight feet across, pushed against him and buckled. The rolls folded onto themselves, raising, toppling, rolling again, up onto the extruder, up towards the rafters, back over the machine. Olin held back thousands of pounds of sponge. He made no sound. He simply lay supine across the steel as the flat blue monster grew too high, flopping down the side of its maker, catching on gears and pulling hoses. The employees watching the slicer didn't notice the trouble. The lack of raw material came as a relief. Maybe it was time for a color change. Maybe the slurry had run out. Whatever. Smoke from jammed, but relentless rollers reached the sensors. Sprinklers and alarms did what no one else cared to do.

Production ceased for two days as employees cleared the mess and repaired the machinery. The estimated loss totaled $400,000. Much more than Olin's worth.

"Why did you do it?" his supervisor asked, as Emory watched.

"I wanted to see what would happen," he replied in a flat, bored tone. It had sounded so distant, Emory thought. As if the real Olin sat deep inside his body and called out his answer through a long tube.

Systems Security came and got him. He complained. That failed to matter. They loaded him in a van two hours post incident. His wife showed up an hour after that; her supervisor made her finish her shift. No one could tell her where her husband had gone or if she'd be able to see him any time soon. Any time at all, really. His cuff had been deactivated. That had given Emory the chills. No one outside of monsters in movies could turn off a bracelet.

Over the months that followed, Emory heard about the wife's struggles. Not reliable information. The usual job-place oral scuttlebutt. Olin had disappeared. Emory didn't give it much thought, as he snuggled into his new job. Then Psych came for him. The feeling he got, having an orderly waiting for him, next to a white, vaguely egg-shaped van, was not terror, exactly, more like that sensation that arrives at the crest of a roller coaster's first hill: anticipation of a stunning, all-encompassing drop.

"We'd like your comments on the test venue we've created," the doctor told Emory when he arrived at Psych's facility. Emory sat in a dark room, looking through one-way glass. The other side consisted of a white room, surrounding a white table, on which sat bins holding various black and white bits of shiny plastic. What where they? Blocks? Lego blocks? In the center of a table Emory noticed a small object. A black and white construct. Kind of three-dimensional star.

Olin came in and sat down. He'd lost weight. Emory hadn't known him that well enough to guess the amount. His cheeks sagged. He could tell they once held more body fat. The doctor pressed a button on the wall and asked Olin to use the Lego to duplicate the object in front of him. They would like to see how many he could make in an hour.

Olin lifted his hands from his lap, examined the snowflakish sculpture and started building. He neither rushed nor dawdled.

"We'd like you to compare this exercise to real world applications," the doctor said.

"Line work? You want to know how this compares to line work?" Emory asked.

"Yes," the doctor answered. "We need a simulacrum of his experience."

"Why?" Emory asked without thinking.

The doctor gave him a look of mild disbelief. "Evaluation."
"You are testing Olin?"

"No," the doctor said. "We are testing the line. We have a subject who suffered an incident. That provides us with a baseline. With the proper technique we can replicate work conditions and limn incident boarders. We can establish better guidelines and policies."

Emory watched Olin take a piece of Lego from his bin and snap it into place, adding towards another duplicate of the original design. He'd made one already. He labored in a relaxed position, moving at a steady pace, but without any vigor or determination. His face had no expression. *A costume*, Emory thought. Olin wore a costume of himself.

"The mental acuity is spot on," Emory said in a voice barely audible. "That's probably about what his job took. The manual dexterity is also pretty close. In terms of problem solving... What are you trying to do?"

"I thought I was clear," the doctor said, staring into the white room. "We want to replicate work conditions."

"You want him to flip out again," Emory said as he realized it. "You want to create a fake job and push him until he flips again."

"What I want," the doctor said in a lower voice, "is to tell your direct report that you were cooperative. I imagine you would like that as well."

Emory watched Olin set a completed object down and draw a fresh, black brick from the bin. Two white ones next. Now four black, at 90 degree angles, followed by four more whites. A small, tight packet of rage coalesced near his heart. *Like a pearl*, Emory thought. *This is how an oyster makes a pearl. Something bothers it so much he needs to soothe it, smooth it. Make it hard and cold because it ain't going away.*

"Baseline." Emory rotated in the word in his head, like a brick. "Where he breaks."

"Becomes unproductive," the doctor said. "Have you experimented with three hour shifts and shorter breaks at the plant?"

"No," Emory said. "The batch vats hold about four hours of slurry. The line workers get a break when the vat operators change mixture or make a repair. The breaks are for the machines."

He'd never said it that way before. You learned it in school, that human assets have more flexibility than capital assets. You learned not to base your schedule on people. You never said it, though. You never codified your hierarchy.

"We alter his schedule daily, but we have yet to induce another incident."

They haven't broken him, Emory thought. *Again, anyway.*

"Are there other cogent factors present in your systems that you don't see here?"

Olin started another unit. A single black brick, two whites, four blacks... The Lego creations looked like large jacks. The kind kids used to snatch up as a ball bounced. Olin's eyes reminded him of marbles. He couldn't watch any longer. He had to get back to work, home, out, the dentist, anyplace in the world but here. He had to say the secret words to egress. He had to give the doctor, and anyone else listening and recording, what they wanted or they'd keep him here until his eyes glassed over and his cheeked sagged, not from lack of lipids, but from lack of concern, and lack of any emotion that might move their muscles up or down or sideways.

"Disassemble," Emory said, lips barely parting.

"Pardon me?"

"Have Olin disassemble the object after it's done. Tell him you want to see how many he can build, then destroy. It's so pointless. The pointlessness will..."

Emory didn't know what else to say. If he had any more words they weren't coming out. His face got too tight, his throat too tiny. He knew, in that moment, that he'd never fully forgive himself for saying what he'd just blurted.

"Em?"

Lillian's voice brought him out of his memory.

"What 'cha doing?"

He jabbed the 'enter' key and posted his milk reports. People all across the Niagara Falls and Buffalo catchments could now check on the freshness and quality of dairy products in their local markets.

❦ · ❦

The pub looked like any of the 1,400 or so McCallum had been in since birth. A thick swirl of beer, cologne and mold hung over an undying din of loud, yammering voices and acoustic guitars from a raggedy band in the back. The crowd averaged a good ten years younger than McCallum and stood packed tight. His parents were Ambyr Consolidated, he'd worked for Ambyr his whole life, so he had rarely been in an establishment of any kind that wasn't part of the company. Even now, after 24 years of service forcing him into all manner of places, he still found another company's watering-hole disconcerting. It looked like an Ambyr place, until you caught the details. Glowing signs for beers you never heard of. TV shows on the monitors that you've never seen. It was all familiar, yet different.

"Hey," he heard from the middle of the bar. Effchek leaned on an elbow, hip out. She raised a brown bottle to him. McCallum felt every mistake he'd made in his adult life slap him in the back of the head. He wove through the crowd. She handed him the beer as he arrived.

"Thanks," he said.

"Least I can do. Your money's no good here."

"It's nice of you to do this."

"For you?" She mocked. "I'm on the clock. We haven't cleared this one yet."

She wasn't all business. Her tone, her head tilts, the way she winked a little with both eyes as if she could telegraph you a secret message. Which she could. When she wanted.

"Any progress?"

"Two steps back," Effchek said. "A couple of kids noticed the vic on the way in. Nobody saw anything through the window."

"Nothing?"

"Fog on the glass. Nobody was looking for anything. Cold night so everyone snuggled in tight."

"Like I should be."

Effchek smiled. "You always were a snuggler."

They both sipped their beers.

"When did you make detective?" McCallum asked. "I hadn't heard. Good news never seems to travel between companies."

"Inspector, we call it. Couple of months. I should've sent you a note."

"It's not like we're—"

"No, but you helped. You were like an inspiration. You got me to put in for the job. You know, aim a little higher."

"I didn't know."

"You couldn't have," she said. "Any other leads?"

"That's too strong a word. I got an engineer, and he's all kinds of twitchy. But I don't like him for it."

"You got a crystal ball?" Rosalie smacked McCallum in the shoulder. "You finally start using a psychic? I knew it."

He couldn't think of anything funny to say back. *Tease away*, he thought. *Put your hand on my shoulder again, if only for a second.* "No, he's just… I don't know."

"I'm sorry. I know you're trying to do your job here."

"No," he let slip. "I mean, yeah, this is the job. I mean you can still make fun of me."

"I will."

They sipped their beers again. McCallum glanced around the room, not wanting to enlarge their moment. Not wanting any more super secret personal information to leak out, to get intercepted by her magical, womanly double wink powers.

"The tip came in anonymously."

"Really?" she left her mouth open, in slight disbelief.

"I know. Hard to pull that off. We've got a whistle, if you know how to use it. Most people don't."

"So you don't like the engineer for the kill because of the way the tip came in."

"Pretty much," McCallum said. "Don't like things handed to me."

"Yep."

If there was more to the sentence, McCallum couldn't make it out. Did she mean he was difficult? The right way and hard way weren't always the same things. Did she—

"You try to trace the tip?" she continued.

"Dead end. Somebody wanted me to know that engineer was there."

"Maybe some upstanding employee."

"Anonymous? I've seen weirder things, but never weird in that way."

Rosalie laughed. "I know. Weird in the weird way."

The band started its next song. Everyone stopped with the first cord. Everyone knew the tune. Even McCallum. Some songs passed the company barriers like a breeze through a screen door.

"You look good," he said.

"Thanks," she returned. "It's the stress. Keeps me young."

The band's lead singer started high and pure.

From the day of your birth
It's bread and water here on earth
To a child of light, to a child of light
But there'll be pie in the sky
By and by when I die
And it'll be alright, it'll be alright

Everyone in the pub raised their glasses and bottles and sang along.

Chapter Seven

SYLVIA DIDN'T LIKE driving. She liked being other places, but getting herself to wherever, in her mind, would be best left to someone else. Still, it was LA catchment. If you didn't have a car, you were helpless. At the mercy of others. And she wasn't ready to hire a driver. She didn't make that much on her last film.

Her silver SAAB bounced and complained over the hard crumblecake that may have once been a road or a racetrack, before it lost its battle with the grasses and shrubs. Each thunk from around the front fender areas made her think the car was going to bend and break and leave her standing in the scrub, waiting for the coyotes to call all their friends and decide what sauce went best with a young, stupid girl.

The grass opened to a large expanse of broken concrete and asphalt. A few hundred yards beyond that, stood what? A long forgotten mausoleum? It sported three domes, with the center one twice the size of its companions. They weren't smooth, though. One had a long hatch. The others might, too. She couldn't tell because of the angle, and she had to drive, through all this silly ass brush.

"Marshall," she said through clenched teeth.

Up near the building, she saw two other modern cars. Teardrops laid sideways. She never could differentiate makes and models like ops could in the movies. 'Late model Chevy.' Ha. It must have been easier in the old days. When cars looked like the one she saw up ahead, that massive black box on black wheels. It looked like a vault, if you overlooked the chrome trim and three-pointed star in a circle on its snout. That was the car you needed to drive up here, on this asinine hill.

"Marshall," she said again.

She parked and walked a path of moss and white rocks— not rocks, but busted concrete she decided. The height and thickness of the plants made her uncomfortable. They stood well above her in certain places.

"*Centaurea solstitialis,*" she sneered. The pretty yellow thistles sat on battlements of hard needles. They could cut and many were cheek high. "You will love it up here, huh." She recognized *aristida purpurea*, some very healthy *leymus condensatus*, with some fescue hanging in there, catching enough light to live. Were she still in the grounds keeping business, this would be her worst nightmare. Not that it wasn't becoming that anyway.

At the fallen spire, she stopped. Marshall couldn't be worth this. Chunks and rubble lay across the path, broken, but not so much that she couldn't tell it had once been a concrete sculpture maybe four-times her height. Stone men had surrounded the base. Their lower portions still stood, atop a pointed pedestal. Their heads and shoulders ruined on the ground.

This place wasn't safe. Not for a woman, all by herself. Probably not for anybody. Time to turn around.

Her wrist tingled. She shook it. "Yes?"

"You're fine." Marshall's voice flooded her left ear. "We've been watching you."

"That doesn't mean I'm fine."

He laughed as she shook her wrist again, telling the bracelet to end the call. She jumped the spire and continued on towards the main structure.

Marshall St. Claire didn't like to meet indoors. At first, Sylvia thought he had an acceptable case of paranoia. His deals were, largely, opportunistic. After a few years, she concluded he simply found more comfort outside, watching people stroll, cars roll, birds, dogs and clouds pass him by. He watched everything as if submerged in a fully holistic movie.

Not that he was an outdoorsman in any sense other than being physically outdoors. Plum-pudding round, forever dressed in bespoke suits, with vests and ascots, he seemed to want to play the part of an old, odd uncle dandy in whatever film it was that he watched all around him all the time.

Today, he'd chosen a dark cinnamon cloth suitable to the season. Thirty — maybe forty — tiny bright buttons up the front of the vest, with more on the jacket, front and sleeves. Many minute buttons would soon be the new thing, in Milan or New

York, she knew. She didn't know if he picked up on trends early, or drove them.

He sat on a bench, a top—

"What is that?" Sylvia said.

"What?" Marshall appeared astonished.

"Get up," she ordered.

He lifted his formidable butt off the green planks. "Is the paint wet?"

Sylvia pointed at the cushion on the bench, thick, quilted, cut from the same fabric of his suit.

"It's a walking suit, dear." He sat back down. "With accoutrement," he added in a poor French accent.

"That means you only brought one."

"I'll give you the name of my tailor." Marshall motioned to the open bench space next to him. "Besides, your tight young tush should have no trouble."

Sylvia plopped down and tossed her head back far enough to see the structure behind her. "What is this place?"

"Griffith Observatory. I'm embarrassed for you having to ask."

"Why should I know a piece of junk so desperate the company didn't even repurpose it?"

"Rebel Without a Cause? Terminator?"

"Old movies I should've seen. I'm sorry. Life's short."

"Ha," Marshall belted out. "Right you are. I'm trying to help preserve it. The property is Ambyr, but hobbyists are making a go at it."

"You come here for sex?"

"Not that kind of hobbyists, dear." He huffed. "Good God. I wouldn't call you to a brothel."

"You would."

"Yes. I would. I didn't in this case, however. These hobbyists are astronomers."

"Fortune tellers?"

"Agh," he belched. "Weren't you, once upon a time, a woman of science?"

"I learned about photosynthesis. What else do you want from me?"

"Astronomers study the stars. They monitor the heavens, plotting where we are in the universe, along with everything else."

"The point being?"

Marshall bowed his head, gripped in a sadness so heavy it had to be fake.

"I'm in trouble," Sylvia said.

"You're telling me."

"No, Marshall. True trouble. I think I've bitten off more than I can put away for the winter."

"That is unimaginable. You devour any challenge."

"This may be my Waterloo."

"Agh!" he belched again. "Napoleonic Wars you know, the difference between astronomers and astrologers eludes you. Did you hire an actor to play you at school?"

"What a great idea," Sylvia said. "If I had thought of it, I would've hired someone to visit you out here in the rubble. I'm not jerking you around. Listen."

"Of course." Marshall put one hand on each of his knees and straightened his back. "Proceed."

"I've taken on a contract for a documentary fully funded with private money."

"Oh." Marshall kept his mouth pulled into a circle. He looked off to the right, like he might want to slowly sidle away.

"I know. They want me to track down the Milkman. Some urban legend—"

"I'm familiar with him, or her as the case may be. My familiarity lacks that level of intimacy."

"You've heard of the Milkman?"

"I have a fondness for people that flout the company."

"Ambyr lets him exist. Lets him report on the viability of its products."

"It would seem so."

"If I do this film and raise his profile, am I going to get checked? Is this guy going to get checked?"

"I don't know. You think the company doesn't mind at his current level of nuisance. They will if he gets louder."

"And there's the money. Can it really be all private? Have you ever done a deal like that?"

"Never. I've come close, but if you can actually raise enough money from someone's personal savings to fund a film, the company suddenly decides it's a good idea and wants in."

"The funding comes from outside, doesn't it." Sylvia flopped herself into a slump, arms to knees, hair hanging straight, hiding her face in a cascade of black. "One of the other companies wants to give Ambyr a tweak. I'm going to rake in huge trouble for what is it? Diversification of species? Is that the policy? Next time you see me, I'll be pruning rose bushes around some grade 10's pool house. Fuck it. I knew it. I freakin' say 'yes' to my impulses far too frequently, lately. Far and away." She sat up and rubbed small circles on her belly.

"I see why you called." Marshall patted Sylvia's knee. "I wish you would have called earlier. Still, now is fine."

"This is bugger shit."

"Whatever. You're a bit wrong around the edges. Ambyr, India Group and BCCA/Hong Kong do, in fact, lob things at each other, but it's usually beachballs, nothing with explosives or shrapnel. They'd never use a film. Do you know why I love film so much? This is not rhetorical."

Sylvia said, "It helps you escape the sad little world you inhabit."

"Wrong. Or, rather, not the answer for which I was searching. Movies are one of the few inter-commercial vehicles left to us. Despite it being highly contrary to company policy, they still find their way across channels. Seen any good IG films this year?"

"Several."

"Despite potential fines and penalties."

"No one cares."

"They would if the message was anti-corporate. BCCA or IG can't fund a film that flicks a middle finger at one corporation, without having to flick the finger at them all."

Sylvia turned to Marshall with a rippled sneer across her brow and down her nose and around her mouth.

"Your problem, my dear, is actually much worse. I'll wager some low grade wants to get over on some other low grade, and you and your Milkman shall be used to do it. You've been drafted into an internal war."

Sylvia wanted to throw up for the fourth time that day.

❦ · ❦

Emory transferred his last message from John Raston to his wall. He watched the enormous fork plunge into Niagara Falls, like it were a slice of watery birthday cake. Lizzie toddled back and forth across the living room floor. She seemed to have to aim or project, just walking, in her arrhythmic, verge of falling kind of way. She had watched the Falls for a bit, then grew bored.

"What are you doing?" Lillian stood in the space between the kitchen and living room, shoulder against wall, arms crossed.

"It's a cryptogram," Emory said.

"That wasn't my question."

"I'm trying to decode it."

"If you're doing it because you like puzzles, fine. I've got no problem with that. But you don't. You're not a puzzle person."

"Sure I am."

"Jesus, Em. The ops questioned you."

"That was about the murder."

"They sent you there. Somebody wanted you there, watching. Don't you get it?"

"No," Emory said. "I don't get it. I don't get why they didn't just call me, or send mail. There's easier ways to get me a message than, you know, by trying to send me a message."

"They want you to stop on your own," Lillian said.

"And you? Do you want me to stop?"

Lillian bowed her head and twisted her left foot into the carpet.

"No one else," Emory said. "Who's going to step up and do this?"

"It's not just you."

"I'm the one posting."

"It's not just you you're putting at risk." Lillian raised her head. "Me. The baby. What are you going to do if the company decides they had enough? What are you — no, what are *we* — going to do if they fire your ass?"

"That's not going to happen."

"You ready to go off line? With a baby? No cuff, no doctors, no money?"

"The company wouldn't do that. They've got too much invested in us."

"Can I see your metrics?" Lillian asked. "What is the Milkman costing the company? You can't compare what they've put into us if you don't have that number."

"It's nothing," Emory said. "I'm costing them very little. Once in a while we find milk that sat too long."

"Then why bother? If you don't find much wrong with the milk, why risk our lives?"

Emory watched Lizzie plop down and push around a small, yellow tractor that made beeps and flashed tiny lights.

"There's something there." Emory pointed to the wall. "John wanted me to know something, but not the company. That's why he didn't use voice or words. He sent me a message."

"Lots of people sending you messages, Em. Any of them getting through?"

Emory watched roaring water fall.

❧ · ❧

McCallum drove north, outside of the Buffalo catchment, into that weird area where the Niagara Falls and Lockport catchments officially overlapped and were unofficially overlooked. Orchards, dairies, farms, all outside his usual haunts. The land, from the road out, belonged to Ambyr Consolidated, so he didn't have worries about jurisdiction or even unfamiliarity. He worried about the cost. How many watts was the car burning? How many hours was he burning? His chief told him to go. No one ignores a call from security. McCallum agreed, he just didn't want it on the Vasquez tab.

He pulled into the long driveway and drove towards the small, flat house. A pick-up truck stood parked at the halfway point. *Who parked midway up a driveway?* McCallum pulled up behind it and told his car to scan it. A Dodge registered to John Raston. His house, his truck.

McCallum pounded on the front door. He watched puffs of his breath vanish while waiting for a response that didn't come. Standard operating procedure would call for an area sweep. He should have headquarters read cuffs in the vicinity. Headquarters could tell him all kinds of things about Raston or others in the area. It would go on the dead girl's tab. Maybe they'd charge 25 dollars. Maybe there were two other visitors from two other companies and the cross charges would tally $500.

Screw it. Standard operating procedures were just that— standard. Usual. Normal. What you should do, not what you had to do. Right?

He decided to walk around back. The grass crunched under his shoes. He found the quiet helpful, but you could have too much of a good thing. Used to the continuous low hum of the city, the silence distracted him. This wasn't stillness, this was a pause, like the world holding its breath.

He peeked through the back window. The kitchen lights were off; the back door was locked. He didn't see any movement in the house. There weren't too many places to hide. He circled to the garage side of the home. That side had a human-sized door around the corner from the truck-sized one. He flicked on the light.

Empty. A big vacant space in the middle of the garage. Plenty of tools. One of those big rolling toolboxes. Lots of cans. Big, red five-gallon ones. The smell of gasoline hung in the cold air. He hadn't smelled gas in years. You didn't forget it, though. He stared for a spell, holding the scene in his eyes. As a picture, it was incomplete. A painting without a subject. The concrete floor reminded him of white Gesso. The canvas had been primed and ready. Or, the center had been washed over. The artist wanted to start new.

McCallum crossed the concrete to the door connecting the garage to the house. This one wasn't locked. He walked into the kitchen.

Ah, he thought, there it is. Over the years he'd become used to his ability — his gift or his curse, depending on his task at the moment — for catching the smallest thing so incredibly out of place. He walked through the kitchen to a small maple table and picked up a brushed aluminum bracelet. He tapped the side and spoke his override. He checked the last call. It was from him.

"Well at least I know why you didn't answer."

CHAPTER EIGHT

EMORY WATCHED THE new people across the street unload their rented truck. He didn't consider himself nosey or gossipy, more of a mind-your-own-business type of guy. Standing in his living room, back far enough from the front picture window that the new neighbors wouldn't see him spying, it occurred to him that it might be time for a bit of personal recalibration. He preached constant vigilance at work. Why would he be any different? If, when a nice couple buys the house across from you and your first thought ponders whether or not they're company surveillance experts sent to watch you, it is time to re-evaluate your life.

"They have a two-year-old girl," Lillian said from somewhere behind him. She moved about, probably picking up loose toys.

"A little buddy for Lizzie," he replied.

"It would be nice. Except…" She paused. Emory paused as well, though he didn't take his eyes from the two men carrying a maple headboard down a bouncing aluminum ramp.

"Except they're snitches," Emory said. "They'll flag us for listening to Woody Guthrie recordings?"

"Relax, cowboy. They're BCCA. That's all."

"Kongers, huh? How do you know?"

"License plates on their rental truck."

Emory looked back and smiled. "How observant."

"I saw them unload a bunch of kid stuff and got excited."

"And now?"

Lillian stopped beside her husband and put a hand on his shoulder. "You know how it goes. It's easy to be friends when you're two. Before, you know, everything else."

Emory tilted his head to the side and rubbed his cheek on her hand. Before everything else, he echoed in his head. Before Lizzie asked Santa for a toy she saw at her friend's, one that he couldn't buy. Before they went off to different schools, with different cliques and started talking in different slang. Before the myths kids spread to other kids about how the other two companies serve puppy in the cafeterias and make kids take gym naked.

"They don't look like saboteurs," Emory said.

"They're probably saying the same thing about us," Lillian replied, leaving off the last part of her thought. The funny part, that wouldn't make Emory laugh.

❧ · ❧

McCallum gave the woman a once over as he pushed the elevator's "7" button. Tall, a decent shape, with a bit of muscle. She seemed alert. Almost too alert. With her dark yellow hair tied back, he swore he could see her ears turn and cup with the direction of every new sound. She wouldn't be a bad partner for someone in a couple of years.

"How long have you been a detective?" he asked.

"43 days, sir."

"Oh don't be doing that."

"Sorry, sir."

"Ed. Sorry Ed."

"Got it."

"Any idea how the tip came in?"

"Employee, unknown, suspected his husband of straying. He convinced a friend of a friend to tap the cuff. That's when he heard it."

"You ran that down like a pro," McCallum said.

"Thank you, ssss…"

The door shushed open.

McCallum lifted his wrist to his face. "Dispatch, we're approaching the room."

"Hey Ed. We'll give her a look," he heard in his ear.

They walked down the hall, past old wooden doors with frosted glass windows. McCallum had never been in this particular office building before. An old one, perfect for this kind of thing.

"We got four in the room."

"Give me a tap."

They stopped just before the door to room 712. The young woman— he couldn't remember her name. He didn't want to at the moment. No idea why. He just didn't want to know.

"…heure est-il," he heard. "Quelle heure est-il."

More than one voice. More than four, he guessed. He looked at his partner. "Francophiles. You take the lead on this."

"Are you sure?"

"This bunch won't be coming at you using their savate."

She nodded. She stepped in front of the door, put her hand on her bracelet and kicked the door in. McCallum followed her into the room.

The office held a mess of folding chairs and not much else. Ten men and woman sat in a circle, various ages, but trending over 50. They all popped like corn in a pan.

"Ambyr Systems Security," the partner announced. ""If you're an employee of Ambyr Consolidated please stand. All others remain seated."

"There must be a mistake." A man stood, knobby green sweater and scarf. McCallum put him at 60 plus and a grade 12 at the most.

The partner said, "Hold your personal telecommunication unit up please."

The man lifted his left arm and showed off a dull gold band. It made no sound, with no blinking light.

"Remain seated, sir," she said.

"What is this about?" he continued. "We're having a therapy session."

"I asked you to sit down."

"I don't see what we're doing that requires security."

McCallum found the man's eyes. He locked onto them and lowed his chin a quarter inch.

The man sat.

"Come on," the woman said. "We know there are four Ambyr employees in the room. Let's keep this civil."

Four members of the group rose, hefted by jerky ropes. They watched each other. And older man and woman, friends McCallum thought, and a couple, around the age when kids go off to college.

"You are in violation of our company's common language policy."

"No," one of the women said. "We're having a group session."

"You can discuss it with a Human Asset Advocate," the partner said. She walked up to the woman and clinked their cuffs together.

The security operative's bracelet sucked out all it needed to know about the woman who wanted to learn french. Name, age, grade, address, occupation, direct supervisor, bank account, all the things that made her her. The things — in most cases the only things — the company cared about.

Was she nice? McCallum wondered for a second. Did she have friends and family that liked her? Did she want to learn French because she had an ancient copy of Les Miserables, passed down to her from her great grandmother, that she longed to read since she was 12?

When McCallum was 12 he saw Paul Gauguin's 'The Yellow Christ' for the first time. It hung at the local Ambry headquarters, the part that stayed open to everyone, to show off he always figured. The painting enthralled him. The shapes were off, but dead on. The colors were wrong, but right. He'd been standing and studying it forever when an old man came up next to him and whispered like it hurt, "'Le Christ Jaune'. That's the real name. That's what the plaque should say."

McCallum's partner made her final data transfer and looked over at him. He shook his head. He wasn't going to make courtesy calls to security professionals he knew in the other two companies. They weren't under any obligation and the future favors, he decided in the moment, could not be worth the toll. He couldn't rat the Konger or the Groupies out for learning French. Not today. It was bad enough he had to write up his fellow employees.

He walked out of the room. There must be, somewhere in the catchment, a better use of his time.

🕊 · 🕊

Sylvia threw a white cashmere sweater into an open steamer trunk.

"This is silly," she called out.

"Taking a sweater north east?" the image of Marshall on the wall asked. He sat at a desk, dressed in a cranberry plaid suit, behind a large, hexagonal microphone, perched in a Y-shaped stand. "It's probably the smartest thing you've done in days."

"Exactly." She put her hands on her hips and faced her open closet. "But what does one wear to someone else's war?"

"I always dress for respect."

"You know what I respect? Information. Facts. Tidbits. You can stay in your footie pajamas all day if you've got something interesting to share."

"Yes. About that." Marshall adjusted his microphone, which didn't adjust, which Sylvia knew full well didn't matter because it wasn't even connected to anything. Judging by the powdery look of the steel, it hadn't been used for its original purpose in a century. "I have yet to unmute my channels."

"Did you check out Gavin?"

"He is what he seems. A man greasing himself to make any kind of slide. He makes deals. He's gotten lucky as of late."

"But no word on his backers."

"Not yet. I'm proceeding cautiously."

Sylvia turned to face the wall displaying Marshall's broadcast. "Timidity?"

"Prudence. I didn't get where I am through use of a single tool. Sometimes one needs a bulldozer, sometimes a sable brush."

"Mmmm sable. Perhaps there is an upside to the Great Lakes in winter. So why the sudden onset of caution"

"I've got money in play. I've always got money in play. Ambyr makes sure of that. They keep the interest rates so achingly low that the only way to build any wealth is investment. I choose movies, mostly. Not exclusively. Never put your nest eggs in one basket."

Sylvia returned to the survey of her closet.

Marshall continued, "As such, whoever may be involved in this Milkman movie could very well be involved in another project with me. Or has been. Or, more pressingly, will be in the future. We all keep our money moving."

"Ah," Sylvia said. "The great we."

"Yourself included. As you make more money on the side, you'll look for ways to nurture it; get it growing."

"I plan to make more movies."

"Man plans, the company laughs."

Sylvia took a pair of black pants from the closet and held them up, stretching the waist out before her. She looked at her slightly swollen belly and tossed them to the side.

"I know you, my peach. What you really want is the ability to finance your own films. Then you don't have to answer to people like Gavin and Gavin's spectral financiers."

"Perhaps," Sylvia said. "But like you said, that's like putting your whole breakfast in one basket."

"Risk is relative. I'm at the point now where the kinds of losses that might devastate some investors don't make me check twice. If I never have another success, I'll still never have to return to my official company position."

"What was that? Do you even remember?"

"Something to do with shoes. Who knows."

"So you don't mind risking two million dollars on a movie?"

"Oh, I mind everything. That's my nature. I'm just saying, my risk is less risky than, well, most. I'm not some grade 10 putting his life insurance into a falafel joint."

Sylvia nipped a pair of white jeans off their hanger. "The ghosts behind this project. Are they like you? Is this just another roll of the dice for them?"

Marshall leaned forward on his desk and clasped his hands in front of the mic. "The people behind this venture are gambling on something else all together. This movie is someone's vara and you are the picador. Your job is to weaken a low grade who is, I surmise, trying to jump even lower."

Sylvia slapped the jeans into her trunk. "The movie's secondary? As in, might not even get seen? It's a… what did you call it?"

"Vara," Marshall answered. "A lance used in bullfighting."

"Like I said. This is silly. I don't know why I'm bothering."

"Because," Marshall said. "You know, and I know, they don't know you."

Sylvia let the left side of her lip curl, just a little, under her nose. "Then I'm going to need a cape. White. Red's not my color."

"Really? I think you can pull it off."

"Be a dear and send one out to me."

"Certainly. I know just the man for the job."

"You always do."

CHAPTER NINE

SYLVIA HELD HER eye glasses in her hand. A fresh pair, bought especially for this project. White whale bone. The interview subject would know they were cameras. Most people didn't. This one would be shrewder than her typical victim and the glasses might create a barrier she didn't need. She slipped them into her pocket.

Samjahnee extended another telescoping pole and unclipped three legs hinged at one end. Sylvia watched. One could tell a great deal about a person by the way they treated equipment. Samjahnee took his time, moved with precision, and seemed to follow a floorplan in his head. The workmanship impressed her. Serial killers needed the same skill set, but, whatever. He placed a globe-shaped camera on the tripod. He set another on the floor beneath it. Sylvia wanted a second video source angled up at the subject, as if she were perched high in a tower, looking down on the audience.

Emily Durante entered the dark room and stopped just outside the growing circle of cameras and lights perched on aluminum stalks. Mid-fifties, gym-trim, Autumnal brown suit with bright yellow blouse. Sylvia approved. A work costume, with just enough 'hey look at me'.

Sylvia rose from her stool and held out her hand. "Very nice to meet you in person."

Emily shook her hand and looked around. "Likewise. I'm a big fan. Love — I mean LOVE — Tobacco Road."

"Thank you. Always nice to be appreciated."

"This is a bit of a departure for you."

"It's good to stay fresh. I'd hate to keep doing the same thing over and over, you know?"

"Oh yes. One of the reasons I enjoy my job."

"Please." Sylvia motioned to the other stool. "You're Vice President of Corporate Response?"

"For Great Lakes Dairy and Dairy Derivatives."

"This is a departure for you, too."

"I've never done a documentary film, no. Lots of interviews, though."

"Good. This should be easy, then." Sylvia glanced at Samjahnee, who nodded once. "What can you tell me about the Milkman?"

Emily exaggerated a startle. She gave off an ersatz chuckle, pressing four fingers to her lips, as if trying to hold back what had to be her well rehearsed and vetted statement.

"A myth," she said.

"So you've heard of him or her?"

"Sure, like any good myth, the story has made the rounds. I've heard of the Loch Ness Monster, as well."

"But the Milkman actually posts, to a site anyone can see, if they know the address."

"We're sure the findings are fabricated. And in many ways, that makes matters worse. This poor soul is presenting false data to the public."

"Why do you think he does it, then."

"I couldn't say. Attention, perhaps?"

"But he's remained anonymous."

"Like I said, I don't understand him. He's troubled."

"And yet you let him continue."

"We live in a free society," Emily said, maintaining a tight, practiced smile.

The real myth, Sylvia said to herself. "If this Milkman is doing harm, though…"

"The dairy products of the Great Lakes region are thoroughly checked and tested. We don't put out anything that would harm any of our fellow employees. We drink it, too. We serve the same milk, butter and ice cream that you get from our fine retailers to our families."

"So there's nothing wrong with the milk."

"Not at all."

"The Milkman posted a high bacteria count from two dairies this past August."

"Unsubstantiated."

"You tested the claim? To make sure there was no substance?" Sylvia watched Emily's eyes. Would she admit it? That they monitor the Milkman and react?

"We test continuously," Emily said. "There is no need for this so-called Milkman."

"Perfect." Sylvia clapped her hands. "You were awesome, Emily. Dead on perfect."

"Thank you," Emily replied, this time genuinely startled. "Did you get what you needed?"

"Plenty." Sylvia rose. Emily followed.

"You are very quick."

"I wish." Sylvia pointed the best way through the field of electronics and trailed Emily out the door. The brightness of the hallway made them both squint.

"Can I ask you something off the record?" Sylvia bent in. She held up her cuff to show its lack of life.

"You can ask," Emily said. "I can't promise an answer."

"Why is this film moving forward?"

"I'm sure I don't know."

"Who gains?"

"No one I know?"

Sylvia turned. She wanted to face Emily square. "This film will make money, but not gobs. Docues never do. It'll be an underground hit, lingering for years and generating tiny deposits. Who gains?"

Emily smiled again. This time, Sylvia thought it different. More real around the corners of the mouth and under the eyes.

"You are asking the wrong question," Emily said. "Or should I say, the right question in the wrong way. It's not who gains. It's who loses."

❧ · ❧

"I don't want to call him," McCallum said out loud. His cuff picked up his voice, cleared away some of the ambient noise and sent it over the airways to his assigned economist.

"Not your call," Clement returned.

"Then I won't."

"You know what I mean. It's not your call not to call him."

"Couldn't you hold out for, I don't know, hold off? Drag your feet?" McCallum sat in the pursuit vehicle, pulled to the side of the road, watching the cars go by. They got slower and slower the longer he sat there. The flat black vehicle always had that effect on drivers. They were all doing something wrong.

"We've been hitting the pause button for more than a month. You don't think this guy's good for the Vasquez murder," Clement said.

"I think this is someone who buys those mouse mazes for his garage because be can't stand the thought of the spring loaded steel bar breaking a little varmint's neck. I bet he catches flies in his hands and lets them out the door."

"Wow. So the whole multiple stab thing is—"

"It ain't right."

"I wish I could help. Fact is Leveski's worth 90 grand a year at his current post. The chain-gang stint is a 50 grand pull. If the company stops paying salary, drops his medical to basics and cuts his cuff, it's a net gain. The company will save about ten thousand dollars a year for every year the poor schmuck's in detention."

"Fine."

"Sorry."

"Not your fault. I just hate calling HA. I'll talk to you later."

McCallum shook his cuff. He clicked it on the steering wheel and brought a workscreen up on the vehicle's monitor. It glowed blue between the driver and passenger seats. He flipped through Emory Leveski's case file, found his Human Assets manager and put through a voice call.

"Whelen," a voice answered.

"Walter Whelen, this is Detective Eddie McCallum, Ambyr Systems Security."

"Yes, Mr. McCallum, I've been expecting your call."

"How do feel about transferring Emory Leveski to a restrictive position."

"I've got just the opening for scum like that. I'm happy to do anything I can to get a killer off the streets."

"Well, he hasn't been convicted of anything yet."

"Yes. I'm sure you'll get that part worked out. Pick him up as soon as possible. We've got an opening."

"Thank you."

McCallum gave his left arm a wide, vicious shake. He sat for a moment. The trees near the car held one leaf for every hundred they had last month. He could see the coldness in the air, the hazy light, the growing grayness. The holiday seasons would start in a few weeks. Thanksgiving, Christmas, New Year's Eve.

He was about to ensure Emory Leveski didn't share any of that with his family.

He poked his screen and requested Emory's whereabouts. A map appeared, with a small red dot inching next to a road. *He's moving too slowly*, McCallum thought. He asked the computer for the signatures within two meters. 'Lillian Leveski' and 'Elizabeth Leveski' appeared, next to dots alongside Emory's.

"Taking the baby out for a walk. Great."

He put the flat black, six-wheeled armored car in drive and pulled out into traffic.

❧ · ❧

Emory tensed a little every time he saw a security car or a uniformed patrolman. He knew he was being ridiculous. He talked to security and nothing happened. They never even asked about the Milkman. He needed to start calming down, enjoying himself. And his first order of business would be ignoring the frighteningly black pancake that had just lumbered by. The small ASS on the side, in the color of blood, wasn't going to bother him at all. He was out for a stroll with his lovely wife and beautiful baby.

"You don't see a lot of those," Lillian said.

"Oh, I don't know," he lied. In their neighborhood, with its white sidewalks, trimmed lawns and cozy box houses, the machine looked like a bullet hole in a stuffed bear. The vehicle stopped and the red lights began to flash. Emory felt each strobe throughout his nervous system.

"Oh crap." Lillian knew. She knew before Emory could assimilate the scene.

McCallum crawled out of the driver's side without hurry. He paused and looked at the three, like he might ask for directions or if he could come in for a beer.

"Mr. Leveski," McCallum said as he walked towards them.

Emory hadn't even been aware they'd stopped walking. He glanced down at the stroller. Lizzie, bundled tightly under layers of coat, hat, and blankets, gazed around, equally interested in everything.

"Mr. Leveski," McCallum said. Emory recognized him. He didn't imagine he'd ever forget the man's face.

"Yes, sir."

"I've got to ask you to come with me."

"No," Lillian said. Her voice twisted the sound, working it into a soft howl.

"Right now?" Emory asked.

McCallum nodded. He pointed to the black machine.

"Oh God, Em. Oh God."

"Shush," he said carefully. "We'll be OK."

"No we won't, Em. Not at all." Lillian looked at McCallum. "Where are you taking him? Why? Why are you taking him?"

"The company will be in touch, Ma'am."

He walked to the car-tank-thing. Emory glanced back at his wife and baby, stopped on the sidewalk. Lillian stood pole straight, shaking, mouth contorted, so red it looked like a flare. Her eyes sealed up from the salty gush. Her tears seemed to flow into his own eyes. The whole scene blurred and curved. He didn't see anything inside the car. A cold, black plastic cave. He grabbed his knees as the door crunched closed and rolled onto his side.

You'll see them again, he drilled into his head, ramming the thought through collapsing thatch and timbre. *You'll see them again real soon.*

CHAPTER TEN

SYLVIA LOVED THE stinging cold. She never had a chance to wear anything like this white ermine trimmed cape. It made her feel regal, taller, even more in control than usual. The softness was pornographic. People must live up north, she thought, just so they can wear sumptuous wraps of fur and fleece. Which also concealed bulging bellies. Like hers. Her subject, Mr. Killington, wouldn't have cared, but her opinion of Samjahnee remained out of focus. Blurry ideas, colors and shapes, lacking sharpness. He could ignore it or he could be reporting her measurements back to their boss pro temp pore.

She also loved her white boots, even though they were a size up, because her feet and legs had taken on a mild sausage like quality. Were she not busy and on location, this would be causing a mild panic. She wanted to have a baby, not change shape. Like she wanted to have a baby and not impale her career. Like she wanted to make a documentary the company didn't want made.

She pushed her bone glasses up her nose. The pressure on the bridge activated the cameras in each lens. Samjahnee's rig automatically recorded everything upon which she cast her gaze.

She stared at the farmer. He looked, as the phrase went, right out of central casting. Sylvia chuckled to herself. The idiom had become relevant again. She could call an Ambyr Entertainment division and have them send her a dozen sea captains, ollies, hobbyists all gussied up, or farmers. The latter would all look like this guy. Thin, leathery creases down the sides of his face and across his forehead, the kind made either by a half-century outdoors or an iron. He leaned back against a green tractor. Its jellybean cabin sat between two rear wheels a few inches taller than the man. The curvature gave off a spike of reflected sunlight that made Samjahnee grumbly. He kept moving the cameras, even as Sylvia ran the interview, trying to keep the flares from interfering with his shots.

"He's an asshole," Nathan Killington of Killington Dairy said.

"So there is a Milkman," Sylvia returned.

"Somebody's trying to make us look like chumps."

"You don't believe the Milkman's serving a greater purpose."

"He's trying to destroy what we've got because he doesn't understand it. When you find him, he'll turn out to be some asshole kid who doesn't know any better."

The left side of Sylvia's lip curled. "You know better, don't you."

"My grandfather owned this farm before the Buy-Ups. My father fought for it during the Buy-Ups. I learned how to clean a shotgun at age six," Killington said. "We defended this place with our blood and guts until we got a decent offer. We earned this deal the hard way."

"The Milkman stands to upset that in some way?"

"He thinks we don't know what we're doing."

"Maybe he thinks you know exactly what you're doing."

Killington folded his arms across his chest and narrowed his eyes. "I'm not sure where you're going with this, Ms. Cho."

"I'm not sure, either. I'm just trying to learn. You take a salary and benefits, like everyone, right?"

"Yep."

"Even though this dairy has your name on it, you're an Ambyr employee, assigned to this site. It's a job."

"A job I do well."

"In the old days, your income would be directly tied to the product. If your milk wasn't good, you'd go hungry."

"The old days? You think milk was safer in the old days? Before market stability? Back then there was a reason to game the system. Like you said, you'd live or die by the price of milk. You could work your ass off and the price could drop and you'd be screwed. You'd do everything you could to produce more."

"And now it doesn't matter how much you produce?"

"No," Killington popped. "We do a good job out here. We produce."

"There's just no incentive."

"Well, there's bonuses and your career track and hell, there's pride in your work! You think we want to put out something bad? Something that'll make people sick?"

"This isn't about what I think," Sylvia said. "But if you want to move down in the company or make bonus, you've got to produce."

"Yep."

"So some dairies — and I'm not implying yours — for some dairies there could be an incentive to let some little things slide. I don't know, cleaning the lines less often or letting the milk sit a wee bit longer than it should. Huh?"

Killington stood. "We're good people. We put out good product."

"You speak for all the dairy farmers in the Niagara catchment."

"No—"

"But the Milkman does."

"That's not right. I don't think I like where you're going with this."

"I'm sorry, Mr. Killington. I'm just trying to get a full understanding of the situation. I'm from Hollywood. You'd be amazed what I don't know."

"I thought we had an agreement. We'd talk about the Milkman."

Sylvia glanced at Samjahnee. The pause made him look up from the small, flat monitor he held in his hand like a mirror, like he was going to brush his hair. He met Sylvia's glance and gave her a thumbs up.

"How about you show me around." Sylvia smiled and walked towards the farmer. His scowl didn't budge. The cameras on her face got full load of it. "I'd love to see the cows."

❦ · ❦

McCallum didn't like being called into work. Some guys loved the overtime. Extra cash never hurt. Or so the saying went. The security business proved the phrase false time and time again. The company never called in more operatives because they thought an operation might go south, or they just wanted to be sure a movement went smoothly. No, if they called up reserves — paying not just overtime, but losing money the ops may have spent during that time in some bar or sporting event or dumping back into the economy through whatever passion they might have — if the company decided to take a double hit, somebody was going to feel the pain.

"I've got better things to do," McCallum grumbled.

Davies, the uniformed op next to him grinned. McCallum grinned back. The kid stood at six foot two and 225 pounds. He wouldn't have to do too much with Davies around. He leaned his shoulder against the concrete wall of the ally they guarded. The main team would raid the blood bank. They'd stop anyone from escaping out the back.

"Don't you have anything better to do?" McCallum asked.

"I'd probably be getting into a fight about now."

"So this is just found money for you."

"Something like that," Davies said. "Any idea what we're busting?"

"Brass said they're running an unauthorized blood bank out of that garage." McCallum pointed up the ally at a gray steel door that looked like it hadn't been opened in five coats of paint.

"I don't get it." He cupped his hands together and huffed in two lungs full of warm air.

"Not everyone likes to give blood."

"It's about the easiest thing you can do."

"Maybe for you. There are people who hate mandatory blood letting so much they're willing to—" McCallum's wrist tingled.

"Analytics at the Sergio. The new show opens Friday," rang in McCallum's ear. He hated ads pushed into ringtones almost as much as forced overtime. At least for Sergio's it was self-advertising. He had less respect for people who announced they wanted to talk to you with "Have a Coke" or "When's the last time you changed your furnace filter?"

"Excuse me," McCallum said to Davies. He shook his wrist and strolled up the ally. "This is McCallum."

"Eddie," Aga Graber's voice stopped the ad. She sounded like she was calling from beneath a pyramid. One she had built for herself 5,000 years ago. "Did I catch you at a wonderful time?"

"It's always wonderful when you ring me," he replied.

"Are you coming to the opening tomorrow night?"

"I'm going to try."

"Try your hardest," Aga said.

"What's so large about this show that gets me a call from the gallery owner herself?"

The metal door at the far end of the ally smashed open, clanging like a broken bell.

"I've got an open slot."

"That sounds like a relationship issue."

"In the show."

Two figures ran out from the back of the garage and towards the ops. Little light made it into the ally, so McCallum had to guess it was a man and woman. They ran stiffly and sloppily, looking back over their shoulders, barely managing any forward momentum. Davies continued to lean back against the wall.

"You want one of my pieces for the show?" McCallum asked.

"I always want one. Now I really *need* one," Aga returned.

"I don't have anything—"

"That acrylic on glass. With the girl. 'Ghost', I think you called it."

"I stopped doing that stuff," McCallum said. "Too kitschy."

Davies pulled away from the wall and filled the alleyway with his frame.

"Out of the way," a man's voice shouted. Older, strained.

Davies ran at the couple.

"That's not my best work," McCallum said.

"You've always got an excuse. I don't even know why you bother making up new ones. You should just say 'insert excuse here'."

McCallum smiled. "My dog ate that painting."

Operative Davies slammed the man against the concrete wall, lifting him clear off his feet. Davies stuck out a leg and tripped the woman trying to pass behind him. She fell to the ground, stifling a yell. A tiny chirp leaked out as her knees and palms skidded on the pavement. McCallum took a few steps and stood over her. The woman's crisp yellow hair cascaded forward. She wobbled to a stand, probably unable to see much of anything. McCallum figured her for late 50s. Thin, but not exactly in shape. She held her palms out, both dirty and bleeding.

He said, "Systems Security."

"Pardon?" Aga said in his ear.

"Sorry," McCallum said. "Working."

"Out apprehending villains?"

"Like everything I do," McCallum said, "it depends on your point of view."

❧ · ❧

65

The supervisors stripped Emory, power-washed him with a freezing blue disinfectant that left him tomato red and numb. They shaved his head. No hair, no lice, the barber was nice enough to explain. His hair would be sold to wig makers. They gave him blue overalls two sizes too big, paper shoes, pajamas woven from a plastic he couldn't identify and a pouch with a jar of toothpaste, an imminently breakable toothbrush and a bar of soap. His day turned out to be much better than his night.

He slept in a room with three other men, so the door squeaked all night, with them coming and going to the men's room. The fact that this particular squeak had not been proceeded by the creeks of another bunk did not alarm him. The hand across his mouth alarmed him, and the ones on his arms and legs. He kicked and felt a sharp chop to his gut, someone trying to break him like a board. They rolled him off the bed and bounced him on the floor. They lost the grip on his mouth.

"What the fu—"

The punch almost took his head off. A hand behind him smashed his face into the mattress. Other hands jammed his pajama pants down. The searing pain prevented him discerning the first item inserted into his rectum. In the morning he'd guess the handle of screwdriver covered in margarine. It felt distinctly different from the four warm, fleshier items that followed. One after another, taking turns wrenching his arms, legs and head into useless positions. They performed quickly and efficiently, in assembly line fashion.

He didn't look as they left. The lack of light made it kind of pointless. The lack of desire to face any of them, absolute. He kept his head buried in the bedding. The scent of disinfectant filled him. Clean, but not pure, the kind of chemical used on filth. The kind they hosed him with that afternoon. They must buy one kind and use it on everything, he thought. Sheets, floors, people— an economy he could respect. One order, one stock item, one lesson in how not to have it burn you and your buddies to the ground. He thought about that for a while, bent over his bed, spit soaking into the rough sheets. He thought about the supply-line efficacies of industrial disinfectant, anxiously hypothesizing the intricacies of comparative benefits.

"Sorry." He heard from the bunk above his.

"What?" Emory raised his head.

"Sorry," the voice doled out. "It's just business."

Chapter Eleven

"I DON'T GET IT, Marshall." Sylvia stretched out her legs, moving them closer to the fire even though she wouldn't feel the warmth through her sweater tights and boots. She wanted to nudge them off and curl into the stuffed, high back chair— a cat in a cottage, all cozy and unimpressed, concerned with nothing but personal comfort. Were she not in a hotel lobby, she'd be half undressed. She had a good view of the Niagara Gorge — the two hundred foot gash in the ground left by millions of years of receding waterfalls — as well as the dancing, soothing, hypnotizing fire. So she put up with the clothes.

"What don't you get?" Marshall's voice filled her left ear. "I can't believe you don't get everything you're after."

"This farmer I interviewed. Total shit. I expected him to have some not-so-secret respect for the Milkman. Farmers are supposed to do things on their own. Cherish their independence. Hate the human calculators from corporate. Not this piece of leather. He loved the company. And I don't think he was faking it for the cameras."

"It's not surprising," Marshall returned. "Commodity producers used to be the play-things of the market. If they produced too little, they didn't have enough to sell. If they produced too much, the price dropped and they did all that work for the same amount of money they would have made had they produced too little. Most benefit from corporate control. You didn't think any dairy farmers were going to help, did you?"

Sylvia flexed her feet. "I don't know. A little 'look the other way' is what I was hoping for."

"I'm afraid the dairymen are playing the part of French aristocracy to this creamy Pimpernel. They are not going to blow the Milkman any kisses."

"Ho hum," she said. "This wouldn't be fun were it easy. What else is on the menu?"

"I knew you didn't call because you missed me."

"I didn't toss a message, either."

"True, true, true…" Marshall's voice trailed off.

"Did you see something shiny? What are you doing?"

"I made a note. Right here. Your previous victim's cryptic expression proved helpful. Called an old friend from blah, blah, blah and, Emily Durante was right. Her boss, Victor Park, is lined up for a monstrous promotion. Director of Consumer Products. Grade 2."

"Oh." Sylvia felt 'Grade 2' slide down the back of her neck, from the regions of the brain that processed the data to the stomach, legs and sphincter that may be called on to react. People became deities at Grade 2, with power over landscapes and lives. Restrained only by the laws of physics, their imaginations and other Grade 2s (maybe the Grade 1s, if they're paying attention). Or so the rumor went. Not a lot of trustworthy information circulated about the lowest grades. They remained largely unseen, beyond the news, unless one died, which seemed rare. There were only a handful of them. Sylvia wasn't sure how many. 300 out of the more than three billion Ambyr employees? What little knowledge did surface bubbled in gossipy legend, a friend of a friend who saw the Director of Medical Services rounding up children for an orgy, the Director of Land Management hunting ollies for sport or the Director of Energy turning off power to Ambyr's third of Mexico City because they beat Rio in soccer.

The highest grade Sylvia had ever met was a Grade 4 and he expected to have his rings kissed. She did not want to contemplate what real, unbridled power did to the psyche. When there's only 11 people left in the world with a higher grade, it must unhinge you. She knew it. Marshall held a grade 5 and entertained his peculiarities with devotion. Of course, he made most of his real money on the side. A good deal of his power buzzed outside the corporate structure. Still, money bought power and power bought indulgence. She could feel it herself, after the tiniest taste of it. More fur, bigger fires, a baby.

"The question now," Marshall said, "is who else is on the bench. I'm tugging on my strings to see who answers the chimes."

"You think another candidate for this Grade 2 post is financing this movie."

"It will embarrass Victor Park. The Milkman is currently under his purview. It looks like he can't control his employees. Which he can't. No one can. It's the videographic evidence that does the harm."

"My movie." Sylvia drew her legs in and sat up. "The Milkman's the bullet, my movie's the gun."

"Bull's-eye." Marshall laughed. "Get it? Bullet, gun, bull's-eye?"

"Yes," Sylvia said. "It's about as funny as a hole in the head. My head. Seriously, if my project might keep this man from becoming a 2…"

"He'll stop at nothing to see it quashed."

Sylvia felt a squirt of acid in her stomach. She'd felt them before, intermittently her whole life, but the baby had begun to encroach on her guts, dimpling them she thought, making things like a squirt of acid so much worse than they'd ever been.

"When were you going to tell me this?" she asked.

"I don't know, dear," Marshall said sans his usual force. "When I figured out how, I guess. Or what to do next. There are other candidates who will stop at nothing to see this movie made."

"So all this gun and bullet shit is nonsense. I'm a fucking nut in a cracker."

"You do have skill with the visual metaphor. Have you ever considered a career in film?"

"I think I want to go back to landscaping."

She twisted in her chair to look out over the gorge.

❧ · ❧

McCallum had never been to Wayne Clement's office before. No reason, really. Everything he needed to know from Econ usually fit in two lines of mail or, on friendlier days, a short oral exchange. A face-to-face? Rare. Discouraged, he always thought, as if too much chumminess between the detectives and the economists might put the company in the back seat; move the bottom line closer to the bottom.

And they were right, McCallum thought. Putting business second absolutely was the reason for this visit. Security professionals caught on to the value of personal appearances before they left the academy. Lean more and learn more, they teach you. He came here for both.

Clement had a nicer office than he'd expected. Ninth floor, with a view of Lake Erie. The exposed pipe work had enough layers of beige paint to give them the texture of elephant skin. The oak desk dated back before the Buy-Ups, probably back before Buffalo was a broke and busted pumping station poaching water from the Great Lakes and pimping it to warmer climes, back when it was a jewel of the Great Lakes. He liked the old world charm of the space, the slight hint of the past— that there *was* a past. Especially the big framed print of Captain Marvel. He figured it at around four feet by three, it dominated the wall behind Clement's desk and represented the kind of information you got not with mail, but with a visit.

Because it took a special kind of confidence to have comic book art in your office. Old comic books stored wealth, McCallum knew, like paper money did in the last century. They had physical presence, outside the companies' electronic realms. As such, they could be exchanged between the corporations. With fine art, it had become nearly impossible. Everybody knew everything's whereabouts. But comic books, baseball cards, first edition Twains— you could always say you found one in your grandma's attic and the company couldn't prove otherwise. McCallum had once investigated bales of copper wire gone missing from a job site and two weeks later found a foreman selling a *Giant-Size X-Men 1* he 'found in his basement.' Unauthorized intra-corporate trade. Not the kind of thing you wanted to advertise in your office at Systems Security headquarters.

He liked the Captain Marvel, though. The simple red figure, with a bold yellow lightning bolt down his chest. Muscles, power, a subliminal phallic symbol. The print had a grainy quality to it. Blown up from the four-color original, no effort had been made to hide the fat dots of the source material. It occurred to McCallum that altering the size had created a new piece of art entirely. Not unlike some of Roy Lichtenstein's pieces. 'Head, Red and Yellow' still resided in town, at Ambyr's city headquarters. He made a point of viewing it any time he found himself in the building.

Clement rested his head on his fist, elbow planted on the desk. He gazed into rows of numbers on his large monitor.

"Shazam," McCallum said as he sat down.

Clement's eyes popped wide. They darted quickly right and left.

McCallum pointed to the print. "That's what Captain Marvel says."

"Didn't take you for a fan."

"Wouldn't have guessed you were one, either. I'm not. I have a professional interest."

"My appreciation is... similar."

"I can imagine," McCallum said. "My beat is theft of material and sabotage. I don't care about much else."

"Nothing else? Nothing on the side?"

McCallum looked away from the print and found Clement's eyes. He knew a probing question when he heard one. He should've figured Clement would expect some give with the take, he just wasn't used to it. System Security Operatives took. They usually just took.

"I knit," he said.

Clement chuckled and looked back at his screen. "I've got to pronounce this John Raston thing dead."

"What?" McCallum sounded more confused than angry.

"They've moved his account from Human Assets to Human Liabilities."

"No fucking way." McCallum inched to the edge of his chair.

"He retired," Clement said. "He started living off his pension and savings. He produced nothing. The company pays for health-care regardless, so he got moved to Liabilities. Now that he's disappeared, he's off the books. There's no budget for a search. The opposite, actually. If you found him, he'd be back on the books. In red."

"He's worth more dead than alive?"

"We all get that way eventually."

"There's no pool to draw from."

"He didn't have an insurance policy to cover any investigation into his death or disappearance. He's got no family to foot the bill. The company's going to get all of his assets."

"What about..." McCallum tapped his head. "What about proving his death? Doesn't the company want to know, so they can seize everything now?"

"Now, later, the company doesn't care. You're right that time is money and the company is so frequently in a hurry. This isn't one of those times. You may not find him dead. He may have gone to another company, or off line, either of which makes things messy. The company is happy not to know until you've got a corpse."

"Off line, huh?" McCallum said. He wasn't in the habit of thinking out loud, but he wondered if Clement had a thought on the matter. "You think Raston decided to go ollie?"

"You tell me, detective," Clement said. "I would've picked dead or defection. What makes you think ollie?"

McCallum thought about Raston's garage and the smell of gasoline and the open space in the middle. The nothing. The place where something had been.

"Can you give me a run down of Raston's purchases over the last year?"

"Sure." Clement nodded towards the screen. "They're all here. Looking for something specific?"

"That would be too easy."

Clement tapped his wristband, stared, mumbled, tapped again and turned his screen so McCallum could see the list of transactions. Dates, costs, places, parties involved. He moved closer, putting his arms on the desk.

"What's this costing me?" he asked.

"The first one's free," Clement answered. "Once we get you hooked, you can't afford it."

"There," McCallum pointed to the monitor. "Auto Trade, what's that?"

"A solenoid. No idea. 80 bucks."

"Me neither. What's Auto Trade?"

Clement tapped on the desk space in front of his monitor.

"It's an Ambyr sanctioned open market for vintage car parts."

"Vintage, like in gasoline?"

"Lots of people restore them. Collect them." Clement thumbed the Captain Marvel print behind him. "Bigger, heavier versions of these."

McCallum nodded. "Any details on this solenoid thing?"

Clement tapped again. And again. "Solenoid 12v 3 terminal, 1955 through 1971 Jeep CJ. Seems to be something that helps start a gasoline engine on an off-road vehicle."

The men looked at each other. Clement turned in his seat, folded his arms and hunched over the desk, leaning in close to McCallum.

"I wish I had some funding, Ed," he said, "I can see what this looks like, but I couldn't squeeze out enough to buy you a beer to cry in."

"It's not your problem."

"It is. It is my problem. I don't want to be one of those assholes in Econ… like mom, telling everyone when to come in. Lights out. Grounding you if you spend your whole allowance. You know what I mean? The only way I can come to work everyday is if I can convince myself, once in a great while, that I facilitated some good. That I didn't yell 'times up' and stopped you all from playing ops just when you were about to catch the robber. If I could be the robber— if I could rob some Peter to pay Paul, I... I need you to know that."

"I know." McCallum leaned back and looked over Clement, out at the blue lake. "That's about the only thing I do know."

❧ · ❧

Lillian Leveski pulled the hem of her daughter's navy blue dress. The girl squirmed in her arms, arching her back, trying to flip out of her mother's grasp.

"Lizzie," she hissed. "Sit up."

"No."

"Don't tell me 'no'. Sit up. You're going to conk your head open. You want to go to the doctor?"

"No."

"Then sit up."

"No." She threw back her arms. The added momentum almost helped her break free. Lillian clutched her back, fingers splayed and hooked, and pushed her back up.

The cafeteria had no food. Round tables, bolted to the floor, shiny plastic dulled from unrelenting use of power disinfectants. The space held 50 tables, a third occupied by couples or small families, huddled, chatting not to be heard. The aggregate of tense whispers and nervous cavil created a low continuous rumble.

Emory entered from the far end of the room. He'd been told the table number, but the tables had no labels. He glanced around until finding his wife and daughter. He couldn't force a smile. He knew he should. That had been his plan. Lie about everything and the lies would start with a smile. He zigged and zagged, stopping at the bamboo chair across from the girls. It didn't feel like it had the heft to support him. He sat anyway.

"Hi," Lillian said.

"You shouldn't have brought her," Emory said.

"That's how you're going to start?"

"No, I just… this is no place for her."

"It's no place for anyone, but I'm not going to let her forget what you look like. She asks for you."

Emory watched Lizzie look at him, then to his left, then farther left, at whatever. "Hi, little lady."

"Daddy," Lizzie said.

Her clear, thin, perfect voice. The kind of tone and timbre every flute strives for and never achieves. It hit him in the eyes. He blinked, sucked and bit the inside of his right cheek.

"Mom was busy and a sitter would've cost me twenty bucks I don't have."

"How are we doing?"

"I'm not going to lie to you. This is failing. We're failing."

"Your salary—"

"Covers the mortgage, com, heat and electricity. Those are up, by the way. Now we've got extra daycare. And did I mention food? No, that's right, because we can't afford any."

"Lil. Our savings."

"Burning through it. Tossing it onto the fire." Lillian sat straight, controlled and calm, as if reading about their lives from a teleprompter on Emory's face. "We won't last much longer. Even with my parents help. It kills me more every time I ask them for anything. Like they've got a massive stash. We were just getting by on two salaries. With yours suspended, were losing to the math."

"I'll see what I can do."

Lillian's face broke into smile. But it wasn't a good smile, Emory thought. The sides of her mouth sliced upwards like two scimitars. Her eyes bulged. "What you can do? Em, have you seen yourself? God, you've got no color, no hair, and lost what? 25 pounds? I'm not the one who needs the help here."

"I'm doing fine."

"Fine at what? Digging sewers?"

"Fine, alright." He slammed his hand down. The slap made Lizzie jump and put a puzzled look on her face. Lillian didn't appear to notice the sound. Emory looked to the corner, where a supervisor stood. The guy didn't seem to notice either. He drew his hand back and shoved both under the table. He couldn't hide his appearance from his wife, though he'd hope he didn't look as bad as she said. He only saw part of his face for couple of minutes in the morning. His hands, though. He didn't want Lillian to glimpse his hands for a second. The 'no touching' rule came as a relief.

"They give you a hearing date yet?" Lillian asked.

"February 6," he answered.

Lizzie hopped down from Lillian's lap. She stood.

"That's crap," Lillian said. "You're stuck here and you can't even get a hearing?"

"It's not that far away now."

"A quarter," Lillian said. "They bounced you into the next quarter. Somebody wants you in this budget or off that budget or the arbitration budget went over. It's crap and it's going to kill us."

"Not us." He started to reach across the table and stopped. He knew the rules. He wouldn't risk it. They looked for reasons to deny visits. He looked forward to them like nothing else in his life, not dessert or Christmas presents or sex. Seeing Lillian's skin, her plump lips. Hearing words and sounds directed at him, because he existed as a person and not some piece of organic machinery. Watching Lizzie fidget and dance, bored from lack of tension, fear, drama. Her lack of attention left him relieved. Happy even, though that word didn't fit. Too large.

Lizzie walked away. Back in the direction from which they'd come.

"Come on, daddy," she said. "Home now."

"Not today, pumpk..." Emory's voice fell apart.

CHAPTER TWELVE

SYLVIA AND SAMJAHNEE sat in their rented all-wheel drive wagon. The vehicle stood tall, and had 13-times the room they needed, but she'd insisted on it. She wanted something rugged, that could subjugate slush and snow without causing her concern. That there wasn't much slush and snow at the moment made no difference. She'd read about the Great Lakes climate. Blinding blizzards without warning. Roads transforming to ice beneath your tires. Wild wind ripping across frozen lakes, kicking out your feet and flying you to a frosty neverland. Legends said winters around here fell far too large and powerful for anyone to fight. They took your control.

She didn't care for that part. She had to at least try to control everything she could or she'd... she didn't know what. She instructed her forward team to set her up with everything she needed to survive in the arctic for two weeks. Starting with a big, bad six-wheeled truck.

In which, Sylvia and Samjahnee sat, looking at the monitor in the center of the truck's dash. It showed a young, blond woman's photograph. Sylvia looked back through the passenger window. The real live version exited a gym.

Samjahnee said, "Our girl's done a wee bit early today."

"Those 'get fit' New Year's resolutions never last." Sylvia watched the woman walk towards them, gym bag over her shoulder. She held the black strap with both hands, presumably not trusting the grip of her enormous fleece mittens. They matched her boots. Sylvia liked the style. Cartoony, but the woman had the body and age to get away with it. In fact, Sylvia thought, she had the looks to get away with a lot. She knew it, too. Only the confident could wear such outsized fuzz.

Sylvia slid her whalebone glasses onto her face. "Are these going to work in this cold? They're not going to frost over or anything are they?"

Samjahnee tapped the monitor and brought up live feed from Sylvia's glasses. "The greatest achievements in science in the last 20 years have been in the area of surveillance cameras."

Sylvia opened the door and pivoted on her seat. The baby bump changed the way she used to exit an automobile. She didn't care for it, or the uncertain feeling of the packed snow that covered every inch of everything up here, or the sting the cold delivered to your nose despite the sun telling your eyes it still worked. She wrapped her ermine cape tight and walked to block the woman's path.

"Patricia Racie?" Sylvia asked.

"Yes." Patricia smiled, but it wasn't friendly.

"Hi, sorry, Sylvia Cho." She didn't hold out her hand.

"Have we met?" She stopped walking.

"No, I just have a couple of questions, if you don't mind."

Patricia locked her knees and straightened to her full height, a few inches taller than Sylvia. Sylvia resisted the urge to step forward, remembering Samjahnee's early suggestions about the distance and angle. What she wanted was a step stool. Patricia looked her up and down. Sylvia knew she didn't look like systems security, so the young woman probably didn't know what to make of her.

"I don't think so," Patricia said.

But she didn't move, Sylvia noticed. The poor thing had no business being a conspirator. She was far too much the scientist.

"You are Patricia Racie, a biologist with Utica Brewing, division of Ambyr Consolidated. You test beer and the machines that make it. You live up in dairy country."

"Not hearing a question."

"You're a member of Localvor."

Patricia's face curled into indignation. "So?"

"Three quarters of your friends are too."

"How do you know that?"

"How hard do you think it is get a look at your little circle? A friend of a friend lets you in, then you go down the list, check it against the other nature loving, local food munching, must-be-fresh-and-friendly types and smash. I'm in."

"Who the hell are you, lady?"

"I told you. Sylvia Cho. C-H-O."

Patricia brought her silver cuff up close to her face. She tapped it a few times and repeated the spelling.

"You live within biking distance of 12 dairy farms," Sylvia continued. "This isn't rocket surgery. You take food quality very seriously. I admire that."

"Do you." Patricia gazed into her cuff's tiny monitor.

"On a bike you're harder to trace, aren't you. If you take your bracelet off. The company doesn't always know exactly where you are, does it, Patricia?"

She looked up, nose pasty red from the cold, mouth in the shape of a mouse hole. "You're a director? A Hollywood movie director?"

"I'm a little disappointed you didn't recognize me right off."

"I'm not into mov... what are you doing here?"

Sylvia said, "You sneak onto dairy farms, take samples and test them. Then you report your findings."

"You sticky bitch." Patricia stepped closer to Sylvia, who now had to lift her head to make eye contact. Sylvia didn't want to back up, that was the wrong non-verbal message, but the cameras on her face were getting little more than a load of wool-covered chest. She stepped to the side and ran her gaze up Patricia's body, stopping at her mouth.

"Either you are the Milkman," Sylvia whispered, "or you work for him."

"I have no idea what you're talking about."

"Then why are you calling me names?"

"Because you're obstructing me."

"All I want is a chance to talk to the Milkman. I need to get in touch with him or her."

"Like I said, I have no idea what you're talking about."

"When this runs, when I've put all the gears into place and given this story a spin, you'll be the tall, blond liar."

Patricia brought her head back a notch, then looked left and right. "You fucking sticky bitch."

"He'll want to talk to me, Patricia."

She caught sight of Samjahnee near the car. He held a parabolic microphone the size of a halved cantaloupe. "ohGodohGod-ohGod." She ducked around Sylvia, hands tight to her gym bag strap and loped down the sidewalk, a deer at the scent of a wolf.

Sylvia turned to follow, at least with the cameras. Running on the snow, six months pregnant, didn't occur to her even for a second. *I hope he's getting that snow sound,* did occur to her. Such a cool sound. Literally. The spongy muffled crunch each time a boot touched down. Sylvia stood still until sure she had enough footage of Patricia's departure. She walked back to the car, as Samjahnee put away his equipment. Both climbed into the truck. Samjahnee turned the heater to 'Full'.

"I think you made a new friend," he said,

Sylvia took off the glasses. "I'm not here to make friends. I'm making a movie."

"You scared that girl."

"I inspired drama," Sylvia said. "That stuff we just shot is going to cut in nicely when we snap this mess together. All cinema — all story — is conflict. Nobody's going to down a copy of this film if it's nothing but a bunch of red-cheeked, butter-eaters flat faced in front of the camera. We need emotions, reactions, people struggling against people, the company, or best of all, against themselves. Like that girl just did. Fight or flight. At war with her own curiosity and indignation. It was too lovely for words... it's why I love movies so much."

Samjahnee narrowed his eyes. He tilted his head just a little to the left, getting a different angle, changing the way the light crossed Sylvia's face from his point-of-view. She looked back, waiting.

"I thought you liked this guy. This Milkman," Samjahnee said.

"I haven't met him," Sylvia replied.

"Whose side are you on?"

"Poor man." Sylvia pursed her lips. "Did you grow up playing soccer and dodgeball? Is everything in your world on one side or another? I honestly believe team sports should be banned. They don't foster a multifaceted point of view. I'm sure I don't have to tell you, there's more than two sides to pretty much everything. Or, if you look at it another way, just one side. Mine."

Samjahnee stared at Sylvia for a moment. She couldn't tell if he wanted to ask another question or lacked the energy to turn and start the car moving.

"Cricket," he finally said. "I grew up playing cricket."

"Well, there you go," Sylvia said. "You ever play with six or seven teams on the field at one time?"

"That wouldn't have worked out too well."

"Maybe not then, but it might have prepared you for now."

❦ · ❦

Emory saw a roll of duct tape on a red metal cart. He never wanted anything more in his life. He never would want anything more, he knew. The tape hit his desire's maximum, the point at which he could not desire more. He'd risk his life for this roll of duct tape.

The tunnel gave you a lot of ways to risk your life. Poisonous gas, explosions, electrocution courtesy of the wet wired power tools and Emory's least favorite: buried alive. This section of the water main ran only 15 feet below the streets of Buffalo. Still, that 15 feet held more than enough crumbling rock, concrete poured near the time of its invention, wooden timbers cut back when they still had to be drawn to the job site by horse teams, and earth, packed and crusty with frost to lay waste to a bunch of men. Palming supplies did not invite a cave-in, he told himself. If the foremen caught him they'd what? Freeze him, beat him, rape him? Too late.

He looked neither left nor right, he just walked into the cart and pushed. He made it look like his job, like he was so freakin' annoyed to have to be pushing this rickety squeaky piece of junk he might fall asleep while doing it. The cart belonged to someone in this tunnel. Someone close. Stealing down here was nuts because there was no place to hide. He could stumble forward in the tunnel or back. He couldn't even rise because they pulled the ladder once the crew descended. After a few yards no one had a direct view. He snatched the duct tape, rammed it into his coveralls and strolled on, in the hunched way everyone moved underground. His bump hat never touched the top and still, like everyone, he stayed bent.

The yellow man-shaped balloon he wore was supposed to keep the near freezing air and water off his skin as he worked in the pipes, but the gaps were so large and numerous that each day below became a battle with frostbite. The cold let you think of little else. Because of Emory's duties, he reached the end of the tunnel before any others. He ripped off squares and patched his suit in a shaky blur. He couldn't mend fast enough. He knew he was saving his skin, his digits, probably his life.

As he worked a jack, forcing a support spar into the ceiling of the tunnel, he noticed the man next to him had similar problems. The gash in his coveralls stretched from his knee down to his ankle. Emory knew from experience that the gash would let water inside his boot, where it could do the most damage. Pooling, burning, numbing and finally killing your toes.

"Here." He handed the roll to the man, motioning at the tear.

The man looked down and took the tape with some hesitation.

"Dry the area first," Emory said. "It'll stick longer."

The man found a rag by the floodlight stand, whipped his leg down, tore off a long strip of duct tape and fixed his rip. He gave the roll back to Emory.

"Thanks," he said. "Campbell."

"Emory."

A chime rang through the tunnel, followed by an old guy with white boxes. He passed them out and all the men dropped to the ground, splashing water out of the way, making butt-sized craters in the soft soil. Cold sandwiches of unclassified meat. An orange. Water laced with enough vitamins to render it milky and metallic tasting. Emory crammed it all in his mouth regardless. The labor took every stored calorie out of him. Dragging, lifting, ramming support beams, and the vibrating— he knew that's what really drained him. His body quivered continuously to shake off the cold.

"What did you do?" Campbell asked.

Emory heard the question far less frequently than he wanted to ask it. No one on this work detail talked much about their infractions. He made a game of guessing. Who failed a drug test, who slugged a superior, who killed a man in a bar fight because he looked at him funny? He wanted to ask all the time, but didn't. They never asked him, adhering to a protocol he failed to fully fathom. Emory could guess why Campbell asked. Emory did not look like he could do anything bad enough to end up on this gang.

"Not sure," Emory answered. It was an honest answer, in its own way. Campbell grunted a half smile. *He understood*, Emory thought, making a good guess at Campbell's policy violation much harder. Tall, in his late fifties, Campbell carried himself like his muscles had abandoned him— under his overalls would be levers and counter weights. He seemed bright, and alive and yet lacked the searching eyes of a man seeking a crack, an edge, a way in or out. Thief, saboteur, smuggler— none of it fit. Plastered with dirt, ensconced in yellow plastic, Emory could only guess he'd been an inventory superintendant or traffic modulator or some such watch-the-numbers job, back up top. In the world. Ago.

"How about you?" Emory asked. "What did you do?"

Campbell swallowed whatever he'd been chewing. "I know the truth and made the mistake of trying to share it with others."

☞ · ☜

The scene didn't look right, McCallum thought. No single detail sat out of place, no scent or sound set him off. He'd lived in this loft for 20 years, the last several alone, and knew when his world had been disturbed. He padded into the center of the space, between the kitchen island and kitchenette. He skipped turning the lights on. He peered into his living area. All his canvases seemed to be where he'd left them, leaning on the couch and coffee table. His recent piece up on an easel, under the skylight — the reason he purchased the place — waiting for the shower of natural light you couldn't really get until winter called it a year. The round table he used as a coat rack remained empty. That left his bedroom. He backed up, and stepped between the island and the kitchen's cupboard-coved back wall. He flipped the faucet lever. Water gushed into the sink with a soothing racket. *If there's no one here, you look like an idiot only to yourself,* he said inside. *If there is someone here...* He rounded the corner and kicked his door in.

"Hey," a man said, snapping his arms into blocking positions.

"Hey." McCallum hopped and kicked again, into the man's midsection. The man knocked the kick aside, turned and took a proper stance.

Fuck, McCallum said inside. *He's got a skill set.*

McCallum punched. The man blocked and punched straight, twisting his fist. Perfect stance and execution. McCallum spun, caught the man's arm, pulled it to his chest and used it as a brace to ram his head into the door jam. The apartment shook. Frames rattled on the walls. McCallum's momentum took him through the doorway, breaking his grip. The man lurched behind McCallum, snaking his forearm under McCallum's chin. *Death hold,* he screamed in his head. He grabbed, rolled right and flipped the guy, smashing him to the kitchen floor.

The man bounced up faster than McCallum expected. They each bent at the knees, turned to limit their profiles and raised their arms. The man wore dull black pants, jacket, turtleneck and watch cap. It hid blond curls. McCallum put him at 5'10", 180, 15 his junior. The spot of blood in the center of his forehead made a tail down his nose. A slick, red tadpole tattoo. McCallum had the advantage. He hopped forward… then back. The man looked confused. He wanted to look around but wouldn't. McCallum inched backward. The man took a chance and spun into the living room. He took the canvas off the easel and raised it above his head.

"No!" McCallum yelled.

"Then don't move." The man's voice confirmed his youth. McCallum heard just a tincture of excitement.

"I'm an op. This isn't going your way."

"This ain't a break in. My superiors gave me the door code."

Fill me with fuck, McCallum thought, but said, "What are you doing here?"

"I'm supposed to be delivering a message."

"They should've sent more than one asshole."

"Not that kind of message," the man returned. "I'm supposed to tell you Emory Leveski is innocent."

"You couldn't call me?" McCallum shook his arms, letting the blood loose in his muscles.

"I'm just the messenger." He stepped forward, keeping the painting high. "Now if you'll step away from the door."

"Who sent you?"

"Right. The door."

McCallum sidestepped to his left. He let the guy pass between him and the island. The man refused to relax. He watched McCallum like this was a match. His arms stayed cocked and tight, waiting for a bell, as if smashing the canvas would win him a stuffed lion.

"So what was your plan?" McCallum asked. "Come at me all tough and scary?"

"It wasn't to tussle, I can tell you that." He arched a hand behind his back and opened the door, lowering the painting, but keeping it between himself and McCallum. His eyes never strayed from where they needed to be. He tossed the canvas. McCallum jumped and caught it with both hands. He examined it to make sure nothing had marred the image; the sweep of black lines, all in the same direction, broken only by the figure of a woman face down on a sidewalk.

McCallum kicked his door closed. Even if he caught up with the man, what would he do? Fight more? Maybe lose? He crossed his loft and returned his art to the easel. He liked this one. He always liked them before they were finished. Then he hated them. He walked around the island and turned off the water.

Emory Leveski was innocent. He wished they'd sent professional muscle into his home to tell him something he didn't already know.

CHAPTER THIRTEEN

THE COMMON ROOM for men assigned to the alternative work detail had no sharp edges. The corners of the walls met in concave joints; every chair rim, table lip and door jam curved. The walls glistened, painted in a peach enamel that Emory believed to be a 'calming color', a hue the industrial psychologist researched, tested and decided would promote tranquility. The high gloss made it easier to clean if the color failed. Two doors stood at opposite sides of the room. No windows. The back wall served as a large monitor. Everyone could watch whatever movie or educational program the company deemed appropriate. Emory had yet to start watching one he could stay with till the end. The films tended to show little action of any kind, unless it was a period piece, usually an old movie about governments trampling citizens.

Most of the films depicted families striving to make an honest living under the tyranny of government regulation. They couldn't plant crops because of arcane land restrictions. They had to shut down the mill because the corrupt government official wanted it for his lazy son. Emory tried to watch all of the native people's movie. Good natured, natural folks, living off the land, rounded up and marched from their homes by the government. The absurdity of the story made him think it might be true. The company didn't have the imagination to manufacture stories that bizarre. In end, he didn't make it. People marched and cried and marched and cried until he fell asleep.

Tonight's feature had to do with different Indians. These lived near what he knew as the Bombay catchment. They wore more clothing, but not much more. Another government army seemed determined to round up more people and march them around.

"It's all true," Campbell said as he sat down. He stretched out his legs, crossing them at the ankles, and folded his arms across his chest.

"The movie?" Emory asked.

"Yep." He nodded once. "The British Islands were once all under the same queen who wanted to rule the world. She used her army and navy, but her real innovation was commerce. She used companies to expand her empire. Not realizing that…" Campbell quickly scanned the room, decided no one but Emory could hear him, and continued "…that the companies would eventually turn on her descendents."

"Is this the truth you're guilty of spreading?"

"A little. The company doesn't mind me talking about how bad the queen was… or the United States of America or the Third Reich or any of those devious old, malfunctioning structures. No, they're fine with that. It's the rest of the story that bothers them."

"What's the rest of the story?"

Campbell turned from the wall monitor to Emory. He looked into his eyes for longer than Emory liked, but he refused to look away. He wanted to see if this guy was insane.

"How'd you end up here?" Campbell asked.

"Don't know," Emory answered. "I honestly don't know."

"But?"

"No buts."

"Aren't you going to say, 'but it's a mistake. I'm innocent. The company's got it all wrong'?"

"Oh no," Emory replied. "I deserve to be here. I just don't know if the company's got the right reason."

Campbell's bottom lip protruded, not in a pout or bout of sadness, but in a way Emory thought projected disappointment. Campbell's own, personal disappointment in not guessing all of Emory's specs from their first, brief encounter. Emory trusted the man on instinct. Of course, he no longer trusted his own instincts, so he decided to refrain from spilling his life's story.

"I haven't killed anyone," Emory said. "How's that?"

"No problem. It's your own business."

Emory snorted and half-smiled. "No such thing."

Campbell smiled back. He panned the room again — all the faces faced the far wall, some asleep, some on the verge — then leaned in closer to Emory. "What did they teach you in school about the Buy-Ups?"

"I don't know," Emory threw out, "Governments borrowed money to fight wars and went bankrupt. The world's corporations stepped in to make sure society didn't collapse. They fed people, maintained police forces and sanitation services and divided the world up so we'd never have another war."

"Very good. You must have been a great student."

"For what it's worth."

"Sadly, you learned history as written by the Public Relations Department. Just like this movie, it's part true, part false, and part missing."

"What makes you think that?" Emory asked.

"I'm not some tin-foil hat wearing alien abductee. You know what I used to do before laying sewer pipe? A datologist, that's what. I specialized in pre-Buy Up code. I translated old information into modern formats. The company decided what should be preserved and what should be destroyed."

"Sounds like a dangerous job."

"A lot more dangerous than crawling around underground."

"If you read all this stuff the company wants erased," Emory said, "why are you still alive?"

"Ha," Campbell chirped. "It's taking them longer to kill me than they first figured. You really don't know much about your situation, do you. It's death by labor."

Emory's stomach curled up on itself. Campbell's smug conviction; his acceptance. Emory played cat's cradle with his hope every day, stretching it, weaving it, reworking it into shapes that fit his changing predicaments. Through all the manipulations, the strung-out hope held. It hadn't snapped and fallen limp. He wouldn't let this crazy asshole pinch it from his fingers and turn it into his life sentence.

"I'm not going to die here," Emory said.

Campbell sighed. He watched the movie for a moment, saying nothing, as if waiting for Emory to catch up to him.

"How long have you been on the chain?" Emory asked.

"Seventeen months," Campbell answered.

"And you're still alive."

"The new line's not done. The companies hate paying for public works. There's no profit in sewage. There's no easy way to make people pay for what they don't use. The fact that all three companies share the main lines really fucks things up. So business centers pool funds and they look for the cheapest labor force they can find. That would be us, in case you're wondering. When this project's done, they'll have less use for us."

"You know what I did before this? I was… I *am* a systems engineer. So I can tell you without a doubt, this project will never be done. It's constant, continuous maintenance. By the time you finish at one end, you'll need to start back at the other. You may be around a lot longer than you anticipate."

"I appreciate your optimism."

"So what do I need to know, Campbell? What's the other history?"

Campbell bent his head and spoke out of the side of his mouth. "The Buy-Ups didn't happen. Not like the companies say. There were no white knight rescues. They foreclosed."

"Foreclosed? Like took over?"

"They decided governments had become… become too wasteful to continue. It didn't matter what kind. Socialist, communist, monarchy, even the great capitalist republics on which the companies themselves had been built all had to go. They didn't collapse under their own foolishness, they were uprooted."

Emory made his doubting face, eyebrows jutting out like plump bookshelves. "All the guns and armies," he motioned to the movie playing on the wall, "they spent all their time frightening people into submission. But you want me to believe a bunch of executives took them over?"

"Those armies didn't run on their bellies," Campbell said. "They ran on their bank accounts. By the time of the Buy-Ups most armies were professional. They worked for a paycheck, just like you and me. They worked for whomever *gave* them the paycheck. It was easy when the checks came from the King's exchequer or the Department of the Treasury. When it came from World Security International Incorporated? Or the Bank of Hong Kong? The lines of command became tangled. And weak.

"The change didn't happen with a big pageant. It took years. A lot of bloody years, according to the stuff I read. The Buy-Ups we know are actually this period, when the companies, and vestigial states, all fought each other for assets. There were thousands of companies at the start. Thousands. Not divisions or branches, but separate companies. Big corporations bought up smaller ones, or forcibly gobbled them up, until there were only three."

"And you read all this? You have this data?"

"They E.M.Peed on my office. While I was sitting there. Lost everything on my cuff. My back ups. Lost everything…"

Emory returned to the movie. Khaki clad soldiers with long, wooden guns stood blocking a throng of skinny men in thin cotton warps from advancing down a street. Emory had no idea what they wanted, but they seemed desperate, determined and destined to die.

"You think I made this up?"

"It doesn't matter," Emory said. "You're here. I'm here."

A man two rows in front of Emory rose. As he passed he tossed two packets of butter into Emory's lap. Emory spun. All he saw was the man's back, nearing the door. He walked fully upright, arms swinging, in no hurry. Emory flicked the butter away like bugs. He glanced at Campbell, who was polite enough to stay focused on the wall monitor, pretending to be entranced by the army raising their guns to their shoulders.

❦ · ❦

The woman said she'd talk to Sylvia so long as it didn't interfere with chores. Sylvia had no idea what that might entail. The woman was 91. Whatever her chores might be, she was sure she could keep up, even in her current roly-poly state. Corrida wore a long twill coat, with lots of hoops and pockets. She waddled through the stalls checking on gauges, fittings, and hoses. She patted the cows on the rump or nose, depending on their orient- ation. Each of the farm hands said good morning to her with a fair degree of reverence.

"If I'm working, they're working," she said. Her voice carried like an accordion. "I shame them into it."

"You run a tight ship, huh?" Sylvia followed behind her.

"Oh, I don't know. As long as everything's working right, I'm OK."

Sylvia waved Samjahnee ahead. She wanted him to film her and the dairymaid approaching, slowly, through the stiles. He skipped around them, stopping to set a globe on a gatepost. It would catch them passing. He could work the shot into the scene in post-production. He kept the other globe to film the old woman and Sylvia moving towards him.

"Do you find the Milkman insulting then?"

"God no, sweetie. Someone wants to take the time to tell everyone how good our milk is, I've got no issue with that.

No issue, none. We put out good milk here. Good milk. This Milkman's helping us."

"So you don't mind that he's questioning your integrity? Isn't he saying that your tests are either ineffective or nonexistent? Isn't he calling you a liar in a way?"

"Insulted? I'm old and fat and I can't remember what I had for breakfast. He's just testing, is all. He's testing to make sure I'm no liar. I'm not insulted somebody wants to test me. I'll tell you this— I've had hard tests. This ain't one."

"You're a proud woman, Corrida. You don't need this guy looking over your shoulder."

Corrida stopped and leaned back against a gate. An enormous heifer, a velvety grayish blue, stuck its nose through, rubbing it right against Corrida's shoulder. Sylvia thought the woman might tumble sideways, but she held. She breathed. Sylvia could hear her breath chug through her airways. She smacked her tongue inside her mouth.

"I fought in the Buy-Ups, you know," Corrida said.

"I didn't," Sylvia replied.

"I commanded a tank recovery vehicle. We were there when the House of Saud fell. A whole mess of us running around, trying to prop up the world while it crumbled like an old barn. You should've seen it."

"I wish."

"You don't. I got shot at by men I thought I was fighting along side. A woman piloting a tank did not go over well with our Arab friends. You ever get shot at by your co-workers?"

"Never even seen a gun."

"That there is the best thing to come out of this. I'll tell you that. Guns were a quick way to do something you can't undo. I was pleased as punch to be done with them, pleased when they sent me to the farm."

"Who sent you?" Sylvia's voice changed. It surprised her. The bite was gone. "How'd you get from the army to the farm?"

"Oh, I don't recall it all. All that craziness. I was only 20 years old. Mostly worried about staying alive. An oil company, I think it was Exxon, bought up my unit's contract from the United States of America. 'You're going private, private!' That was the joke back then. Then I think it was Unilever next? Or was it Pepsi? I think it was PepsiCo, as they were called at the time. When the fighting died down they sent we soldiers all over. I could drive big stuff, so I ended up on a farm in Davenport Catchment. I liked it there. I liked the new quiet."

Sylvia glanced at Samjahnee. He kept the camera on them. She didn't know if any of this had any value, but she wanted it. Every drop.

"When did you come here?" Sylvia asked.

"To Niagara? Let me see…" the woman tapped her puffed and spotted chin. "I got posted here about five years ago. The company wanted me to whip these boys into shape. Get production up."

"You got transferred at age 86," Sylvia said slowly. "Your family?"

"Scattered. You know how it goes. None of us got low enough to have any juice. We go where the company blows us."

"It doesn't seem to bother you."

Corrida chuckled. "Like I said about the Milkman, it's a all a matter of perceptive. Your generation doesn't quite get what it was like before. You don't fully get how good you have it. We worked that farm 12 hours a day every day. We didn't have sick days. You broke your arm, you worked. You couldn't work, there was always somebody around who could. Somebody who wanted to eat."

"Didn't everyone have a job?"

"Eventually. It took years for everything to settle down. All kinds of folk didn't know what to do and the companies didn't know what to do with them. I taught four accountants how to drive combines. You know what an accountant is?"

"Can't say as I do," Sylvia said.

"Not combine drivers, that's all I ever figured out. The Buy-Ups weren't all about battles and whatnot. Not like the movies. It was mostly about surviving. For a while there, a gallon of milk cost three days pay. You'd work all week for some oranges and a loaf of bread."

Sylvia touched her glasses. She wanted to zoom in on the woman's face. See if she could be any glint of fluid in her eyes. "So not being near your family doesn't hurt?"

Corrida stood straight, turned slightly and ran her hands through the cow's top most tuft of hair. "They are alive and well. That's something."

Sylvia patted the nose of the cow. "Belgian Blue."

"You know your cows."

"I did my homework. These are the prettiest."

"They make milk. Like you, soon enough." The old woman laughed.

❧ · ❧

Wayne Clement rowed on a machine in the Systems Security Gym every day (almost) at 11:45 a.m. Finding that in his personnel file took McCallum less than a second; deciding to look it up took a few days. Every search left a trail leading from that fact back to him. He didn't like trails. At least not to himself. McCallum quickly moved on to another file, a man associated with some sanitation removal case he was supposed to be working. If ever asked, he could claim an error. He had no reason to see Clement, so he had to run into him. By chance. Casually. As he did with nearly everyone else in the building when he didn't want to.

McCallum's workout times tended to be in the morning. He sparred with other ops, then swam a few hundred meters. Just enough to keep his medical coverage current. The last thing an active op needed was a lapse in health insurance. Visiting the gym in the middle of the day would be unusual if somebody was paying attention, but wouldn't set off any bells. So he changed into his shorts and T-shirt and walked towards the weights, by way of the rowing contraptions.

"Hey, Wayne," he said as he passed.

"Detective." Clement's voice came out clearly. No gasps or grunts.

McCallum knelt down next to the machine. Clement stopped cranking and sliding.

"I don't usually see you here." Clement dabbed his forehead with a small, red towel.

"I don't like to intimidate the rookies," McCallum said.

"What brings you here now?"

"You." McCallum lowered his voice. "I've got a question I didn't feel like digitizing."

Clement paused for a moment, face blank. Then he said, "This is a noisy place, isn't it?"

"Makes it easy to talk."

"Go oral, my friend. I'm already intrigued."

"You remember that Vasquez case?"

"Like my middle name. It never came together right."

"I got visited by a messenger the other night who's sole purpose was to inform me I'd written up the wrong man."

"You believe him."

"That's the easy part. I never thought the guy I tagged for the murder did it."

"There's a hard part?" Clement picked up a water bottle and snapped open the cap.

"I can't reclude the file without a revenue source."

"Ah." Clement took a long sip of his water.

"I know I'm stretching things thin, but if there's any potential..."

Clement turned in his seat and put his arms across his bent knees. "One of the worst parts of this system we've got is our shared ignorance. Ambyr decides it wants you to be a security operative, so they teach what they think you need to know and very little else. I'm no different. A couple of years ago my son told me plants take in carbon dioxide and give off oxygen. I thought he was messing with me. We argued about it until he convinced me to search it. Man, did I feel like an idiot. I've got my masters in economics and don't know how plants grow. I don't say this to insult you. Or me. It's just the way it is."

"I've picked up a few things along the way," McCallum said. "The job demands it."

Clement nodded. "You're a good man. You've stayed curious. I'm lamenting the mysteries of my profession. They shouldn't be mysteries. Of course, if everyone were an economist, the economy would cease to function."

"We've all got our place on the rope," McCallum said.

"Something like that." Clement ticked off a humorless snicker. "Do you think the girl was killed by someone from India Group or BCCA Hong Kong?"

"Not enough information."

"That's about the only way the company might make some money. Even then, it's a fight they don't always want to pick. Is the murderer going to kill again?"

"Don't know that either."

"That would drive up the opportunity cost of allowing the killer to remain in the marketplace. Other than that, I've got nothing."

"I hoped you might know some other trick."

"Ah, now I get it. Your world is short-cuts and scams. People trying to beat the system. That's your base of knowledge." Clement stretched his back and rolled his head around, stretching his neck muscles, popping the gases trapped in his spine.

"You know how the world works," Clement said. "You know all about bottom lines and who pays for what. What you don't know is why the world works the way it does and that's why you believe in tricks. My rules — the laws of supply and demand, the infinite repetitiveness of human choice — they can't be fooled. There are no tricks. I understand you are used to people bending policies, but these rules. They're structural."

McCallum sat back on the floor of the gym. "What don't I understand here?"

"Your problem is one of externalities. In that there aren't any anymore. For the company, with rare exceptions, all costs are internal."

"Including the cost of a young woman's life."

"In the old days you could have…" Clement held up his bottle of water. "A mining company, let's say. It mines iron efficiently, but there's a by-product. A nasty chemical that gets thrown into the river. It made people sick, but whatever. The company generated profit by mining iron.

"Now suppose that company's employees only drank water from the river they polluted? Suppose the company paid for their health care and sick time. Suppose the company educated all their employees from birth? Now that external cost of poisoning the river is forced inside. It's internal. They bear it. Ambyr and the others are just like that now. Every problem is their problem. They can't shove anything off onto anyone else."

"Murder's like poisoning those employees. The company doesn't profit from murder."

"The company doesn't profit from punishment, either."

"The girl had value."

"Whoever took her life has value, too. Odds are, the company paid for the killer's birth, education, dental care— everything it takes to create a decent worker. What are they going to do with that? Throw it away and double the cost of the girl's death?"

"The alternative work details. The chain gangs."

"They're deterrents. I guess. You'd know better than me. But they don't maximize productivity for everyone assigned. What if the killer's an aeronautics engineer? Or a neurosurgeon? It doesn't make sense to have employees with that level of education and skill filling potholes on the road. Not to mention the cost of removing a consumer from the market. Men and women on alternative work details aren't buying new sweaters or tickets to hockey games. They're not contributing to the economy to their fullest extent."

"So the company doesn't want my guy on the chain gang?" McCallum let a bit of hop into his voice.

"No," Clement said. "For the most part, they don't. They've found over the years that they need carrots *and* sticks. You're the stick. Ultimately, what they want is for the *right* people to be on chain gangs. The ones who *should* be painting the tops of bridges. If the company found someone to blame for the Vasquez murder, and they can extract equitable value from that person in a manner alternative to the open work place, they're made whole."

"There's a chance the real killer is from another company or is a lesser grade to the guy I tagged."

"Not a good chance. The first thing I did was consult an actuary. I looked at the odds on who committed the murder. You know the rest."

McCallum crossed his legs into a pretzel shape and straightened his back. He breathed in through his mouth and out through his nose, like his martial arts teacher had instructed him years ago. Clement took another sip from his bottle.

"It's not right," McCallum said.

"It's not meant to be," Clement replied. "It's profit maximization. Right and wrong are irrelevant."

"That is the why?" McCallum asked.

"Yes," Clement said.

"The only one?"

"I can't be drinking water and have that conversation. That sounds like a bourbon kind of talk."

McCallum almost smiled. Then he thought, and subsequently said, "I've got no way to free an innocent man."

Clement nodded. "None."

Chapter Fourteen

EMORY TRIED SLEEPING in a stall in the men's room. In many ways — in separate ways — the anticipation of the gang rapes were worse than the rapes themselves. Once an evening's attack began, he knew they'd be over soon. His stomach could untwist. He'd cease twitching at every creak and shuffle. His neck and shoulders could release their unrelenting hunch and the ache could seep away. So he tried the lavatory. Cold, brightly lit and with every surface hard enough to cut off blood from parts pressed too tight to the porcelain, the environment fought sleep in every way he could imagine. Other men came and went, knocking him out of whatever hazy state of pseudo-slumber he achieved through exhaustion.

He gave up twice, but returning to his cot made him sick. While being raped he tried to blank his mind. He didn't want to think of his family or Christmas or a warm, lush creek side. He didn't want to associate things he loved with the violation for fear that he wouldn't be able to uncouple them later. In freedom. When he had his real life back. The smell, however, had a main line to his memory. The scent of chemicals and sweat, the male-ness other than his own, it triggered revulsion as quickly and efficiently as the smell of rotting flesh, sulfur or spoiled milk.

Spoiled milk. He hated his own bed because of spoiled milk. Everyday he worked until his body gave out. Some nights he barely had strength enough to get soup into his mouth. If he didn't dip his bread, it was too hard to chew. Then he tumbled onto his cot and the smell reminded him of being rousted and rolled onto his knees. That op said he'd murdered a girl. The thought would be laughable, if it weren't so serious. No. He was here because of the milk.

Although even that didn't make a whole lot of sense. Ambyr Consolidated could have shut him down at any time. He always figured some day he'd go to post and find his access denied. The company owned the network, the storage, the satellites, towers and power to make it all function. They could bar him from doing anything they wanted with a few keystrokes. Why this? It's not like they needed a systems guy to help fix the sewers. They'd be better off snatching some civil engineers, if that's what they needed.

He darted into the men's room. Balancing on the toilet and trying to sleep was near impossible. Still, he thought it worth a try.

He thought wrong. He knew as the men's room door opened and multiple footsteps echoed on the tile. At night, men didn't travel in groups. Late night potty breaks were a singular call. They smashed open the stall door. It sounded like thunder when the lighting hits just inches away. They hauled him out. Four of them. He saw their faces. He didn't want to. He tried to close his eyes tight, waiting for the storm to pass. Every swirl and spin exacted a peek. He saw each one, in complete detail.

Clark was the leader. Lean and mean, he was in his fifties, and it looked like all of them had been hard. Gem could have been two Emories put together. Conner and Teddy were young. He didn't know much about them. During the day he didn't notice them much at all. Quiet and surly, which were not attributes that made one stand out on the chain gang.

The hardness of the tile floor hurt their knees as they took him from behind. The third guy dug his knees into Emory's calves, creating a whole new level of pain. In the morning, he struggled with the yellow plastic suit, legs refusing to bend enough, joints on fire, his rectum still moist with blood.

❧ · ❧

"I'm only trying to do right by my baby, you know?" The woman said, bouncing the child on her thigh, keeping him close to her chest. He looked at the lights, smiling, Sylvia thought, though it was a matter of opinion. His tiny mouth bowed open like a wet flower. Samjahnee's lights made the baby's enormous eyes sparkle like sapphires. The lights delighted him, the blue mound of sweater. So happy…

"Certainly," Sylvia said. "You want to make sure your baby's getting good, wholesome milk. Because he didn't always."

97

The mom's mouth opened. Her eyebrows rose. She seemed so much younger when surprised, Sylvia thought. And the younger the better. People have inherent sympathy for mothers like this one, pretty in a plain way, unadorned by jewelry or obvious makeup, wearing a pink sweater and jeans you could buy in any catchment on the continent. Her curly brown hair would have looked amazing, if she didn't devote all her time to her baby. People sense those things, and find them comforting.

Let's keep her shocked and looking 16.

"Little Ian, there," Sylvia said. "His medical records indicate a nasty bacterial infection around his first birthday. After you stopped breast feeding."

"How did you—"

"I bought his medical records. I bought records for a lot of children in the region. Those with intestinal problems that could have been milk related, my staff cross-checked with the pur-chasing records of their parents. You, for instance. Since the illness you've been driving 26 miles out of your way to buy milk approved by the Milkman. The speed limit is 35, so that means you put an hour into your milk purchasing, when there's a store four minutes from your house."

"I'm choosey."

"So it seems. Did you know 18 other people reported sickness after consuming the milk you used to buy?"

"I didn't know that."

"Nobody wants you to know that. Except the Milkman."

"Why are you doing this?"

"Don't worry. There's no policy against viewing the Milkman's posts."

"No." The woman clutched her baby, pumping her leg as if blowing up a ball. "I mean this is never going to make it into the movie. Why are you even bothering? The company's going to kill this thing faster than you can say 'screw you lady'."

Sylvia grinned. The mom had plenty of spunk. She hoped Samjahnee wasn't getting any shadows on her face. She needed this woman to look pure, not spooky. Shadows would make people doubt her.

"I'm just trying to collect background," Sylvia said. "Get an understanding as to what the Milkman does, why it might be important. Why someone might want to read his posts."

"You don't know?" She diverted her eyes to Sylvia's belly. She looked back up at Sylvia and bobbed her head forward, eyes wide again, mouth saying 'huh?' sans sound.

"Cut," Sylvia said.

"Seriously, Ms. Cho. How far along are you?"

"That's not part of this." Sylvia spun her head towards Samjahnee. He sat on a folding stool a meter behind her, gazing into a thin, flat monitor. He rubbed his chin, looking up when he realized the conversation had stopped.

"Did you hear me say cut?"

He pressed his right index finger to the lower left corner of the monitor. "We're clear."

"Sorry," the mom said. "I just figured, you know… babies don't come with an instruction video."

"Perhaps that will be my next project," Sylvia slipped.

The woman forced a smile at Sylvia and turned her attention to her son. She patted him on his head and told him he was a good boy in a cooing, cascading voice.

"After I find this god damned Milkman," Sylvia said, mostly to herself.

"It must be your first." The mom didn't look at Sylvia. She played with her baby. "You'd be asking different questions if you had a child."

"Really," Sylvia snapped. "You learn all kinds of motherly secrets when the little things pop out."

"Not right away, but you learn. Don't we little guy? We learn."

"And what questions would you ask?"

"Not if I visited the Milkman's post, I can tell you that. Why wouldn't you? The question is whether or not it matters. Are the reports good and usable? Has the Milkman, you know, saved you and your family from getting sick?"

"Such wisdom. Did any of this—"

"The break that refreshes," played in her ear. A deep male voice with soulless guitar music behind it. "Coke."

"Arrr." She had told her cuff to hold calls, notes, messages of any kind. She jerked it in front of her face like she might bite it. The thumbnail-sized screen flashed red. She slapped it, bolted up and stomped towards the front door of the house.

"Yes," she blasted out into the cold.

"Ms. Cho, this is Walter Whelen. Human Assets."

"Yes," she stretched out with lots of extra breadth, ensuring Walter Whelen knew she was already quite bored with him.

"You're being recalled."

"What?"

"You need to report to Mortimer Clive's office Thursday morning for your new assignment."

"What the fuck are you talking about?"

"Your supervisor, Ms. Cho. You are being returned to the grounds keeping crew at the Vermillion Office Complex."

❦ · ❦

McCallum knew why the test funneled him into police work. Testing was one of the few things the companies did well. Growing up, he never considered becoming an op for a second, not even in pre-teen years, when every boy gets model armored cars, gold badges and hollow plastic truncheons to wail away on each other, burning off boyish energy and aggression. Little Eddie never bothered with that stuff. He liked to draw.

Not that he didn't have his share of boyish energy and aggression. He ran, jumped and played with other kids in the neighborhood. He loved hide'n seek. He won that game more than any other kid he knew, maybe more than any other in the Buffalo catchment. They had to make special rules for him, to make things more fair. You couldn't hide more than five feet off or under the ground. Eddie had the ability to scan an area and see things before a count of ten that other kids would never see. He couldn't have known his talent would be spotted and slotted, as they say in the human assets business.

McCallum saw, in any scene, both the detailed and the abstract, the real and the possible, the nuts and bolts and the high purpose of their conjoining. He nurtured and grew the talent, from doodles, to sketches, to large oil on canvas works that brought his first art teacher to tears. He didn't figure out why she cried until about two years later, when Human Assets gave him his track. The company recognized his ability to put together big pictures from small details, to fill in the blanks, connect the dots, follow not the clues left behind by some tea-drinking writer in a cottage outside Sheffield, but the scraps left in a stupid, messy policy breach. The company didn't need any artists, it needed ops. If Eddie wanted to doodle, he could do it on his own time.

Like usual, the company was right and wrong at the same time. He knew his art had merit. If he had more time, more feedback, more training, he knew he could kick art ass. They were wrong not to let him pursue it. They were right about him being a good op. He knew when something didn't look right.

Emory Leveski didn't murder Geri Vasquez or John Raston. He had the nagging feeling that the latter wasn't even dead. The gleaming white of that unpainted corner, that place in the painting reserved for John Raston kept him awake at night, like a streetlight through your hotel window. It pulled his mind from other focal points, the way a fleck of white fuzz can ruin an old photo. Tugging the eye, pulling the eye, always diverting attention to itself. John Raston and his gasoline powered off-road vehicle. The asshole needed a conversation.

All he had to do was find him.

McCallum was supposed to be investigating a possible theft of services from a refuse crew. An Ambyr restaurant split a building with one owned by BCCA/Hong Kong Holdings, common but never a good idea from corporate's perspective. In this case, the Ambyr restaurant seemed to be cranking out 40 percent more trash than the waste systems department expected. The garbage squad could easily be picking up BCCA trash and getting some kind of pay back under the table. They requested a detective be assigned. The missing person, the dead girl, the pitiful schlub on a chain gang for no reason… no. None of that required one of Ambyr Systems Security's top detectives. Eight extra bags of trash per week? That demanded his complete and immediate attention.

He remembered Lillian's Leveski's car from reading her dossier four months ago. He had no idea why details like that stuck with him, but it came in handy. He didn't want a file search to register with headquarters. No records were the best records. He chuckled to himself. The margin between ops and robbers was so thin they couldn't help wobbling back and forth over it most of the time. It probably never occurred to the company that the traits of a young artist or future safety operative, could also make for an excellent arch insubordinate.

The Leveski woman had recently purchased a Mahindra Civet. It had two electric motors, the type of upgrade young couples purchased when they have recently started to keep a little bit more money than they brought in, when they thought they could see farther down the road and everything looked smooth and bright. Silver, shaped like raindrop sliding on glass, the car had a natural, organic prettiness McCallum found acceptable. They must have figured their careers were tracking upward.

The car passed him. McCallum pulled his pursuit vehicle out into traffic. Non-reflective black, a hunting knife with a shiny hilt, McCallum answered more questions about the pursuit vehicle than any other part of his job. Did he buzz it out every chance he got? Did he want to be op just so he could drive it? Did it really do 60 miles per hour? He made up answers depending on the questioner. Some guys got to hear how it sucked onto the road, all four motors working together made it handle like a train. And it could actually spin in place if needed. Some guys got the truth. It had all the comforts of a dentist's chair, fit like an oversized hockey helmet and let you see as much of the world around you as a hangover. He found it amazing that he saw Lillian's car at all through the thin strips of glass.

McCallum flipped the light-bar switch. Red and blue strobes blasted across the top of the op car. Confident that she'd done nothing wrong, it took Lillian almost a mile to pull over. He pulled in behind and got out. The cold snapped at McCallum as he approached the side of the car. He wore jeans and a pea-coat, so he figured the poor woman might not lower the window right away. He tried to make his walk casual, knowing for all 25 feet that he could very well be making things worse.

The curved glass slid into the curved door. Lillian looked at him, stern, then puzzled, then horrified a lot faster than McCallum planned.

"You," she spat. "You?"

"I've sorry, Mrs. Leveski—" McCallum started.

"Sorry? For stealing my husband?"

"For stopping you now. This way. I guess you remember me."

"I'll remember your face for the rest of my life. Have I done something wrong? I'm going to call for a female op, if you don't mind." Lillian raised her left wrist, turning her band.

"I do," he said. "If you can give me a moment."

Lillian's finger lingered over the 'on' button.

"I don't think your husband killed anyone."

"You got that right."

"I've got no budget line for an investigation. It's cleared."

"I don't... You want money?"

"Do you have any?"

"Jesus Christ, this is a shakedown? You should've dug into the data, sir. I'm broke. Beyond broke. We bought the house and had the baby on two incomes. Now it's one. Less than one. Did you know the company still draws pension funds, even though Emory's income's been suspended? I'm about to lose the house. Every month that he's on the chain gang is another we go deeper in debt. We're already buried and he hasn't even had his hearing yet." Her voice rose to a screech. "He hasn't even had his hearing yet! Sir!"

McCallum let the 'sir' reverberate and settle into the swish of the passing traffic. "Do you know John Raston?"

"Yes," Lillian said. "I know him."

"I'm looking for him."

"And..." She didn't understand; McCallum did.

"He doesn't have his bracelet."

Lillian faced forward, eyes focusing out through her front windshield. "Old crusty jerk-wad."

"Mrs. Leveski?"

"I always knew he'd get Emory into some trouble. I knew it, just not how... and I never figured anything like this. You see, sir, they weren't matched up well. Emory had so much going for him. John Raston had nothing."

"Can you help me find him?" McCallum asked. "Do you have any idea where he might have gone?"

"God help him if I did." She looked back at McCallum. "He's gone off line. He's been prepping to be an ollie for years. Maybe his whole life."

An ollie, McCallum said to himself. Off into the wilderness. No communication, no money, no trace.

"Thank you for your time," McCallum walked back to his car. He couldn't be around Lillian Leveski any more. He saw people getting chewed in the cogs of society every day. He usually escaped feeling like one of the teeth. She didn't allow that and he couldn't blame her.

CHAPTER FIFTEEN

EMORY HAD TROUBLE grasping his plastic spork. His skin had grown so dry his joints cracked along the sides when he closed his hands. White-toped crevasses, red and pink beneath, he could peer into them, amazed that so much burning pain could emanate from such tiny fractures, amazed that the cuts even existed. To work all day in the wet, only to have your skin desiccate to the point of cracking. Not fair. Not fair. Not fair.

"The nurse will give you cream." Campbell sat down across from Emory. He placed his tray on the table.

"Never thought to ask," Emory said. "They ignore everything."

"Unless it interferes with your productivity. If you get to where you can't pick up a tool, they'll give you some cream."

"Splendid." Emory sporked some gray, mashed potatoesque substance into his mouth. He had to be careful not to let this batch stick to the roof of his mouth. The last one almost killed him. About 50 other men sat in the big room, eating what the company called dinner, Emory didn't think one of them would notice him choking, or, if they did, leave their food to save him. Except maybe Campbell.

"They can't escape healthcare." Campbell studied his tray like a puzzle. "Right down to the moisturizer."

"So I've got that going for me."

"Health care's funny that way. They pretty much have to provide it. You can't have people curling up and dying on the street."

"We pay for it," Emory said.

"Oh sure. They turned it into a revenue draw. I haven't figured out how it started. If one of the three companies offered it, the other two had to fall in or fall out. Or, they absorbed huge healthcare companies in the Buy-Ups and momentum took over. I never found any definitive data."

"Maybe it was both," Emory picked up the shingle of brown protein and ripped off a chunk with his canines.

"Probably both," Campbell said. "Much of what happened during that time had more than one cause. You don't have paradigm switches that big without a large number of factors in play."

"The world is a complex system," Emory said.

Campbell ate some of his potato stuff.

"Like that." Emory pointed his spork at Campbell's mouth. "You need to eat smaller bites or you'll never get it down, where your stomach can start breaking it down to even smaller parts."

"True. You break healthcare down, it gets simple. You're born into a company, they educate you, they develop an interest in keeping you alive while you're useful."

Emory said. "It's a closed system."

"Yes. Once the companies established complete control it was just that. Complete. The good and the bad."

"You think they bit off more than they can chew?" Emory made a tiny smile at his own joke. The right corner of his lip cracked, like his knuckles. He had not smiled in a while.

Campbell made a light, listless chuckle. "In a way, I think you're right. In the old days, companies could shed what they didn't like, or no longer needed, in their striving for profit and growth. When they reached the end, they lost the abilities that got them that far. They now have everything and can rid themselves of nothing."

"A system can't really work that way." Emory finished his peach slice, the best part. The taste you wanted to be last in your mouth. "Nothing is perpetual. There's always waste."

"Yeah." Campbell spread his arms and rotated at the hips. "And you're looking at it."

They both glanced around, forever wary of a tussle, an advance, a change in the fragile balance of each moment. The Alternative Work Detail resembled a closed system, Emory learned. No one, not the workers, not the supervisors, had a way out. It busted in on itself every so often. A fight. A protest. A boiling in everyone, at the same time, that blew apart the brief periods of peace. He mused over possible repairs. Moving guys around, chopping shifts, acknowledging holidays — humans seemed to need pivotal points in time — or the occasional party. He knew of an auto-parts factory in the Hamilton catchment that brought in hobbyists for company-sponsored sex parties. The plant saw increased output numbers that far outweighed the costs.

That wasn't going to happen here. None of it would happen here. Emory had ended up in a place with no ideas.

"Suicide," Campbell said.

"That's not an answer," Emory said. "That's quitting."

"Not us, capitalism," Campbell continued. "That system couldn't last either. It had to kill itself."

"I thought this was capitalism?" Emory ran an up-turned palm in a semicircle, displaying the room.

"I don't know what this is. It's not the capitalism that's in the files, though. It's nothing like the pre-Buy Up era. It couldn't be. That was my point."

"Capitalism committed suicide," Emory conferred.

"Self-destructed, would be a better term." Campbell nodded at his own correction. "It had to. It was based on competition and competitions eventually come to an end."

Emory lifted a spork full of gray goo and held it in front of his mouth. "They ate each other up until there were just three fat corporations with nothing left to eat." He put the goo in his mouth.

"Capitalism ate itself to death." Campbell laughed.

"Not a bad way to go," Emory said.

"I can think of worse ways."

"So what do we have now?" Emory asked. "What system do we have?"

"I don't know. Nobody talks about it. There's no market for that kind of thinking. There's no school for strictly intellectual pursuits."

"Just a hobbyist, then. One of those philosophers with his own post or one of those anthropology clubs. Maybe some hobbyist has a name for this system."

"Oh," Campbell said, "That kind of hobbyist."

"There's only one kind," Emory said. "Believe me. There's only one kind."

❦ · ❦

"I had to get on the train because I wasn't going to make it to Atlanta otherwise," Sylvia said through a mouth so thin and tight the words ricocheted. They caught other passengers in the car. They couldn't help but look her way, which made her even angrier. Public arguments were unseemly. Low class. Worse than riding coach on a train speeding across a frozen countryside of concrete slab buildings, industrial towers, conveyors and other crap she didn't care to see.

"Where is Samjahnee?" Gavin Stoll's voice entered her ear.

"You should be more worried about where I am."

"You are the least of my worries," Gavin said. "We'll straighten this out."

"I left Sam in the Lockport catchment, with the truck. He'll collect B-roll while I ride the rails like some hobo." She re-crossed her legs and smoothed out her cashmere skirt. The older couple across from her went back to their monitors, watching some tripe about spies or pirates, she imagined. At least trains had legroom. She couldn't imagine cramming this belly of hers into the last seat on an airship.

"We're checking things right now," Gavin continued. "According to our records, your assigned employer, Vermillion Holdings, has accepted the last six pay differentials. They are, in fact, 10 percent more than the man they've got filling your position. We shouldn't be hearing a dribble from these bastards. They're going to lose money taking you back."

"Is this a milking?"

"Pun intended?"

"Do they want more, Gavin. Is a 10 percent differential not enough?"

"They didn't tell us otherwise. We tagged onto the same agreement you established with Marshall. We pay them off so we can have you. They never complained. If this is a leveraging move, they don't appear to know what they're doing. You don't call Human Assets first. God, you never call them at all if you can help it."

"You've got to fix this, Gavin. I'm not going back to land-scaping. I'm not. Ever."

"We don't want you to." His voice sounded like salve, Sylvia thought. Too soothing. She'd tell him to dial it back if she were directing this scene, which she wasn't and that fact made her angrier than all the other facts combined.

"Then take it up a notch," she said. "Call our investors and get this guy juiced. I was almost done up there, you know."

"I know."

You do? Sylvia thought. *Save for later.* "I had a couple of beefy leads on this Milkman. A few more days and I would have…"

"What?"

"Nothing," she said. How stupid. Did she think it would be that easy? Like finding a lost earring? The Milkman would sit and wait as if this were a great game of hide and seek. She'd find him under the stairs and they'd laugh and have lemonade and she'd capture it all on video.

"Forget the whole thing," Sylvia said. "What a silly lark."

"I don't understand."

"The movie, Gav. The movie was going nowhere."

"You just said—"

"I just said I didn't want to go back to landscaping, but that's my true calling. Putting it off any longer isn't going to help."

"B—"

"Don't bother with Mister… what's his name?"

"I don't know. Clive?"

"Clive. Yes. I'll see him soon enough. You get out, enjoy the sun. What's the weather like on the coast?"

"Fine. 72, like always."

"I'm headed for some heat myself. And looking forward to it. I'll be in touch."

Sylvia slapped her index finger across her bracelet. Then she slapped it again. And again. She slapped it 12 times — until it stung too much — as the couple across from her watched.

❧ · ❧

The bamboo framed out a box big enough to hold a man, if your intention was to get him to turn on his friends after a few days. Thin nylon fishing line crossed through the structure, meeting occasionally in fat, elaborate knots. The knots caught the ambient light, making them much more visible than the line. Standing back, looking through, the knots formed undulating patterns. A calm wave? A snake? A woman on her side, satisfied? All three?

McCallum loved it. He couldn't imagine how long the piece must have taken. His beer grew warm as he strolled around it, wanting to view if from every possible angle, forgetting to sip. The intricacy. The statement. He couldn't move on to the rest of the works, fully aware they could be even better.

"Hypnotic, isn't it?" That voice from a crypt. McCallum turned, panning the gallery spotted with people mingling, nibbling, trying not to spill their red wine on the white everything, none of whom were addressing him. Then he looked down. Aga Graber looked up, holding a partially filled brandy snifter with two hands. Five foot in heels, she wore a floor-length black crepe gown. Her curly salt and pepper hair lay flat and wide across her head, making her look, at the moment, like a mushroom, McCallum thought.

The thought made him smile. "Can't part from it."

"Then buy it," Aga said. "That's what it's for."

"I don't think it's in my area of affordability."

"Eh, you'd be amazed. She's young and poor. No name yet. It would be a good investment."

"I'm sure," McCallum turned back to the sculpture. "Still outside an op's salary."

"I suspect the real reason may be your loft is already filled to the shingles with art."

"That is also true." McCallum smiled again.

"I can help you with that."

"I know."

"I've been asking for years."

"I know."

"Someday I'm going to stop asking and then what are you going to do?"

McCallum turned. His grin popped, leaving his lips parted and curled.

"You're an artist, Eddie."

"And an op," he added. "Who dabbles in art."

"It should be the other way around."

"Being a professional artist would be no better. I can't imagine having a boss tell me what to paint and how to paint or not to paint at all. I couldn't function properly. I couldn't do my best work working for the company."

"Can any of us?"

What a great question, McCallum thought, peering through the strings and knots at the intersections of balled, glossy spectrums. *Can you do your best work for the company or do you need to leave to achieve greatness? To get something done that is complex and hard? Something the company simply won't let you do?*

One could connect those knots in so many different ways. The curve of the helix, the arc of the sun. The artist had had to get right in there, into the web and work her way out, envisioning the whole project first, crafting backward. The meticulous tying and stringing. He couldn't see any short cuts. It took true devotion to create a piece of art like this.

"You are right," McCallum said. "About the dabbling. Nothing profound was ever done by dabbling."

CHAPTER SIXTEEN

WINTER HAD ITS upside. Every aspect of the sewer rebuild moved slower. The ice and cold weighed on the electric winches, cranes, forklifts and trucks, even more so on the human operators. Even the foreman who reveled in pushing and pushing and pushing the alternative work force let their shouting and growling trail off as cables snapped, pipes cracked, mud froze in the extruder, constipating the entire operation. Emory would not have picked the dim, frigid tunnels for his breaks. Sitting down on the cold, concave, soiled surfaces provided almost as many challenges as working. Still, you rested where and when offered. Plopping down in salty snow slush was better than shoveling it.

Like most days, Campbell and Emory sat alone, at the farthest most portion of the pipe. Their job involved placing the struts and beams that reinforced the walls and ceiling, preparing the way for the rest of the crew. Today, no one followed. No one seemed to move much at all.

"They must hate you." Campbell lay curled like a fetus under a tarp. The wrapping's murky, wet translucence made a plastic womb.

"Why?" Emory asked, laying back on a brace he decided not to install. It fit so nicely in that curve of his neck, between the back of his head and his shoulders. "Because they paired me with you?"

"Yes. We've got the most dangerous job on the detail. Most floods and cave-ins happen before you jim jam it."

"Maybe they think we're the best," Emory said. "The best of the worst."

"You get it on with some low grade's wife?"

"I killed a man for asking too many questions."

Campbell chuckled. "No... something bad, though."

All the prying. The nosiness. Emory understood it. You put a bunch of guys together, all the time, with little else to occupy them besides chiseling dirt and conversations weave and wander. He didn't like it, though. He didn't like Campbell's persistence. *Curiosity,* he wondered. Or more? No. Stupid thought. The company wouldn't plant someone here to extract information from him. They'd torture him, right? Of course, this felt an awful lot like torture and they got some value out of it. They could have made a deal with Campbell. Time off for information on Emory, the Milkman and the enterprise he created.

Time to change the subject. "How did the Buy-Ups happen?" Emory asked.

"Oh, now you're interested."

"No. I'd like to be playing with my baby," Emory said. "Or drinking coffee in bed with my wife. But you're what I've got."

Campbell sat up, keeping the tarp tight under his neck. "A confluence of events, my friend. A confluence. I told you how the boundaries between public and private interests broke down. Security was the big one, but services morphed as well. The mail, sanitation and regulation of all sorts got handed over to private firms. The government had less and less to do, but the price tag still grew. At the same time, these companies wanted more and more rights. They paid taxes, so they figured they should get to act like citizens. Big, fat citizens with multiple addresses, crossing international borders. You understand about borders?"

"Yeah," Emory said. "Like big fences that kept people separated. Rulers had so much land and so many people and that's how it all got marked off."

"Except for multinational corporations. They had influence across borders."

"Which made them bigger than the rulers."

"Right," Campbell said. "These rulers became nothing more than middle men. Companies gave the orders, governments carried them out. But it wasn't a very efficient system. Sometimes the rulers didn't listen. They started wars when they weren't supposed to, or ended them too soon. Failed to protect shipping lanes or opened them up. Company control was indirect. More importantly, it was expensive. They realized they had all these presidents, representatives and members of parliament on payroll, paid to act like mouthpieces and they weren't even all that good at it. What was the point?"

Emory shook his head. "Didn't people like their governments? I mean, it was them, right? Not the kings and queens, but the other kind. The kind with elections. That was anybody, right?"

Campbell shrugged his shoulders. The tarp warped. New troughs sent new trickles of water down from Campbell's head. "I think it started out that way. Didn't seem to work, though."

"Maintenance," Emory said, mostly to himself. "Every system needs monitoring and maintenance. Nothing's perpetual."

"Change," Campbell said. "Change is perpetual."

"Entropy feels that way."

"Entropy?"

"The decay of order. It's the enemy of any system— biological, astronomical, political. Everything."

"What kind of engineer did you say you were?"

"There's the kind that prevents trouble," Emory said. "And there's the kind that deals with it. I graduated from the latter."

"I could've taught there."

Emory laughed. Just two chuckles. It took too much energy to really open up and guffaw. They both paused and listened to the clanking of other men, down the pipe. Long gaps stretched out between cracks of metal on metal.

"You didn't answer my question," Emory said. "I've studied large, complex systems and while they tend to wear, they also tend to evolve. The bigger the system, the more entrenched. How did the companies finally take over from established governments?"

"That's what I spent a long time studying. How did we get from there to here? The thing I didn't see... the thing most people don't see, is that there's no one step. There's no enormous knife switch the companies threw and 'click' everything changes ownership. Like all insubordinations, this one had a means, motive and opportunity. The motive was always clear. All companies want profit, stability and growth. Takeovers have always been great options. The opportunity came as corporate power and government debt intersected. You should see some of the prices I saw on military hardware. You wouldn't believe me. It took me years to believe them myself. A billion dollars an airplane? I thought maybe money had different values back then, but no. A billion is the annual salary of 28,000 people. That's the number of people it took to build one plane for the purpose of shooting down some other government's plane that took 28,000 people a year to build."

Emory huffed. "The governments sound as screwed up as the companies."

"Pretty much. At least, when they weren't playing nice with each other. Anyway, that brings us to the means. And it's a lot simpler than you think." Campbell waited.

Emory didn't guess. He didn't have a good guess or the energy to try to create one.

"It's on everyone's wrist." Campbell held up his scuffed, white ceramic bracelet, the one the company gave him when they assigned him to the alternative work detail. "Commerce and communication. Once they got together, the world changed."

"That's the weapon of revolution? The wrist phone?"

"It's more than that. It's your link with society. Your strongest link. Think about it, man. Can you prove who you are without it? Can you buy anything? Talk to anyone out of ear's reach? Do you know what's going on in the world? Your body is only a part of your life. A little part, and not even the most important part. You're a ball of numbers to the company— and to everyone else you're not actually touching. Whoever controls that link, that bridle, can jerk you around like an old pony. A puppet."

"A puppet pony," Emory said.

"Go and live with the off-liners for a while. You'll see what a marionette looks like once the strings have been cut. Governments used to print money and stamp coins. They used to provide postal services and regulate telegrams, telephones and television. Once they gave that up... it was giving up."

"I'm not disagreeing with you. I miss my cuff. I miss it more than I could have imagined, but it's not a chain."

"You're glib." Campbell rolled over, rustling his tarp.

"I'm cold and tired and hungry," Emory replied.

"What's to prevent you from getting up and walking away? Huh?" Campbell sat upright, pointing at Emory. "Anybody keeping guard back there? Anybody tell you today you can't just start running wee wee wee all the way home? There's no dog or fence or big beefy guy with a halberd? Know what I'm saying? No. Those things would stop the fleshy you, which no one even cares about. The non-corporeal you— that's what you're protecting. That's what they've got captive."

"I can't—"

"Sure you can," Campbell cut in. "Get up. Go see your wife and baby."

"It's not that—"

"Go. You love them. You miss them. Go. Walk home."

"You know it can't be done."

"Get out!"

"Drop it."

"Get out. Go!"

"I said drop it!"

"Pathetic shell of a man."

"Crazy fuck."

"You asked me how the companies took over," Campbell said. "Now you know. They took over everything and everyone the same way they took over you. They gave you everything you wanted."

❦ · ❦

Atlanta was chillier than Sylvia expected, but she couldn't get away with an ermine coat. Which suited her just fine, she decided. She'd let her new boss see her new belly. Pregnancy threw people off a bit. Men more so. She strolled into the management offices of the Vermillion Office Complex in a simple white wool jacket, left to fly open as she advanced.

"Ms. Cho?" the assistant asked as she pushed through the glass doors. Young, male, nondescript.

"You must be Todd," she said, dropping her coat from her shoulders.

"A… no, it's Rog—"

"I'm used to calling the shots. Naming the names, you know what I mean, Todd?"

"Rog—"

"Ra, Ra, right you are. I'm a team player, too. You'll see. So is the coach in?"

"A… yes. He's waiting for—"

"I don't wait myself. I make things happen." Sylvia continued past the desk into the office.

Mortimer Clive sat behind a gray steel desk so dull Sylvia smiled. She would've hugged the set designer who provided this piece for a movie about a lifeless bureaucrat. The desk held nothing but two monitors — the kind you picked up and held in your hand — and a streaked and spotted coffee cup. Yet, somehow, it still looked unorganized. Thinning black hair swept back in a wave of gooey product, Clive peered over steepled fingers, as if deep in thought. He had a trim, black moustache and goatee. And a black, short-sleeve turtleneck sweater. It made the whole trip worth it. A short-sleeve turtleneck. The smile that started when she saw the desk broke into a full-faced beam.

"Mr. Clive, it is very nice to meet you." Sylvia shot her hand across the desk.

He didn't rise. "Charmed." But shook her hand.

Sylvia motioned to one of the two chairs facing the desk. Gray, steel, a thin pad of brown plastic on the seats and backs, she figured she better make this quick. Either of these would make her ass numb up in seconds. Clive nodded. She sat.

"Ms. Cho, I know this must be awkward," Clive said.

"What?" Sylvia returned.

"Being recalled. I was told you were in the middle of another project."

"It doesn't have to be awkward for you, Mr. Clive. And please, call me Sylvia. I don't imagine you were the one to reassign me. Getting me pulled off a major motion picture takes a great deal of juice. I mean no offense, but this is below your pay grade. Mine too. You and I are furniture being moved about the room, Mr. Clive."

"Mortimer, will be fine."

"How about Morty?"

"That would be... Let's wait on that."

"Like I told your boy out there, I'm not much of a waiter. For instance, who was it? Who told you to call me in?"

Clive's head recoiled a quarter-inch. "I'm not at liberty to say."

"Well we'll have to liberate that. The saying." She winked. "My new assignment. Let's talk about it."

"Right." Clive placed a splayed hand over one of the two monitors and slid it across the desktop. Sylvia took it up and thumbed it on. "We're in the design phase now. We're preparing for spring. The parameters and budget are there."

"How is that possible?" Sylvia asked.

"They're in the memory."

"I thought you said we were in the design phase?"

"Right."

"And you brought me several hundred miles to participate in the design?"

"Right."

"Then how could the budget and parameters be set? Whoever chose me to design the grounds for this building just jerked aside another project worth millions, because he or she wanted Sylvia Cho. They worked their magic, played whatever corporate chips they had, to leverage me into this spot. They want to be able to say to everyone at their club that a world famous director decided where to put their peach trees and marigolds. The low grade that did this is a show-off. He or she deals in prestige. Prestige is the coin of the realm. The new black. And there's nothing quite as prestigious as making people do something they otherwise would not. Like me. Sitting here. So the fucking end product better look fucking good, don't you think?"

Mortimer Clive sat back and pressed his finger tips back together into a pointy sculpture. He studied her, she thought, like a presentation. A 3D diorama that would tell him how the project would proceed.

Head lowered, eyes over the peaks of his fingers, he said, "I like my coffee with cream and one sugar."

❧ · ❧

The string sculpture inspired McCallum. He always thought that acts of insubordination, sabotage, or breaches in policy were works of art. Not good art. Not pleasant art. But they were crafts, sometimes simple, other times intricate, that made one thing look like another. As smudges of charcoal on parchment could call to mind a meadow in winter or a woman pondering her missteps, a guy could look like he was doing his job all day, not dropping every one-thousandth tube of toothpaste coming off his line into his boot.

And if indiscretions could be art, perhaps he could make one. Any decent artist could — maybe should — be insubordinate on occasion.

He told his chief he'd received a tip that someone might be skimming gasoline from the emergency generator supply at the water plant. It was an oral tip. In high confidence. No traces. No one liked to mess with the water supply, so the chief gave him a slush-line budget to investigate. $1,200. Tops. McCallum told him that would be fine for a cursory look see.

The funds gave him enough time and cover to run video checks for gasoline-powered vehicles on the shared roads. He started near John Raston's house, six months in the past, and spiraled out.

Raston was a god damned ferret. The computer could pick out human faces from partial profiles behind tinted glass passing at 35 miles per hour. It couldn't find a single red Jeep. McCallum knew he'd left at night, and the vehicle had no need of roads. He didn't think the man could miss all the cameras, though. Not all 24,000 on the roads alone. Even sticking to fields and ditches could only get you so far. You couldn't go ten miles in this region without needing to cross a bridge.

Unless he didn't run that far? McCallum initially figured Raston was hundreds of miles from home by now. Maybe thousands. Maybe he figured wrong. John could've run and hid in the area he knew best. All that farm country and woods just south of Lake Ontario. John could be living less than 25 miles from his house.

McCallum expanded the timeline of the search. No way that Jeep carried enough supplies for six months. John may have used it this winter to build up his stores.

Two hours later the computer had a hit. McCallum's monitor showed him a few seconds of a Jeep, possibly red, with a canvas roof and side drapes, crossing a bridge up in the greater Niagara Falls catchment. It had a Christmas tree tied to the top.

McCallum checked his budget. $567. Not enough to raise anyone's eyebrows. He sent a message to his chief that the gasoline thing was dead. Then, for the first time in recent memory, he asked for a week of vacation.

— Chapter Seventeen —

THE WHOLE OF the modern world works for me, Sylvia told an interviewer back at the start of the new year. She had tried for bravado without arrogance. She wasn't quite sure she had pulled it off. The sentiment held true, though. Everyones' lives lie spread open for the world to peruse. Everyone had a story, plain to see, if you took the time to look. She did. Then she shaped those stories into documentary films. A term she still used, even though reels and developing and silver nitrate were so far in the past she knew them only from the pictures. Moving pictures.

She sat in a café that offered free monitor use. Order a cup of tea, tap your cuff on the port and you didn't have to look at the tiny screen on your bracelet. The noise and meandering people were a welcome by-product. She liked watching people almost as much as she liked watching movies. She liked trying to puzzle out their personal stories from the way they dressed, walked, tried not to look at that gorgeous boy two tables over who seemed oh-so-ever alone.

Today, she wanted to look into a couple of lives that required a bit of digging. Another term she liked — digging. Her two jobs were not that different, down at the ground level. Scratch, plant, grow and hope people gain from the results.

She searched out friends of Patricia Racie, the brittle young woman she'd interviewed in Niagara Falls. Sylvia databased everyone Patricia associated with. She couldn't get into her private circles and knew that's where the good stuff hid. She isolated Patricia's closest, most frequent friends and set them up in a separate list. She summoned up dossiers on each and crossed them against Gavin's data. No matches. No one ran in the same crowds as Gavin or worked for divisions to which he had some attachment.

She opened Marshall's curriculum vitae and cross-checked. Finally, she got a commonality. Marshall sat on the board of directors of an architectural firm, employing one of Patricia's dearest friends, James Nygyn.

Message to Marshall: Need access to James Nygyn's personal accounts. He works for Camphore, Lumberson and Park. You sit on the board, in case you don't remember.

Sylvia ordered another cup of chamomile with lemon.

From Marshall: Good God, it's Sunday. The day of rest.

Message to Marshall: No rest for the wicked.

Muscling into private lives wasn't her favorite tool. She hated the fact that someone had probably used it on her recently, resulting in her forced decampment to Atlanta. It had given her this idea, though. Fire with fire and all that. If they were going to push her around, she'd push someone else. Maybe, in the process, she'd get to push back.

The café had a polished feel that left it looking so ten-minutes-ago she couldn't imagine ever returning. It was the type of faux maple contraption that corporate could, and probably did, construct all around the planet. Dark greens and peach tones. Brass trinkets here and there. It lacked a sense of being Atlantian. No history. No elevation beyond being a café. This entire city seemed to her like one big, freaking hotel.

Message from Marshall: Here you go. Hope it's worth it.

Sylvia took the codes and entered Patricia Racie's more personal world disguised as her good friend James.

As expected, Patricia's messages and posts to her friends were a vapid mixture of daily grief and miniscule joys. She quickly extracted a list of everyone she communicated with, ever. She databased that list and gave it a good look. Friends from school, from work, from her neighborhood and her extended family. Only one name didn't fit, a man with whom she appeared to have nothing in common: John Raston.

John Raston did not allow 'James' access into his private stuff. Sylvia would need a new sheep's coding.

More lists.

Finding friends of John Raston proved more difficult than she expected. He didn't have many. He didn't have much contact with the world at all. None in the past six months. None? That was a story. The kind she liked.

John's slow reclusion from society began two years ago, with the death of his husband, Roger Gow. Fascinating. She looked into Roger Gow's history and realized they hadn't been together when he passed. He'd been transferred a year earlier. The company didn't make it a habit of splitting up married couples, but they were non-procreating, so the rules weren't as stringent.

Roger Gow's cache of memories survived him. She opened up his life, which he hadn't been too concerned with keeping secret. Roger had spent the last year of his life in a beryllium plant. Dangerous work. The company sent him there after he'd been diagnosed with pancreatic cancer. If you need people to work in an environment that may cause cancer, why not send workers that already have it? Sylvia could see the company's logic.

"That would make a good movie," she said out loud.

Not that it would ever get made, she said to herself.

Roger had hundreds of photos in his core memory. Sylvia wanted to see what this John Raston looked like. She opened the pictures starting with the most recent. And there they were.

John Raston could have been made of reeds. His glasses were the thickest thing about him. They didn't obscure the intelligence in his eyes. Roger had the sagging skin of rapid weight loss. She could tell he'd been handsome in the years leading up to the illness. Bone structure never lied. They had been happy together. Arms on shoulders, smiling. Lots of photos of wine glasses and barrels, shot at outdoor tables, with vines behind them.

She flicked though photos and flicked and flicked and stopped. That wasn't like any winery she'd ever seen. The long walls and old, old stone buildings. Square parapets and a big body of water on the other side. She'd never seen anything like it on the west coast. In one photo John and Roger held up glasses of deep yellow wine, grinning, with a field of shacks and tents in the background. A tramp camp.

"Ollies," Sylvia said. They'd visited an off-the-grid vineyard. What a grand place to hide.

She copied all of the winery photos and sent them to Samjahnee. Message to Samjahnee: Find this place. Now.

❦ · ❦

"They want the baby," Lillian said in a dead calm that chilled the back of Emory's neck.

"What?" he replied. *Go away. Get out*, he ordered her in his head.

"Lizzie," Lillian continued. "The bank told me they'd found a family that will give me eight thousand dollars for her."

"Why are you telling me this?" Emory glanced around the common room, chipped and worn, tables, chains and occupants alike.

"Because I can't keep the house. The bank said we could discuss options and that's what they gave me."

"You've got... we can't."

"We'll sell," Lillian said.

"My parents?"

"Your parents are tapped out. My parents are tapped out."

"Did you call John?"

Lillian's face crunched. Emory could see the tendons in her neck strain against her jaw.

"You think John's the answer to everything? Is that what you think? He's the problem, Em. Not the solution. John was no wizard. He had a couple of tricks and he fooled you with them."

Emory clenched his hands. They hurt. He opened them and clenched them again. Harder.

"Don't worry. I'll sell the house. I'll probably have to take the transfer corporate offered. Tel Aviv. Figures, right? An ocean away."

"But research, it can be done anywhere."

"Anywhere the company wants. Our marriage no longer registers. I'm in heavy debt. They can send me to the Artic."

Emory pressed his hands together in front of him. He didn't know what else to do with them. He didn't know what else to do with any part of him.

"I..." he didn't know what to say, either. He closed his mouth, afraid that if he opened it again he might just howl. A coyote in a trap.

"John's gone," Lillian said. "He disappeared the night our troubles started."

"How do you know? Did you try contacting—"

"Of course I tried. Just to scream at him I tried. The ASS ops can't even find him."

"He might be able to..."

"To do nothing. He's gone off line. That's what that stupid message was. That last one he sent you."

"The video bit?"

"Yeah. The fork in Niagara Falls. Fork Niagara. Get it?"

"Fork Niagara..." Emory wanted to bring his brain back around. He used to be bright. Really clever. That's why he could... that's why he was here, on the chain gang. A place between too smart and not smart enough.

❦ · ❦

As far as McCallum knew, there were two types of ollies: those in hiding and those the company wanted hid. Both cases tended to fall outside his job description. The company didn't care about the latter and lost interest in the former. Spending money to get somebody back on the payroll didn't make a whole lot of business sense most of the time. In his whole career he'd only tracked down one off-liner and that was because the man's brother thought he might be a decent kidney donor. That story did not have a happy ending. McCallum didn't think this one would, either.

He pulled into the convenience store anyway. A dreary concrete box marked off by trees on three sides. Mostly naked. He got out of his car and stared for a spell at a row of pines that were not. Green, holding on to bales of melting snow. They looked like the opposing team. They'd won on the home team's field and didn't want to celebrate with too much vigor. He liked the mix of species up here in the Niagara Falls catchment. He didn't think to bring his sketchpad even though he told anyone who asked that he'd be doing just that. The evergreens had a timid pride about them. We held out against the harsh northern winter. We didn't shed half our body mass. We gave up nothing. The three of us stood strong, if a bit prickly, because that's the way to survive. McCallum held up his wrist and took a picture, despite the weak lighting.

He turned as another car pulled up. Long, lean, yellow. Black windows. Silent, save for the tires popping on the pavement. He didn't know the make, as it wasn't an Ambyr car. He knew luxury, though. This was a decent vehicle and he didn't need a set of ads to convince him. Rosalie got out of the passenger side, jeans and a short leather jacket. She tossed her hair over her shoulder, not because it hung in her way, he knew, but because of the presentation. The effect it had on him. As Ambyr Incorporated had picked McCallum to be an op due to his observational abilities, India Group had made Rosalie an op because she could twist men into tiny, useless knots.

"If you're looking to get back together, I'm thinking you picked the wrong place." She stopped in front of McCallum and put her hands on her hips.

"Wrong place, wrong time," McCallum said. "Kind of my thing."

"How you been?"

"Spring is in the air. You look good."

"Thanks, Eddie. You too," Rosalie said. "So I'm the only person you know in the ISS?"

"The only one I trust," McCallum said.

"All right," Rosalie started towards the front door of the convenience store.

McCallum glanced back at the yellow car and wondered what kind of driver sat behind the wheel.

The woman behind the counter eyed them as they entered. Two young boys in the back corner stood in a trance, holding open the door of a 20-foot drink cooler, filled with beer, malt-liquor, wine-soda pop mixes that gave McCallum a headache just looking in their direction. He figured the woman held a stake in the shop, because she bothered to glance back and forth between the kids and the surveillance monitors on her counter. She had more pounds than she needed, less brownish hair and the posture of a laundry sack. In the city, this kind of store wouldn't warrant a full time clerk. Out here, McCallum guessed things were different.

"Hi." Rosalie approached the counter. McCallum followed.

"Can I help you?" the woman asked.

"I'm hopin' so…" Rosalie glanced at her cuff, then up to the woman. "Mrs. Margery Ealing, manager and operating partner of the Large Mouth Mini Mart, division of India Group."

Margery took a large, shoulder-pumping huff, crossed her arms and drew a thoroughly fake smile across her mouth. "You the new sheriff? 'Cuz you're gonna have to palm a lot of cream horns to catch up to the last one."

"No," Rosalie said. "I'm here on a special."

Margery's smile dropped. She gave McCallum the once over. "This takes two of you? What's that costing?"

Rosalie held up her bracelet. "Mind a bump?"

"I have a choice?"

"We all have choices." Rosalie clinked her cuff against the woman's. "You're making the right one."

Margery tapped her bracelet, then flicked her finger across the top. She looked at the monitor embedded in her counter. McCallum looked back at the two teenagers. They each selected a beverage and closed the frosty door.

"Have you seen this man?" Rosalie asked.

"Can't say as he rings any bells."

"You sure? Why don't you give him a good long look?"

Margery ran her eyes over the monitor too fast to focus. "Nope," she told Rosalie.

"You sell gasoline?" Rosalie asked.

"You tell me."

"I'm thinking this man, John Raston. He buys gasoline and he doesn't use a cuff."

"Well that would be against company policy now, wouldn't it."

McCallum pretended not to pay attention to the boys walking out of the store.

"I don't care if you're trading monkeys for moonshine, I just want to know if you've ever seen this man."

McCallum followed the boys out of the store. The two kids walked fast, bottles dangling in their hands. Before they rounded the corner of the store, they both looked back.

"Ahem," McCallum said. They flinched, the both of them. They each had the inclination to bolt but stifled it. The flinch told McCallum almost everything he needed to know. Almost.

"Boys," he said. "If you don't mind a moment."

They looked terrified. He guessed local system security operatives must keep the leashes tight in this neighborhood.

"I'm looking for an ollie," McCallum said. "With an off-roader. An old Jeep. Runs on gas."

"Yeah, we don't know what you're talking about," the taller one said. String bean kids, McCallum thought. Both in need of a hair cut. They'd picked Bourberry— a combination of fruit juice and whiskey. They were 14 or 15, he figured. Right at that age when they want much more than they can have, that phase of out growing the kiddie stuff and not fully understanding grown-up games. You don't start drinking at 10 in the morning if you want to finish the day upright.

"Neither one of you, huh?" McCallum said.

"We don't know anything," the shorter one ventured.

McCallum took a step forward. The kids didn't move. "You ever see me around here before?"

"No," they both said.

"You suspect why that is?"

They shook their heads.

"I'm a different kind of op," McCallum said. "I don't patrol mini marts looking for double baggers or in-store eaters. I don't care if you're taking a personal day from school. I'm the kind of op that should something happen, like you get caught with your pants down somewhere, maybe doing something that ain't exactly policy, you want me owing you a favor."

The boys looked at each other. The taller one shook his head, but the other pecked a little, like he was punctuating a sentence that hadn't been said out loud. The taller one shook his head harder.

"What does it matter?" the shorter one asked.

"It's trouble," the tall one answered.

"It's like an extra life, man. I'm taking it. Cost me nothing. Besides," he turned to McCallum. "He's not going to like it anyway."

Rosalie approached from behind him. He knew her walk, her rhythm. "Find a couple of new drinking buddies?"

"I make friends wherever I go," McCallum said. "Now, boys, where have you seen the gas Jeep?"

The short one cracked open his bottle of candied bourbon. "You ever hear of Fort Niagara?"

CHAPTER EIGHTEEN

AN ICY SPRAY of excrement, urine, water, grime, with chunks and blobs Emory couldn't indentify, plunged through the left tunnel, kicking his legs out from under him. He tumbled into freezing slurry, too startled to even yell anything but a single 'oh'. He shut his mouth tight after that. And his eyes. He used one hand to catch the tunnel floor and the other to cinch up his suit under his neck. You didn't want this stuff inside your coveralls. You didn't want this stuff outside them, either, he thought as he tried to regain his footing.

Too slippery. The current pushed, where? Down the tunnel? The new section. Air. He needed air. He flapped for the wall. It had to be here. The junction was only six feet across. He rolled, hit the side, felt the water taking him and a squeeze on his forearm. Fingers. He swung his other arm over and grabbed the arm holding him.

Campbell hoisted him out of the torrent of crap. He pressed him to the wall with one arm, holding the edge of the tunnel opening with the other.

They said nothing. No stupid "are you Ok" which would have meant opening our mouth and awarding a creature stuck on your lip the chance to crawl in. They weren't OK and they both knew it. They stood at the bottom of life, just above freezing, immune systems fighting on forty fronts, tired, hungry, and now unable to move as their senses shut down. The water drowned their work lamps, flooding them with darkness. They heard nothing but the roar of the sewer. Their noses plugged with snot in an attempt to keep out the millions of microbes scurrying the nostril rims. Their senses of touch quickly gave way to numbness.

Emory's bracelet tingled. He looked at the face to see who called. A reflex. Silly. As if he were going to chat on the phone right now. Only the company had his number anyway.

"Tell them," Campbell said.

Emory gave his wrist a quick twist and the foreman's voice shot into his ear. "...ck's happening up there? Can you hear me? What the fuck's happened up there?

"It's Leveski. We're alive."

"Not what I asked," the foreman shouted.

"I don't know."

"You must've seen something. Sewage pouring in? You didn't see a couple tons of raw sewage you fuckwad?"

"Yeah," Emory returned. "From the west tunnel."

"Fucking BCCA. The BCCA..." Emory could tell the foreman now shouted at someone else. "They opened up early. Get'em a message."

Click.

☙ · ❧

McCallum had heard of Fort Niagara. He had a vague idea it sat somewhere north of the Niagara Falls catchment, at the end of the Niagara River. He learned about it in grade school, though the details had faded with sine and cosine and how to diagram a sentence. He didn't want to do a search on the topic, because it could be traced later, if the company had the desire. They'd know he had an interest and no other historical inquires in which to hide it. He decided to research the Niagara Gorge — any landscape artist within 500 miles would — and hope he found a plausible tributary running to the Fort.

The gorge was a deep cut in the earth, running from Niagara Falls to Lake Ontario. Seven miles of declining ridge, starting at about almost 200 feet. Steep walls of rock and shale, the waters roared and swirled at the bottom, rolling over rocks, churning in whirlpools. He imagined it would be interesting to paint. Natural energy always commanded attention. Nature stood as the companies' last obstacle.

The end of the river made two corners of land. One side had a village, the other an old fort. Not the kind with high walls and towers and parapets that a grade three investment technician would have taken over. Fort Niagara laid low in the ground, with chunky stone walls built into thick mounds of earth. To

128

McCallum they looked like giant, fat, lazy basset hounds asleep for so long moss had grown over their backs. The front of the fort, as approached by land, formed a long, foreboding point. If you were attacking on foot, with a gun that held one little ball of lead, he could see how the place might be defensible. You'd have to run up hill across open fields as the resident enemy fired at you from the shed-like buildings dotting the ramparts.

Inside the walls, behind the lumps of green, was what they called the parade grounds. The army paraded around? With no one watching? McCallum didn't fully understand the term, but he could figure out the purpose. Stone buildings lined the field. Those were the warm, safe places. Where the higher-ups lived. Generals and colonels and the people they liked best. The foot soldiers, cannoniers, blacksmiths and cooks, they lived out in the open, in tents, in winters white and withering.

The photos he saw of the fort were decades old. He knew no one had bothered with the places since the Buy-Ups. Many modern military properties went to the weeds. 300-year-old stone and mud ruts designed to fend off muskets? They became the perfect place to hide.

McCallum almost called up the most recent satellite image of the Fort. His finger circled the command button on his cuff like a hawk. His inquiring would leave an electronic trail, electron breadcrumbs leading them to him.

Them, he chuckled. He was them. Under other circumstances, at least. He stood up from his recliner and stepped back. The drawing of the fort filled his wall, blue lines on cream. Rough, but full. All the right and necessary details. Artists given such assignments never seemed to get any credit, even when their work is done so well it survives centuries, from paper to graphic file, from pen stroke to streams of ones and zeros.

He turned and looked at the easel in the middle of his living room. Charcoal arcs across canvas, of a young woman face down in the street. He had sketched the bar into the background. Frosty windows. He'd make them glow warm and friendly when he painted. People drinking, touching, unwinding, rewinding—oblivious to the horror outside? Ignorant?

They don't care to see, McCallum said to himself.

No one wants to know what's living in Fort Niagara. All the psychotic, delusional, disturbed minds that proved too much for the company. Too much time, too much money, too much care. Care didn't figure too heavily into anything. Except his painting.

The dead girl lay prostrate, right arm off the curb, in the gutter. Bubbly orange jacket hacked to raged strands, flaps of her skin pulled up through the rubbery material. It looked as if she might bounce back up at any moment. Just joking. A bad horror movie. Her young flesh and hip coat so resilient death ricocheted like a tennis ball.

McCallum reached for his case of oil paints. He'd make the outerwear and wounds appear wet, a billiard ball effect. The death would shine. This would be his best painting in years. He could see it all now, as if the canvas painted itself and now all his hand merely had to catch up.

And Aga Graber would love it. And it would anchor his first solo show. And posters would rave about his haunted captivating vision and toss photos of his work around the globe, as offers came in for this piece, and others, and commissions from low grades who wanted a McCallum over their baby grand pianos, to point at with Champagne flutes and smile because they were now so fucking cool to own an original. All thanks to that pretty dead girl on the street.

McCallum smashed the canvas on the top of the easel, where the three legs met in a point. The thin wooded spires tore through the cloth and charcoal like a knife through a back.

⚞ · ⚟

Sylvia sat behind her bamboo desk, up on the edge of her seat, legs slightly spread, per the baby's dictates. How to sit, where to sit, duration and why all came from the baby. Her other new boss. Which infuriated her. Life is a ladder of bosses. Life's purpose is escape. Climb as many runs as you can, trying to get to the place where you stand all wobbly with nothing but the wind and weather to worry you. It's everyone's raison d'être: break the shackles. Parents, educators, supervisors. Freedom is not your potential or goal, it is your duty.

Now here she sat with not one, but two insidious, illogical supervisors telling her where, how and when to sit, like she was a well-dressed malamute.

And her jeans didn't fit and her boots strangled her calves. She wore a white T-shirt, because the office had the temperature of an orchid house. It smelled like soil. Not a scent that bothered her, on its own, but here it reminded her that her office also served as a potting shed. Mortimer Clive put her desk in a room also used to repot plants, mix fertilizer and store chemicals, tools and pieces of crap no one had the guts to toss.

"You've got to get me out of here," Sylvia said into the monitor. The sheet of glass sat propped by an easel on the desk. Marshall St. Claire's face filled half the screen.

"I'm doing everything I can, dear," Marshall said, fist against his cheek, already tired two minutes into their call. "What's Gavin doing? He can't be happy."

"Who knows what jollies him up. Besides, Samjahnee's doing the rough edits as we speak, so Gavin feels the movie's progressing. Even though I should be there, making the decisions, making sure he's not fucking things up beyond belief. I'm sure he's trashing gold right now. I know it. He's got the narrative sense of a cabbage."

"I thought you liked him."

"As a camera man. He gets shots. But stringing the shots together?"

"Only the great Sylvia Cho can do that."

"On the nose," Sylvia said. "On the fucking nose. This little detour is draining my soul."

"Is it that bad?"

"I had to wash the tractor."

"Ha," Marshall belched. He shot upright and laughed through his astonishment.

"Mortimer figures the low grade who plopped me here just wants my name on the project. The fact that I don't pick out a single begonia or blade of grass matters not. As long as I worked here, this was a Sylvia Cho production."

"Amy Beauregard," Marshall said. "The low grade who's responsible for the building."

"That's my fan who hates me, huh?"

"It is a strange sort of love."

"Have you pinged her?"

"Not directly," Marshall said. "I'm still putting together a dossier."

"What else do you need to know?" Sylvia huffed. "I'm here. She did it. Can we get her to do something else now."

"Exactly. Can we? I'd lose my small fortune betting on the motivations of the fairer sex. I'm not convinced I understand

Ms. Beauregard. I'm quite convinced the benefactors behind your film project already tried to pry you loose. So something else is at work."

"The world is not that dramatic." Sylvia slumped back in her chair. "That's why it needs people like me. To give it shape and dynamic. The boring, petty little plays people live through. She saw my name on her list one day and plucked me like the juiciest grape on the vine."

"Perhaps," Marshall said. "Or pruned you. Did she place you here or take you away from someplace else?"

That concept made Sylvia stop.

"Either way," Mortimer's voice came through the speakers. "She works for me."

Sylvia iced up. She shook, frightened. The fright turned to anger. She'd let someone like Mortimer frighten her? Embarrassing. Now. How much had he heard? Did it matter? Did he listen in on all of her calls, read her mail and messages?

Marshall said, "That is about the rudest thing I've ever—"

"Then try this," Mortimer said. Marshall's image on Sylvia's screen went black. "I'd like the soil sample report by 11 a.m."

Sylvia's screen returned to a chart showing acidity rates.

━━ Chapter Nineteen ━━

EMORY HAD NEARLY finished his pudding when a man in his early twenties walked up to his table. Campbell stopped talking. Which was a kind of special moment all in itself.

"Come with me," he said.

"I don't think so." Emory went back to his pudding.

"Go with Frank," sounded in Emory's ear. He spit out his pudding.

"You OK?" Campbell asked.

Emory wiped a paper napkin across his mouth and nodded. "I guess I'm going with Frank."

The young man led him out of the common room, down the hall, into the elevator. They went to the first floor. Instead of heading for the garage, they turned left and walked into a part of the barracks Emory hadn't ever considered. A dim, yellowing shadow of a hall. Long, quiet, ending in a steel door that looked like it could take about 40,000 pounds of pressure per square foot before giving way. It shushed open as they approached. The young man stepped aside and Emory continued in.

Familiarity set in as the door closed behind him. This office suite looked like 40 or 50 others he'd visited in his life. Beige felt sectioned off with strips of aluminum. Glass and plastic placed without care, without purpose. This entrance area had enough room for two opposing couches, dull and inviting as crates. An older woman entered and beckoned him forward. Emory walked down another shorter hall and into an office.

The man behind the bamboo desk was the offspring of a swine and a bear. Pale skin, red cheeks, next to no hair. Emory figured late forties. His faded striped shirt fit like hot dog casing, ready to burst. He considered Emory as he entered and with an elaborate, deliberately showy gesture, put a finger to his bracelet. He suspended the cuff's functions, as one might at the theatre, or if they were having an affair. The act would have made the old Emory nervous. This current one shrugged it off.

"I'm Chief Supervisor Valient," the man said. "Sorry we haven't met but I don't like to mix with you people."

"Understandable," Emory said. He stood, hands folded in front of him.

"I'm not going to ask how things are going. I know. This detail is punishing. I make it that way." Valient interlaced his hands and leaned his large head back into them. "I can make it not so punishing, too. Would you have any interest in that, Mr. Leveski?"

"Please, call me Emory."

"I can make your time here a little easier, Emory. Especially the night time."

Emory's stomach twanged. A guitar string, out of tune, running from his glottis to his anus, vibrated. *Why'd he suspend his cuff?*

"Would you like that, Emory?"

"I imagine so," he mumbled.

"Barter is technically against company policy, but helping each other out, that's OK, don't you think? I help you, you help me?"

"What did you have in mind, sir?"

"I want you to kill Jeffery Campbell. Make it look like a cave-in or some such thing. Can you do that for me?"

❧ · ❧

"Meet me at the service door," Mortimer said via voice call, directly into Sylvia's ears. She couldn't tell much from his tone, as his default state seemed to be sour. He certainly enjoyed giving orders, bare of any niceties, fake or phony.

Seeing Mortimer just inside the service door didn't give her any more clues. As usual, his face said he'd just bitten into a fresh Meyer lemon. He wore khaki cargo pants that appeared to actually have cargo in the various side pockets. Tools or meters or something, she couldn't tell. His shirt was like a waist-length kimono, rough black silk, with a plunge deeper than she'd wear to the office. It tied on the side with a thin bow.

"That's a wrap," she said as she approached.

"What?"

"Your blouse. It's a wrap."

"It's a Laotian war shirt."

"That wrap. I love it."

"Thank you. It provides great freedom of movement."

"Ironic," Sylvia said.

Mortimer pondered her for a moment, forehead like a freshly plowed field. "On you," he replied. "Greater freedom of movement would be ironic on you."

"Suit yourself," Sylvia grinned. "But I don't think you've got much more freedom than I do. I know you didn't hire me for this job."

"On that we are in full agreement." Mortimer pushed open the dented, steel service door and motioned for Sylvia to exit.

Seven photographers greeted her with whirls and clicks.

"Miss Cho!" "Miss Cho!" several voices from several different directions. A gaggle of posters. She hadn't seen one since the opening of her last film, more than a year ago now.

"What are you working on, Miss Cho?"

"Is it secret? Can you tell us anything?"

"Are you shooting inside? Is Jamie Grant in there with you?"

Jamie who? That actor that looks like a boy and girl simultaneously? Ah, Sylvia sighed in her head, *the rumorous wind of the posters.*

She glanced at Mortimer. He smiled broadly, like this was a beautiful morning for touring the back forty. She'd never seen anything like that kind of expression on his face. He almost looked good with a smile. Fully human, anyway.

"Let's take a walk, shall we?" He pointed towards the berm and the run-off gully that would be the most challenging aspect of the grounds re-design. It meant she'd be walking up an incline. Huff. They'd get some good shots of her.

Cameras buzzed. Men and woman, dressed for adventure, moved about, careful not to get within twenty feet or her or her boss.

"If you'll excuse us?" Mortimer said to the press as they strolled.

The posters continued to shout questions, shuffle, side-step and trail the two. They crossed the driveway and started up the small hill.

"I'm thinking of covering this with artificial grass," Mortimer said.

"You'll lose some of the binding action of the real turf," Sylvia replied.

"What if we add in poplars? Across the top."

Sylvia looked up and down the length of the berm. The idea wasn't bad. The short berm could stand with a little height. Poplars sent big roots everywhere. The trees would block wind, create shade, put oxygen in the air.

"Not bad," she said. "Are they in your budget?"

"I've been growing them from cuttings for the last five years, on another property."

"Huh."

They reached the top. The posters stayed at the bottom, snapping photos of Sylvia against the hazy azure sky. She put her hands on her hips and straightened her back. She flipped her hair back, catching the breeze. If they were fast, they'd get a picture of it streaming behind her like a pennant.

"Over there," Mortimer pointed to the front of the building. "I'm going to pull out the main walkway and put in a spiral. I want to fill it with lemon grass, mint, some other local herbs."

"Really?"

"The main entrance is low traffic. Most people enter through the sides, close to the parking lot. A more circuitous path won't injure productivity or cause much complaint. Especially after people realize they can clip some fresh Thai basil on their way home from work."

"Wonderful," Sylvia said without moving her mouth much.

"Don't sound so surprised."

"I'm not, I just..."

"This project has been in the back of my head for several years."

"I see," Sylvia said.

"Do you?"

"I'm not going to interfere."

"No, you're not," he said. "You're not going to help, either, are you." He jutted his chin down at the posters, adjusting their cameras and tapping into their wristbands.

"That's not my fault," Sylvia said.

"Sure it is. They're here taking pictures and writing posts about Sylvia Cho, the movie director. Not Sylvia Cho, the landscape architect. No one cares much about *that* art form. Not even you."

Sylvia turned and put a hand on Mortimer's shoulder, as she would with an old friend or child. "You don't know me and shouldn't presume to. Yes, the company arranged a marriage between me and landscaping, but I came to love it."

"Until something more glamorous came along."

"Nothing ever came along. I went and got it. You of all people should understand that. Things don't come along. You need to dig, haul and water. You need to plan, prepare and create. Oh and then get lucky. It's all the same, you know. Movies, books, painting, creating a natural space around some completely unnatural office complex. All art is the same. It's a struggle between acceptance and understanding, leading to moments of supreme reward — those rushes you get when it's right and you know it. Four or five other people whose opinions really matter know it too. That's all you can ask for. It's all the same."

Sylvia put her hand over her eyes to shield the sun. She peered at the lawn in front of the building.

"The herb garden idea is inspired," she said. "But have you thought of maybe an onion design instead of a spiral? It would give people the option of walking directly to the front doors, or taking a little detour."

"An onion?" Mortimer asked.

"You know, a bulb shape, with parallel lines. Walkways in this case."

"Interesting."

"I'm sorry," Sylvia said. "I shouldn't have presumed to know you either. I thought you were simply an asshole. Being an asshole for your art, that is highly different and wholly acceptable."

"I thought you were a pretentious prima donna," Mortimer said.

"There is that," Sylvia said. "In general, you should go with your first impression.

"Did you send for these people?" Mortimer pointed to the posters.

"I've been obfuscating my location for the last few months. The secrecy built a buzz wave. When I finally surfaced —"

"You posted your location?"

"When I fin —"

Sylvia's wrist tingled. She pumped a small smile and tapped her bracelet. "Yes?"

"What is that?" Gavin Stoll's voice. Odd. It couldn't have been much passed eight o'clock in the L.A. catchment. Much too early for movie producers to rise.

"What is what?" she sailed back.

"On your waist," Gavin spat. "You look pregnant, which we both know could not possibly be the case as I told you to take care of the matter six months ago."

Sylvia glanced over at the coterie of posters, watching her through palm-sized monitors linked to fruit-sized, and fruit colored, cameras.

She waved and smiled.

❦ · ❦

The two guys in the waiting room didn't talk. Sitting with their arms on their knees, heads hung low, as if slurping out of an unseen trough, they glanced at each other every few minutes, wanting to talk, wanting to ask 'what the fuck is he doing here?'

Or so McCallum figured. He knew this kind of young men. Guilty of so many things they weren't sure what to say or do that wouldn't make their situations worse. They knew he was an op and an op shouldn't have been in this waiting room after hours, so the whole scene poked them, pinched them, refused to let them sit back and own the room as they would their pub or street corner or back car of their train.

McCallum let them squirm. He tapped through messages on his cuff, called up the news, and waited.

"Ed?" came a voice from behind the door. McCallum stood and walked into the exam room. He could hear the young men sigh in relief.

Dr. Majum sat on a stool next to the exam chair, under the bright light dome, next to spit the sink and tray of picks and loops and brushes. Short, thin but sturdy, McCallum's records said she was 72 years old. He'd checked, because it was hard to tell. She'd been his dentist for all his life, but she didn't seem ancient. At least not anymore. It seemed to him like he was catching up to her.

"I really appreciate this." McCallum reclined into the chair and closed his eyes. Too much light.

"It's my pleasure," Dr. Majum said. "I mean, who doesn't want a security operative owing them a favor, right?" She chuckled.

McCallum smiled.

"So you'll be away for your scheduled appointment?" She fastened a bib under his chin.

"That's the plan. A last minute thing."

"Not, I take it, official business."

"No," McCallum said. "My pleasure, I guess you'd say."

Dr. Majum produced a small mirror and pick and began to look around inside McCallum's mouth.

"Next week I'll mark you down as having made your appointment. Nobody wants to be out of compliance. Not even ops, I imagine."

He nodded. The only acknowledgement he could manage.

"Those two yokels out there are in the same boat," Dr. Majum said. "They didn't show for their mandatory well exams. Who knows what they were doing. They both got hit with a garnish for more than they bring home in a month. That got their attention. I'm going to retro them. Claim it was a clerical error."

McCallum leaned over the sink, spit and returned. "That's nice of you."

"Not at all. I'm going to have them clean my gutters." She put her hand over her mouth and feigned a startled expression. "Not that I should be telling you."

"I'll haul you in when the moment's right."

"I won't go willingly," she returned. "Do ops — and I don't mean you by any means — do ops do a lot of moonlighting?"

"Smmummm," McCallum grunted as Dr. Majum dug around in his mouth.

"I would assume. Everyone's got bills to pay. There are probably all manner of people who need extra security now and again. I'll get a speeding ticket someday. Or I'll cut the lawn of the people across the street and they'll be furious. They keep it so long. Then I'll need your help."

"Oh ay," McCallum said mostly through his nose.

Dr. Majum pulled her hands out of his mouth.

"Tell those boys to cut the lawn," McCallum said. "Never do the nasty jobs yourself."

Dr. Majum chuckled again. "Never thought of that. So used to doing my own dirty work."

"That's not how the low grades do it."

McCallum relaxed back into the long, squeaky chair and closed his eyes to fight the small sun Dr. Majum had for a work lamp.

Take your own advice, he said to himself. A joke. Because he never did.

━━ CHAPTER TWENTY ━━

EMORY KNEELED ON the ground, arms limp to the side, head hung so low his chin pressed on his chest. Four other men worked around him, clearing debris from the tunnel section they'd just removed. He had a few minutes before he had to take down the braces and move up the line. He should've helped them. He wanted to, but couldn't move. They knew, by looking, not to ask. They'd seen the gray face and dark pillow eyes on others.

Emory's joints ached. When he closed his eyes, he could feel the heat multiply where his eyelids met. The fever put a drag on any movement and boiled him if he stayed still. His thoughts came slowly, like butter through a pipe. In the 76 days that he'd served on the alternative work detail, he hadn't gotten sick, despite the wet, cold, bone breaking work, stress and lack of sleep. Oh, and the rapes. He'd lost count at 40. He told himself they were losing their impact; he was becoming desensitized. The assaults were now routine. Part of life. His ancient ancestors on the Serengeti were constantly under attack from lions and cheetahs and snakes and bugs. They survived. The race survived. Famine, ice ages, plagues and wars. He'd be fine. So they turned him into a rag doll once a week for 45 minutes. He'd be fine. Damn fucking fine. Humanity had lived through worse.

He wanted to die.

The fever had been through about half the detail, workers and foremen alike. The isolation of the group prevented a lot of common ailments from breaking in. Unfortunately, when one did, it broke out.

The nurse told Emory to ride it out. Drink plenty of fluids. Report for work, but take it easy. Easy, you know, as in don't lug 60-pound jacks over broken concrete and muck, lift 40-pound pneumatic braces above your head and pound them into place with a sledge. Stay out of the cold. Don't climb ladders, crawl through tunnels on the verge of collapse or subject your lungs to filthy, grit filled air.

This fever would kill him. He'd never again have to worry about when the attacks would come, when the brace would give out or when some young, out-of-luck idiot might get called down to the chief supervisor's office for a chat on Emory's recent lack of usefulness.

"We've got this one," Campbell said.

What was that other guy's name? Stewart? They carried his jack, brace and sledge in addition to their own stuff. Heavy on heavy. He stood, shaking for a second as his blood flow tried to catch up to his new height.

"You'll make it, pal," Campbell said over his shoulder. "You're doing great."

What Campbell should have done was leave Emory in the mud. Helping him added to an already impossible day. Working in broken sewers did not get easier with practice. Everyday brought some new challenge. No power. Deadly gas leaks. Live wires no one knew about until they sparked against a saw blade. The cave-ins were the worst. Not so much because they took the most lives. They didn't. They didn't kill you all at once, like a good, clean zapping. Caves usually crushed part of you and let you think about the pain until you died. An old fashioned stoning. The kind of punishment once reserved for heretics. The kind of death they wanted for Campbell.

"They," Emory mumbled.

Was it the company? As a rule, they didn't kill people. A bit of value always lingered, waiting to be squeezed out. Even saboteurs like Olin Cassavetti, mindlessly wrecking his mindless sponge making machines, could be probed and prodded for the rest of his life. Emory knew, in a way, he'd been lucky to be placed on a chain gang. Some employees caught in breach of company policy ended up in the labs, serving as test beds for pharmaceutical research, establishing the length of time it takes mercury to cross the blood-brain barrier or how much asbestos in the lungs is truly too much.

He wouldn't mind the drug studies now. Thanks. Had enough. Got to go now.

Emory collapsed face-first into a new section of pipe, splashing the inch deep trough of runoff.

❧ · ❧

From the outside, the old fort retained a shred of majesty. The walls and towers stayed sturdy and purposeful. McCallum liked the lack of uniformity in the stones. The builders took what they found and made it work. They did such a careful job, the ramparts still seemed ready to repel canon balls, even though the smoke rising from three points inside made it seem like a couple had gotten through.

McCallum ran his thumb down the right strap of his backpack and walked to the front gate. One of the 10-foot halves had swung inwards enough for two people to pass side-by-side. He got a good whiff of the open fires as he entered. He got a good whiff of all kinds of things he would have taken a pass on, given the choice. With the temperature inching above freezing, stuff frozen and forgotten during the winter loosened and glistened and let its stink melt into the air.

The parade grounds inside covered a triangular acre. Battlements ringed the sides. A couple of stone buildings stood in the back. He'd seen it all in his research. He hadn't seen what had grown in the middle of the fort. A junk city. A mash-up of anything wide and flat that could possibly be lashed to something else in the hope of creating a shape large enough to hide one or two sleeping humans. McCallum couldn't name all the shapes— cubes, pyramids, rhomboids, bulging polygons that flashed a middle finger at gravity and the wind. Colors made the shapes even harder to discern. White, clay, yellow striped, green speckled foam-wood predominated, but paled by the side-ways traffic signs, orange tarps and gray corrugated steel, spotted with dirt, rust and sometimes pink spray-on insulation. He estimated 25 huts, guessing where one ended and another began

The ground consisted mostly of mud. Paths of rough pebbles made the earth somewhat passable. His boots stuck to them as he walked. After four steps he sounded like a lazy tap dancer. Not that anyone noticed. Two men sat by an open fire, tending an open pot. They had empty mugs waiting. Another walked aimlessly away from him. All three were well past middle age. He decided to walk straight through the center lane, aimed at

142

the old headquarters on the other side of the parade grounds. If anyone had any kind of control of this place, he'd find them there.

Two women hung clothes on a rope strung between two shanties. It reminded him of a painting— what was it called? Women Tending the Laundry, Pissarro— but with more grime, more stench. He passed another man, this one in his thirties, crouched on the ground next to a stack of empty egg cartons and a box of seed.

"Twelve, two times six, three times four," he said to himself, dropped fistfuls of potting soil into the cups that used to hold eggs. "Two, four, six, eight, ten, twelve."

The man glanced at McCallum and chose not to stop his work. McCallum held no interest for him. McCallum understood. He smiled and kept walking. He'd intended to look around the fixed buildings and decided against it. He wasn't here to ask permission. He circled the shanties, found a fairly dry spot on the north-western edge and threw down his pack. He took out his tent and popped it to life. A milky blue half-bubble big enough for him to sleep in, keep the rest of his pack dry and little else. He took a Bristol board and a case of charcoal pencils from his pack and walked to the back wall. He climbed to the top of the battlement and peered out over the end of the Niagara River and the start of Lake Ontario.

Rock and patches of grass, green and brown, covered the angles of land. The water had a bright sapphire sheen, three shades darker than the sky. This angle had no particular drama to it; no inherent story. What he wanted was to be over there, on the other side, viewing his current location. He turned and looked back at the collection of hovels and, for the first time in months, felt the wave, that inner surge, a welcomed and unstoppable urge to draw.

He worked for about an hour, roughing in a sketch of the grounds before him. Ramshackle huts, set up in the shape of a town, as if 25 groups of boys decided to all move their clubhouses to the same open field. Tree houses without trees. McCallum needed a wider canvas. He wanted to frame the mess in the walls of the fort-a larger, older, more official kind of playhouse for boys.

A woman crossed the field and stopped on the grass under McCallum. He tried not to give her the obvious once-over. He kept drawing, stealing glimpses between strokes. She had no problem standing and staring at him like he was a new and peculiar work of art. Five and a half feet tall, he couldn't tell much about her build under that big brown cowboy coat. He guessed slim, like someone who spent a good deal of time outdoors, on the move. Her green Wellies held several grades of mud. She had a solid stance, confident, with energy enough to stand straight and alert. He saw a black ponytail every so often. A wide brimmed hat hid her head and shaded her face. On purpose, he noted. All her garments were chosen to disguise the person underneath. Were he on the job, which he wasn't, he would have taken her for a famous actress who didn't want to be noticed or someone who was about two minutes away from holding up a jewelry store.

After a good ten minutes, McCallum got curious as to how long she might stare at him without making contact. What kind of person stared like that? A patient three-year-old? Which, of course, didn't exist. She shifted her weight once in a while, leaning back on one foot, then the next. She kept her hands in her coat's deep pockets. He started to think she was a bit addled, like the guy counting seeds into egg cartons. One of the mentally challenged the company lets drift out to the fringes. He'd dealt with enough of them in his career. The people who couldn't go outside. The people huddled in a corner because their office walls got painted, because they could see germs spread or the noises in their heads ran so high they couldn't hear you begging them to calm down. The ones who snapped, wrecking sponge-making machines or themselves or anyone in their flailing range.

This woman didn't fit, McCallum decided. She didn't seem as odd as she acted. This brought an end to his drawing. He stared back at the woman for a while.

"Can I have a look?" she asked.

"Sure," McCallum replied. "Hop on up."

The woman walked away. McCallum assessed his drawing, smudging a little, to work in some of the shadows he'd been seeing earlier, but had now faded as the sun moved directly overhead. His hands were cold. He'd have to stop soon or screw up what he'd already done. He put his pencil back in the case as the woman walked across the wall, in his direction.

She smiled at him, thin and long and caught him up in rolling cheekbones under eyes the color of chocolate. They angled up at the corners, pointed like cherry tree leaves. They made mischief just glancing around. Olive toned skin, smooth and unadorned. She'd hit 30, but not too many years after that. His mouth opened a bit and he faked a yawn to hide it.

She stood next to him and looked at his drawing. "Huh?" came immediately. "You can actually draw."

McCallum couldn't place her accent. Spanish, in flavor, but geography wasn't his thing. "Why do you sound so surprised?" he asked.

"Made you for an op not an artist."

"Maybe I'm both."

"Hadn't thought of that."

"What do you get more of up here, ops or artists?"

"Ops. There is no question. Each of the three companies represents equally."

"Why? Do you have a lot of troublemakers?"

"Yeah," the woman said, "the ops."

McCallum chuckled and held out his hand. "My name is Ed."

The woman took it — warmer and rougher than he'd expected — and shook it. "In Fort, they call me Snyder. If you're here to bring me back, let's get it over with."

❦ · ❦

Another hotel room that looked like a hotel room. Sylvia hated it. They all looked so similar she could never remember where she was. Why didn't anyone take just a few extra minutes and at least try to give it some identity? Even disastrous, out-of-touch style would be preferable to none. A picture of dogs playing poker, a flaming skull, purple and aqua— anything that she wasn't used to seeing would be embraced. Didn't anyone involved in making hotels have any pride in workmanship?

Or was there no workmanship. Did little off-white rooms like this, with their splatter-pattern rugs and formless lamps and brown featureless features simply appear out of a collective, with no one actually making any over-arching decisions? Hotel rooms by committee, but a committee that never met. Hotels grew, she decided. They appeared like pale mushrooms in the vast corporate loam that had become the world. No vision. No dream. Space like this coalesced around need. Plaster, vertical blinds and oil paintings of fruit bowls gathered and poof. A hotel.

"You've got to get me out of here!" Sylvia said to an image of Marshall projected on to the ceiling over her bed.

"That should be forthcoming, dear," he returned.

Sylvia reclined between two sets of pillows, one elevated her feet, the other her head. Her cuff alerted her to another call. "Hold on." She waved her hand and Marshall's image shrank by half, making way for Samjahnee.

"Sam the man," Sylvia said.

"Samjahnee come lately," Marshall said. "What's flappin'."

"When are you returning?" he asked, presumably to Sylvia, face blank.

"I can't decide if you want me back or you're worried I'm on my way."

"Yes," he said. Marshall laughed.

"I've offered to pay my salary plus 15 percent, but the offer didn't even get opened."

"Up the bid," Marshall said.

Sylvia rolled her eyes. "They don't even know what the first was. They didn't open the message. They don't want to negotiate. Besides, Gavin cut me off. I've got no additional income stream."

"Astonishing," Samjahnee said.

"Thanks," Sylvia said. "Glad you see the entertainment value."

"Everything you do is interesting," Marshall kicked in. "Even nothing."

"This is not the good kind of interesting," Sylvia said. "This is a 'white spot on your x-ray' interesting or a 'file you didn't download to your core memory' interesting. Gavin wants the movie. Now."

"He can wait," Marshall said.

"He's angry about the baby."

"So?"

"So, it's a breach of contract. Getting rid of the baby was a term of extraneous employment. He don't owe me shit."

"But he wants his movie," Samjahnee added.

"Sure. I guess. It's not like he'll stop being mean to me to get it, but sure, everyone wants me to complete the meaningful project, the first really important one in my life. Before…"

Sylvia looked away from the images on the ceiling. Her eyes hurt from squinting her tear ducts shut. Her neck spasmed. It all came up on her suddenly, like an earthquake on the inside, shaking her from the belly out. She wanted to roll over, cover up and scream.

"Before what, dear?" Marshall asked.

"Nothing. Before nothing."

"Before the child," Samjahnee said. "You believe the child will interfere with your directorial career."

"Don't you?" she spat, returning her face to the projections.

"I don't know," he replied.

"Then why did you even call? What gave you the urge to disturb me face-to-face?"

Samjahnee said, "We found the Milkman."

— Chapter Twenty-One —

"HOW ARE YOU FEELING?"

Emory opened his eyes. The lids left a trail of goo across each, spattering the light, making his surroundings bend and blur. He tried to raise both hands to wring the sleep away. Only the right eye obeyed. The left arm refused.

"Feeling," Emory said. He rubbed his eyes and looked at his left wrist. A nylon belt tied it to the bamboo rail of a hospital bed. A small-bore plastic tube ran into the same arm, confined by a few wraps of white bandaging.

"You think you're smart getting yourself in here?"

Emory raised his head. Valient sat on the edge of his bed, turned at the waist, leaning back on a large spotted knockwurst of an arm.

"You think you're the first to try this?" he continued.

"I'm sick," Emory said as he realized it. The exact nature of his sickness escaped him. He remembered the fever and the cave closing in on him, like he was being cobbled back into a womb. Something about a bed, flying through clouds, with a head gazing down on him. Inspectors, tinkering with a broken… him, he guessed, now, through the fuzz in his frontal lobe.

"I'm sorry." An automatic response. He still operated on automatic. The rest of him stood back making notes, checking diagnostics. Energy levels? 10 percent. Processing speed? 50 percent. Mobility? Zeroed out.

"The doc says once you get enough juice in you, we'll be fine. I don't use 'we' like they do. I really mean you and me. As soon as you get off your ass, you're going to do your little chore and you and me will be fine."

"I don't even know… anything."

148

"They think some stool got in your bloodstream. I think you figured a way to fool the thermometer, you being a fancy engineer and all."

"They do any other tests I might have faked?"

"Don't know," Valient said. "Just popped in to make sure you didn't think you'd fallen off my to-do list."

Each sentence acted like a windshield wiper, clearing away the bacteria or drugs keeping him from navigating this conversation.

"I'm delirious from the drugs. Who are you?"

"I'm you." Valient patted Emory's shin. "I know why you killed that girl. Not exactly why, mind you. I've been there is all I'm saying."

"You've been where? And if that's all you're saying, why are you still here?"

Valient bared his teeth and leaned forward, leaning on his arm, elbow tucked into Emory's rib cage. "I extinguished the life of a young woman. A moment I regret. She didn't listen. I digress. I started on this alternative work assignment 18 years ago in much the position you are now. I worked my way into the position I am in now. You could work your way into a different position."

"18 years?"

"What gets measured, gets done." Valient sat up. "You ever heard that?"

"In systems engineering? Never. We're all 'hope for the best', 'life takes care of itself' kind of guys. You know?"

"You're not as respectful as I'd like. I'm going to throw some of it off as the drugs. If I turn off the drugs, do you think I'll get more respect?" Valient said, more than asked. "Results. That is why I'm the super. They measure my results with two metrics: productivity of the crew and productivity of the men who leave my crew. They judge me on how well behaved my men are once they leave here. That may not seem all that fair. I didn't always believe so. The metric is important, though. The company wants good employees who understand policy. They want employees who never want to be put back on my detail. Are you following me?"

Emory thought about his next word choice. He would not follow this guy anywhere. He decided on, "I understand."

"You think Campbell is going to keep to himself if he returns to regular duty? You think he's going to follow the policies of

Ambyr Incorporated and refrain from discussing confidential duties? I'm not inclined to think so."

"So you want me to kill him—"

"I am hoping for an accident. Killing is against policy."

"Let me get this right," Emory said, staring at the ceiling. "You want me to kill Campbell to keep your numbers up?"

❦ · ❦

The room had a bed, a wardrobe with clothing in, out and around its open doors, a table, two chairs and a damp warmth McCallum found foreign. He had no idea what heated the space — he guessed the building predated furnaces by a century or two — and the fireplace sat dark. Something kept the frost out of the room and the whole stone building. He'd removed his jacket the moment he entered, downstairs. Up here, in Snyder's room, it was even warmer.

He sat in a simple wooden chair, elbows on a plank table barely large enough for two place settings. Through the thick, gate-like windows he could see the whole of the parade grounds. He saw his tent easily. The scene didn't help center him, though. The view, the feel, the scent of the place displaced him.

Snyder entered with two unmatched mugs, steam streaming from their open heads. She set them down and removed her hat. Licorice black hair fell to the side. She slid the big duster coat off. It hit the bare wood floor with a knock, its waxy fabric kept its body shape even as it tumbled to the side. McCallum didn't watch. He pretended to stare out the window, using Snyder's pale, ghostly reflection to size up her body, which turned out to be pretty much as he... suspected? Hoped? Dreamed?

He sipped his coffee.

"No way your name's Snyder," he said.

"Sure it is," she said. "A name's just what we call each other, right?"

"I suppose so. It's not like it makes a whole lot of difference. It's all in the cuff."

"For those that have them." She sat down, bending a bit towards the window. She clasped her mug with both hands.

"You haven't had one for a while, huh?"

"What makes you say that?"

"No tan line, no gap in the fine hair of your wrist, and you don't shake your hand for no reason." McCallum made a drilling motion with his fist. "A lot of people do it, without noticing. The bracelets tend to settle and people don't like it. People tend to continue the habit for a while, even if they don't have a cuff"

"Settling?"

"The sameness," McCallum said. "The body needs change."

"That's a lot of insight for a landscape artist."

"Art's a process. The first step is observation."

Snyder's upper lip twitched, a miniscule motion, a quick and decisive fight with a smile, McCallum thought.

"So what else have you observed?" she asked.

"You've got the best living space in the fort. You're the leader here, like the mayor I bet, even if it's de facto. You don't have too many personal items around, but you didn't get here yesterday. Your clothes aren't packed, so you're not leaving tomorrow. You didn't come here with much, but that's not the real reason for the austerity."

McCallum sipped his coffee.

"What?" Snyder asked.

"What?" McCallum peered back out the window.

"You're saying I live like a nun."

"You live on the run," McCallum said. "Did, anyway. You're taking a breather here. I don't blame you. Judging by your accent, if you keep running in the direction you've been going it gets even colder. You didn't grow up in the cold."

Snyder's face hardened. McCallum tried to soften his.

"How long have you been here?" he asked.

"You don't know?"

"I'm sorry. I haven't stayed up on my conversation skills."

"Yeah," she looked into McCallum's eyes. It gave him a small but serious shock. "That's common here."

McCallum glanced at his left wrist. A habit formed from years of checking the cuff's face for news, messages, time or alerts. He saw nothing but skin.

"I'm not the leader," Snyder said. "I'm just together. You know? Most of them are touched. Not all. We've got drifters, hiders and haters, too."

"Haters?" McCallum feigned ignorance.

"Ollies who hate the companies so much they give up everything and come here to live like they're camping for the rest of their lives."

You're no ideologue, McCallum said himself. "You do seem together," he said aloud.

"Thanks." She almost smiled again. "You seem together yourself. You're not jabbering or counting every brick you pass by. You haven't mentioned devils and you're not wrapped in aluminum foil. You haven't spouted off about the companies and how they're destroying the world."

"You haven't either."

"Why bother. It's like saying the sky is blue. So Ed," Snyder leaned forward, raised her mug and blew across the top. "How do you like the fort so far?"

"My best vacation in years."

"You always vacation without your cuff?"

McCallum looked down at his bare wrist. "That is the vacation, Snyder. Getting away from it all."

"I should've broken out the Riesling instead of the coffee."

"The day's young," McCallum said. "And neither one of us seems to be going anywhere."

❦ · ❦

"Move it up the ladder," Sylvia said.

"Where are you?" Gavin's voice entered her ears. "Why no video feed? I'm staring at a three-year-old glamour shot of you that I find rather insulting."

Sylvia sat on a bale of peat moss outside the loading dock. She found the dirty, wet scent soothing and the peat moss itself firm and comfy. She'd made a kind of recliner out of 14 bales. A 700 pound throne. She wouldn't have minded Gavin seeing that part, all earthy and regal. She didn't want Gavin to see her swollen face, crabapple cheeks and flat hair. She couldn't call up all her powers looking like an old ollie, begging on the street. 'Empty bottle, sir? Can I return that cup for you?'

"I'm serious," she said. "You've got to bring the juice."

"You see? Here's the perfect illustration of my problem. I ask a question, you pretend like it never happened."

"It doesn't matter," Sylvia said. "What matters is how much muscle you can flex. How much, Gavin? How high up do your backers go? High enough to pry me out of Atlanta? Because this is the moment."

"I had a simple request," Gavin said. "Clear your schedule."

"I worked on this project day and night."

152

"Clear. Your. Schedule."

"A baby is not a schedule."

"You still don't get it. I made a request. I expected it to be followed."

"It was unreasonable."

"Besides the point. I asked you to do something. That should be the end of it."

"Who the fuck do you think you are?"

"Your boss," Gavin hissed.

"Exactly," she hissed back. "My boss. And if you were my boss, you could have me reassigned. So what is it, Gavin? Are you really my boss? Do you really call the shots? Large and in charge? Huh?"

She heard air passing through nostrils, quickly and powerfully. Like Gavin was having her baby, she thought. Only with his mouth closed.

"Fine," Gavin said. "I'll reach up the ladder. Because you're going to give me something."

"What?"

"I asked for two things. I'll settle for one. A movie or a baby."

━ CHAPTER TWENTY-TWO ━

SYLVIA DECIDED, SHOULD she ever obtain the means, she may very well live permanently in the first class section of an airship. Spotless, plush, silent. The windows angled up and out. Larger than king-sized mattresses, they inspired an Olympian sensation. Not the running, jumping, sweating kind— the Gods. One could stand, especially — up in the prow of the ship — and soak in the full sensation of skimming across the world. Of looking down. On everyone.

She sat in her lounge chair now, with more room than she'd ever need for her out-stretched legs, and watched the endless field of sparkle and shadow roll out beneath her. The rising and falling strings of lights, the occasional cluster of yellow-orange dazzle marking off a town or factory. Constellations passed below. What an exhilarating thought. Who got to float above the constellations if not the Gods?

The dead, she answered herself. Then she went to work. She tapped her cuff on the monitor fitted into the back of the chair in front of her and opened her mailbox.

Message to Gavin: Flight on schedule.

Message to Samjahnee: Will arrive at Niagara Falls Seneca Tower at 4:18 AM. Be ready with the truck.

Message to Niagara Falls Hilton: Will arrive at 4:35 AM and want my usual room. How's availability?

Message to general post: Riding in the belly of a blimp, like a shrimp in a whale, only without all the digestive acids and such.

She poked the file Samjahnee had sent. Lots of b-roll of the country in and around Niagara Falls. The Falls themselves held her interest for a moment. They were huge. The play of the mist rising from the water's endless collision with the rocks below

154

mesmerized her. She also liked Samjahnee's shots of the whirlpools. She hadn't seen those before. The massive crash of water and earth sent the constant torrent gushing, sometimes back in on itself. The water turned and turned, full of power, with no place to go. What a delicious metaphor. Feedback. That's what the Milkman was all about. She'd expected to use endless video of cows grazing. These whirlpools had much more appeal, Maybe they could—

"Fell and Morse Productions" slithered into her ear. "Content that's never content."

Sylvia rapped her cuff. "Yes, Gavin?"

"Hope you're happy with my arrangements."

Message from Niagara Falls Hilton: Awaiting your arrival, Ms. Cho. Your standard package is available.

"It's all about you," Sylvia said. "If I'm happy, it will eventually trickle down and you'll be happy."

"Notify me when you've made contact."

"What else would I do?"

Gavin's voice feed went dead.

Message from Samjahnee: Why the truck?

Sylvia pushed the dictate button on her cuff and said, "To get me from the tower to the hotel." Message to Samjahnee. Send.

Message from Samjahnee: For three blocks? Isn't there a shuttle?

Sylvia ignored the reply. She thought about bouncing more messages back and forth, just to keep Samjahnee from sleep, but the steward entered the cabin, in his cute little sky blue jumper, sporting a dreamy smile. He held a basket of fruit in the crux of his arm.

"Ms. Cho?" He bent and offered.

Bananas. She gasped. She hadn't seen bananas in years. Back when she did see them, it was just that— seeing. She couldn't actually afford to eat one.

"Thank you," she took one as she might a tissue. Forcefully blasé.

"We just got them in tonight," the steward said. "Apparently there's not a shortage everywhere."

"It's a big world." Sylvia sniffed the fruit. "About to get bigger. I am eating for two."

She took another.

The steward winked and moved on.

'Message from Marshall' appeared on the monitor. Sylvia tapped the mail open and began peeling her first banana.

Message from Marshall: Enjoying your flight?

She called up a keyboard so she wouldn't have to talk with her mouth full. She typed: Immensely. This is the only way to travel.

Message from Marshall: You should do a film about dirigibles. How governments outlawed them in deference to the airplane and oil industries. It would be great follow up to Tobacco Road. The flip side. Governments peddled a poison product while withholding one so wonderful.

She smiled. She nodded. That place in her brain reactive to new projects lit up. She wrote: Nifty idea. Lots of potential for the footage. Big airships, chasing clouds. You're onto something. Think we can dig up any old footage?

Message from Marshall: Uncertain. Never saw anything on pre-Buy-Up airships. I only know they existed at all in the past because the company's always saying how great it is that we have them now. You know that tale— government bad, company good.

Sylvia sent: I wrote that tale. I'm going to clean up this milk thing first. Then we'll see if I'm ever allowed to work again.

Message from Marshall: Don't furrow that brow. Perchance I'll back your next feature, regardless of how this one flops or flies.

Sylvia typed: Large of you. Thought you were fully extended.

Message from Marshall: I'm blushing.

Sylvia typed: On you that would be called a stroke. Get to a hospital.

Message from Marshall: My last project channeled new funds. I'm flush and full of fun.

Sylvia almost asked about his last project, then stopped herself. Why ask the question if you don't want the answer.

She typed: Working now.

Message from Marshall: Huff.

She ate her last banana as slowly as she could possible stand. She thought about making a general post about the fruit and how heavenly it tasted and decided against it. She wanted it all to herself. Even the idea of it.

❦ · ❦

Emory tried to remember what his little girl looked like. He closed his eyes and called up all the parts of her face. The tiny pink lips, the crystalline blue eyes and shaggy, crazy, refuse-to-behave hair of gold wildness. He had tried ... months ago ... when he could ... anything at all to make her laugh. Her face blossomed and body bounced. She laughed with everything. He thought, anyway. That's how he remembered it. Ago. In a different time stream, in a different universe. He couldn't count on his memory now. He didn't have a good check on his recollections, a baseline to which he could match his mental vision. And he needed it. At this precise moment, he needed to see his little girl. Not his wife or his mother or anyone else. Now. Elizabeth. Not a flawed facsimile from his poor and wasting imagination.

He jammed the cross brace into the wall. Jagged teeth bit into the earth. He hefted the central cylinder, held it with one hand and cranked its wheel with the other. The brace elongated, pressed the other foot into the other side of the tunnel. Campbell readied a post beneath it.

Emory gazed down the tunnel, into the moist blackness. The other team had yet to descend. Waiting, wisely, for the supports to take. The moment had arrived. Campbell crouched beneath him and the 60-pound steel brace with its saw-like foot. The back of his pale head could have been a mushroom. Inhuman. Not his friend. Not a man who wanted to tell people things he knew because man should be fair and honest and not a chump, submitting to the shaft of crap the company crammed into you from age four until death. The edge of the metal plate at the end of the brace would shatter the skull, driving into the brain, taking pieces of the bone along for the ride. Campbell would feel a prick, a flood of warmth, presaging a faint. Then nothing.

Could he look Lizzie in the face? Would the chief supervisor let him live at home, with his family? And if he sat cross-legged on the floor, watching her stumble towards him, could he look her in the face?

"If not you, someone else," the chief had said.

Or not, Emory wanted to say back. Everyone could make the right choice? Right? Couldn't the world work that way, with one guy setting the brace and the other guy setting the support, and the next guy bringing in the new section of pipe so that everyone moves ahead? Everyone lives?

Emory's arms hurt from being aloft for so long. The blood drained and the cells screamed, cut off and starving. He held his breath. The tunnel sent down no human sounds, nothing but dripping. He closed his eyes.

"Campbell," he said in a harsh whisper.

The man looked up from his crouch, leaning on the steel support beam he'd readied.

"They want me to kill you," Emory said. His face tingled. He felt himself pass from once place to another, through a field of bioelectric moral relativity nonsense. It charged his cheeks and ears and neck. In all his time on the chain gang, he'd felt innocent. He'd wrap himself in that from time to time. He'd crossed to guilty, now. Conspiratorial.

He felt like the Milkman.

"Are you gonna?" Campbell asked from his knees, staring up with his head cocked back so much he couldn't comfortably close his mouth.

"No." Emory finished fitting the brace. "That means the chief will ask somebody else." He knelt down in the puddle, collected by the curve of the mud. "You've got to get out of here."

"He'll know you warned me." Campbell jammed the metal pole under the back.

"He wants you dead. Because you talk too much."

"He's not wrong about that now, is he."

"Just run for it. Lot's of people live off line."

"Lots?"

"Some. A few."

"Ever meet any of them?"

"That's not the point."

"The crazy ass guys who talk to themselves all the time. Or the ones that stand around all day shouting Jesus is going set fire to the world. How about the ones that wander around begging for the last bite of your sandwich or sip of your coffee? You want me to be one of those?"

"You wouldn't be one of those," Emory said. "And you'd be alive."

"Would you come with me?" Campbell asked.

Emory paused. All the talk in his head had been about convincing Campbell to leave. He hadn't thought about going off line himself.

"Abandon my family?" Emory asked.

"You're not with 'em now."

"But... I could be. I hoped..."

"Then you should've killed me. You should have stuck that joist so deep in my head I never would have known another thing."

☞ · ☜

McCallum didn't want to move his arm. He'd let it go all numb and even necrotic before he pulled it out from under Snyder, or whatever she wanted to call herself. Her head on his chest, her leg laid over his, the feel of her back, down the length of his forearm filled him in, gave color to the pencil sketch of his life. Screw the circulatory system. This was bigger than blood flow.

And thirst and the need to visit a bathroom and maybe pop a mint. He'd fight it all. Even the sun, starting to blare in through the multi-pane windows. The leaded glass made the sunlight split and shine with more viciousness than normal. The wine didn't help. When did he ever drink that much wine? White? What did Snyder call it? Ice wine?

"You're still here," she said, with a mushy, sticky mouth.

"You've got me pinned."

"Yeah." Snyder pushed up on her arm. "That was my plan. Trap you here forever."

"Your plan is working." McCallum kissed her just a little. "Maybe better than you thought. I'm not moving a thing."

"You don't have to." She sat up. "Not for me."

She stretched, pushing her fists in a high 'v', with no concern for her nakedness. Not that she should've been, he figured. Not now, not ever, really. He shouldn't be, either. They'd been over it. Each other. At night, after a bottle of wine.

Snyder rolled over and straddled him. "I don't know what you're doing here, Eduardo McCallum, but I'm glad you came."

He snickered. "Likewise." He rolled her, tangling up the sheets and the quilt. She laughed and pretended to fight him off.

"Coffee," Snyder giggled. "Let me go and I promise you coffee."

"Persuasive."

"I can be."

McCallum rolled off Snyder and laid back. "So how does it work, here? I don't imagine there's room service."

"The service is not great. I know, because I'm the service."

"So far, I've got no complaints."

"It's not my morning for breakfast. Thank you Jesus, it's not my morning for breakfast. I'd have a lot of upset ollies down there. It would not be pretty."

"You all take turns?"

"Some of us. Some can, some can't. There are a few who need to do the same thing everyday. There are a few who cannot be trusted to do anything any day. The rest of us do the rest."

"And you all lived here through the winter."

"Winter is difficult."

"It's warm enough in this room."

"Somebody sometime put geothermal pumps in. They work even if we don't want them to. The summer can be worse than the winter."

McCallum rolled to his side. Snyder's profile held him for a moment. The scalene triangle of her nose, erected beside a sumptuous cheekbone hill, near a dark brown pond, feeding bent black reeds, lashing in a breeze. He wanted to live there, paint there, lie in rest in that tiny world next to him. Away and calm and free from desire.

Snyder said, "It had been a while, huh."

McCallum rested his head back down on the pillow. "You could tell?"

She rolled and pecked him on the lips. "You did nothing wrong. That's not what I meant. No, you did nothing wrong at all. I could just tell. That's all. Like you knew I wasn't from around here."

"I make love with an accent?"

Snyder smiled. "Everyone does. Most people are not as good as reading them as me."

"That's quite a skill."

She put her palm on the side of McCallum's face. Her eyes focused on his, unblinking, her mouth parted and he knew he would hear something important.

Snyder closed her mouth and her eyes and sat up. "I promised you coffee."

"Can I go? I don't—"

A rumbling sound grew on the far side of the parade grounds. A machine. Metal and movement. McCallum couldn't place it at first. A garbage disposal, with a spoon stuck in its maw? He walked naked to the window and followed the sound as it rounded the tents and huts and approached.

A red Jeep, with a tan colored top chugged into view, propelled, he guessed, by a gasoline burning motor. It drove without haste skirting the shantytown and pulled up not too far from the window.

"Fuck." McCallum backed up, remembering his lack of clothing. "My ride's here."

▬ Chapter Twenty-Three ▬

MCCALLUM EMERGED FROM the oak door, still stuffing his red cotton shirt into his jeans. He carried his jacket in his teeth. He took the time to tie his boots. As a patrolman, he learned never to short change the footwear. He walked up to the Jeep. Its tailgate swung open and the back window was rolled up and fastened with a strap. A man unloaded boxes of canned goods and sacks of rice. Tan work pants, a fur-lined coat an airship pilot might wear, with a matching leather hat. He had glasses, black plastic, thick enough to use as a pry bar if needed. Whip thin, he moved with jittery speed and precision.

"Let me help," McCallum said.

The man glanced at him. "I won't say no."

"I'm Ed." McCallum went to the back of the vehicle and grabbed a burlap sack.

"John."

McCallum lifted out the last of the boxes and set it down on the grass. "Where do these go?"

"I'll show you." John tossed a sack over his shoulder and went back through the oak door McCallum had just exited. McCallum followed, toting a case of cans.

Once inside, they turned left and stopped in a long, narrow kitchen. Mismatched shelves and sinks. Two steel tables, with various pots and pans leaning in loose stacks or hanging above. The scent of fresh coffee filled the room. John dropped his rice on the first table and continued to a stainless steel coffee machine, an industrial grade four-potter. He grabbed a mug as McCallum set his box down.

"You passing through?" John poured.

"Probably." McCallum took a mug and waited.

"We appreciate the help just the same."

"Least I can do."

John sat down on a stool. He cuddled his coffee cup in both hands and watched McCallum find a stool on the opposite side of the table.

"Is that your tent out there?" John asked.

"You're very observant," McCallum answered.

"It stuck out. We haven't had any new homesteads in a while."

"Spring is in the air," McCallum said. "I like your Jeep."

"Junior? Thanks. The restoration took me 15 years."

"And now you use it to haul groceries."

John grinned. "I think, sometimes, it was the plan all along. Even if I didn't know it."

"You all seem to have survived the winter just fine."

"Lost two to TB. Lucky it wasn't more."

"TB?" McCallum pondered. "Tuberculosis. Didn't think that still made the rounds."

"Not in the corporate world. Out here, I've seen folks die of cuts and bruises."

"Awful."

"Eh," John said. "Some of them died happy. Free of that final tether. They didn't die hostages."

"Doesn't sound like they had to die at all." McCallum took a big swig of his coffee.

John leaned forward over the table, studying McCallum like he'd switched lenses on a microscope. He'd selected a stronger set. McCallum studied him right back. He'd met killers in his career and they all surprised him in some way. Hidden anger or hidden remorse, a pall of pride in a unique accomplishment or an off-handed iciness. Human appliances, he came to call the latter. Human-shaped dehumidifiers that kill. If John Raston was a killer, he'd be the most surprising one ever.

"Ollies don't take to prying," John said. "A man's business is his own. That's an unwritten policy. Just about the only one. But if I may be so presumptuous, let me give you a piece of what I've learned off line. Healthcare makes you a hostage. That fantasy the companies give you about a lasting, perfect life holds no more water than a leprechaun's pot. It's pixie dust. Something's going to get you. Not even Grade Ones live forever. But you've got to understand that to let it go. The doctors and drugs. If you can't say goodbye to them, you can't be an ollie. You're going to have to strap on your kneepads, go back to whatever job you despised, and grovel."

"If I may be so presumptuous," McCallum said. "That's some kind of pain."

"Pain's the kin that knows us," Snyder said. She walked like a cat. None of McCallum's senses warned him she was coming. Green work pants, tight white shirt, she tied her still wet hair in a tail as she neared. McCallum couldn't do anything but stare.

"Pain's the wind that blows us," John sang.

"It seems you're getting along with John." She took a mug and filled it with coffee.

John said, "You make that sound like a miracle."

Snyder sat down. "Sometimes men a…" She splayed the fingers on both her hands and meshed them together like cogs. "…click. Sometimes, not so much."

"How about you?" John mimicked her gesture. "You two clicking?"

Snyder turned to McCallum and curled her lips into a wavy smile. "He'll do."

"Do what?"

"I'll wait to see what comes next," Snyder said.

McCallum raised the coffee mug to his mouth and said, "me too" before he took another long, warm, invigorating sip.

❦ · ❦

The Ambyr educational system recognized Emory's talents from the tests he took at age twelve. He planned. He organized. Their tests discovered his innate propensity for hierarchy and mathematical methodology. They put him on track to be a systems engineer at age 13. He never struggled with his destiny. He actually found some comfort in it, the regimen and the logic.

Now that logic told him to run.

"We will never have a chance like this again," Campbell said. He stood in grimy yellow overalls, black plastic boots pulled up over them, his face wet with underground moisture and nervous perspiration, holding specs of sewer waste like glue.

Emory peered back down the pipe. The next crew had yet to start out. He held up his bracelet. Egg white ceramic, an inch thick, he knew it was supposed to survive a cave-in. It would tell the company where the trouble lay when the workers were uncommunicative paste.

Emory reached up and released the cross brace. The bar retracted into itself a few inches. He lowered it to his shoulder and put his left wrist against the chipped, curving wall of the tunnel.

"Crank it," he said.

Campbell reached across him and turned the winch-like lever, pressing the foot of the brace against Emory's cuff. The crack startled them both. Emory pulled his hand out and they switched positions. He crushed Campbell's ceramic band and it fell to the puddle at the bottom of the tunnel, next to his.

"We've got about four minutes," Emory said. Campbell started back down the sewer pipe. Emory grabbed his arm. "That's what they'd expect." He started running into the old section of the sewer, the section to be replaced over the next few weeks.

"A... yeah," Campbell said. "Because it's the only way out."

"Actually, I think there's no way out. But it's too late now."

Emory had charted out exactly how he'd ask Lillian to marry him, determining the perfect time and location to generate maximum romance. He chose the swings, on her school's playground, at dusk, in autumn. The scent of fallen leaves in the crisp air. Now, he concentrated on that smell, pulling it hard from the back of his memory. He could, by the power of his will, overcome the stench of crap. Urine, feces and rot filled his nose, splashed up by their running feet. Their flashlights slashed back and forth across walls, barely cutting the darkness. Emory's heart fought his breastbone. His mouth sucked itself dry. He stumbled, recovered, caught the reflective eyes of a rat in his light, and kept running.

"You... know...," Campbell huffed, "there's a cut off. A... barrier."

"And..." Emory squeezed out.

A rusty slab of metal cut across the tunnel. A large, riveted ring edged the pipe. Little streams of water shimmered and fell from two spots around the top. Emory ran right to it, turned and bent over. He grabbed his knees, giving himself a moment to breathe.

"A ladder." Campbell panted next to him.

"Figured," Emory said. "Hoped, really."

Emory climbed the iron rungs embedded in the concrete, next to the seven-foot valve. The round iron plate covered the top of the manhole. He managed to jostle it, but couldn't get the lid up out of its impression.

"Can't," he said.

Campbell climbed the ladder, as Emory swung to the side. They both grunted, pushed and lifted the round, waffled hatch out of its nest. They slid it sideways, skidding it on the pavement.

A car screeched. They heard a bang. The twinkle of a glass shower. The light blinded them. They scrambled out, as people— two men maybe — shouted. They emerged into an intersection, downtown. Cars paused at the corners, some obeying the traffic lights, others blocked by the accident.

"Hey!" Emory heard, directed at them. He paid no attention. He saw a parking garage a block back in the direction they had just come, but above ground.

"This way," he told Campbell.

"That's back towards the dorm."

"You arguing with me now?"

"Your luck's gonna run out."

They ran down the sidewalk. The city air tasted wonderful. Emory felt the prick of sun on his cheeks and, even though his stomach shrank and wanted to throw out what little it had left and his lungs had become pincushions, he felt it. The good in it.

They ran halfway into the parking garage, snuck between two sedans and collapsed. Emory looked at Campbell, his dirty face, a long string of drool clinging to his lower lip. They both heaved huge amounts of air in and out.

After his breathing steadied, Emory stripped off his yellow overalls. He rolled them in a ball and put the mass under his arm. He might need them. The temperature couldn't have been 50. The concrete began to leach out the heat he'd generated in his run. Campbell looked ready for a nap.

"We can't stay here," Emory said.

"Where we gonna go?" Campbell rubbed his eyes.

"Aren't you the one who said we could walk away whenever we wanted? We always had the right to quit and go home?"

"Technically."

"I know. I know. The numbers. The chief would rather have two accidental deaths than two resignations."

"I don't even have a home to go to," Campbell said.

Home, Emory thought. That's the other thing they'll do. He said, "The chief will send somebody to my house."

"It'll be all right."

"No, it won't, but there's nothing I can do. Nothing. I'm worse than useless. I'm making trouble."

"No," Campbell said. "You saved my life."

Emory took that in. Like the air and the light, the tiny scent of spring eking its way through the city.

"Those assholes are going to my house," Emory said.

Campbell nodded. Emory cupped his hands over his face. He wanted to punch the door of the car behind him. Such a waste of energy, though. He couldn't waste the energy.

▬ Chapter Twenty-Four ▬

MCCALLUM FOUND JOHN Raston on the wall, river side, next to a small pile of clothes and a cooler; the kind McCallum would've used to keep beer cold at a beach. John ran a pair of jeans up and down a piece of corrugated steel, spraying suds.

"What are you doing?" McCallum asked as he approached.

"Washing my clothes," he replied.

"Was that another company chain? The washing machine?"

"Of a sort," John said. "Everything is. Every material thing. You get my age and you hate them all a little. Once the shine wears off." He put a wet shirt in a plastic bag and picked up a pair of jeans. He began running them up on and down the bumpy board, working up more foam. "Synder says you're an artist."

"Aspirational."

"This is a good place for that. There's time and beauty. You don't find those two cohabitating everywhere."

"It does seem seductive."

"We could certainly use you. I can't trust a lot of these guys with the wine."

"You've got a lot of boozers."

"Some. Not too many," John said. "It's the distribution that's more the problem. Bottling, loading, driving around, that type of thing."

McCallum let his surprise show. "How much wine are we talking?"

"150 barrels. We collect surplus grapes from the local wineries. It's much easier for them to claim a few acres of vine didn't produce than they lost a barrel or two. We make the juice ourselves, then make the wine. We donate some back to the vineyards. We trade the rest for food and supplies."

"Barter?"

"Yep. The big 'B', as in the best way I know to kick the companies."

"Plural? You're kicking the companies?"

"You shave a little from all three and you reduce your chances of getting noticed. They each have holdings in the area, so it's pretty damn easy. Grapes are grapes."

"It's elaborate."

"It's work. A lot of work. Especially with a bunch like this." John nodded towards the parade grounds. "The companies don't care that any of them are here for a reason. Snyder's good, though. She finds a way for every whack-job out there to pitch in."

McCallum gazed out over the huts and tents and trails of mud. A man near the gate sat on a log slicing his hands back and forth over each other. An older woman walked by tossing her hands in the air. Others sat in little groups, sewing, whittling, fidgeting in ways McCallum couldn't discern through the distance.

"Is it worth it?" he asked.

"Hell yes," John said. He put his jeans in the bag with the shirt and picked up another pair for washing. "When you're with a company, everything you do you do for them. There's no other choice. I'm not talking the work. That's the obvious part. I'm talking about every call you make, note you send, every meal, every sip of water is to their benefit. Even protests, weak and pitiful as they are, generate activity, which generates revenue. Let's say you post a complaint. A mess of people glom on. That makes the evening news happy, whipping up interest, which is great for the advertisers. Let's say the complaint really touches people, so much that they want to protest. That brings security. Maybe even overtime. The ops are thrilled. Maybe one guy buys a motorcycle with his extra dollars. From the same company that started the whole problem in the first place." John shook his head, running wads of soaked denim across the corrugated steel. "It's all theirs. All you can do is try and get out."

"But why go ollie? Why not just enjoy your retirement?"

John stopped washing and looked up at McCallum. The look poked him, McCallum thought.

"The velocity of money," John said. "In the economy, I'd still be spending, even if it was all for my own pleasure, not to mention survival. Every dollar you spend is worth several to your masters. You know why they don't work people day and night anymore?

You know why they offer vacations and personal days? Holidays? They need to keep the money churning. They need consumers as much as they need workers. They need people like you to go to the store and buy paints. They want people to buy your paintings. Circulate that dollar. They need the guy at the paint store to watch a movie and they need that movie actor to buy a boat. There's no more growth for the companies. That ended with the last Buy Up. They can try to take from each other, but they end up giving just as much to do that. The whole natural world strives for equilibrium, including the economic one. I think they've reached it."

"There's always something new," McCallum said. "That's growth, isn't it?"

"New doesn't mean revenue," John said. "I'm an engineer. Trust me on that one. Innovation used to give companies a shot at profit. Not any more. You invent something, the other two swipe it. You sell it to your own employees, but that probably means they stop buying something else. Some Grade 5 smiles, as people buy his whatsit. Another frowns, as people stop buying hers. There's no new money. Only the velocity of the money we've got."

McCallum said, "So you don't spend."

John nodded. "Get off line. Freedom. The only way to fight."

John Raston wasn't in hiding, McCallum realized. He wasn't holed up in this ancient fort because he killed a girl. He chose this. Planned this. John Raston was making a stand. Rebelling.

McCallum had a picture in his head that didn't work, didn't resolve. Maybe the Vasquez girl decided not to run off with him? Maybe she knew too much about this enclave and its black market? Had Vasquez and Raston ever had contact before the stabbing? McCallum had never established any connection and connections were hard to hide.

Were this on canvas, he'd squeeze out some Gesso, white it all out and start over.

"What made you think I'm retired?" John asked.

McCallum lowered his head to meet the man's eyes.

❧ · ❧

"That's a Ford Thunderbird," Campbell said. "A BCCA brand. I like our chances."

Emory did not. Running from the chain gang was one thing, assaulting an innocent person was quite another. Stealing cars, kidnapping people, forcing them into servitude— it never worked. Not in real life. People were too connected.

"Connected," Emory said. He couldn't hijack a person and a car. He could ask for a voice call. "This way," he told Campbell.

They walked to the edge of the parking ramp. People strolled past. Couples. Small groups. A few singles. Harsh daylight made him uncomfortable. Their clothes reeked of chain gang and sewer and desperation. Any semi-intelligent person would press and hold their cuff seeing Emory and Campbell from twenty-feet out.

So they couldn't be seen. Emory pointed to either side of the human-sized entrance to the parking ramp and they waited. Standing, unable to lean relaxed against the concrete wall, Emory felt the wait in his insides. Bugs, flesh-eating termites gnawing and scratching his guts. He had to reach Lillian. They were coming for her. A select group of deviants from the Alternative Work Detail, so thrilled to be out in the fresh air, seeing a woman for the first time in months, years, a life time. The Chief's men. Emory knew them intimately. Their musky smells, their calloused hands. The way they slapped, crushed and coupled. And they were headed for Lillian. And Elizabeth. His sad, unsuspecting family. His girls, who didn't even know the horrors that lived under the city. Innocent. Sweet. Doomed. The bugs ate into his lungs and he had to breathe faster to get more air to make up for the leaks in the holes they chewed.

"Hey," Campbell said, glancing over his shoulder.

Emory clenched and unclenched his fists.

A woman strolled into the ramp. Mid-forties, fit, a professional skirt and jacket, all prim and blue. Her heels tapped the pavement quickly.

"Excuse me," Emory said. She turned, crossing her feet, almost falling over. Her mouth, shielded in glossy pink lipstick, formed a tight circle. She recovered and kept going, watching to see if Emory followed.

"We just need you to make a call." Campbell stepped in front of her.

"Oh, sure," she said from a trembling mouth, as if this were a normal request. As if everyone in the world didn't have a phone strapped to their wrist all the time making this akin to asking for some air or a share of sunlight. She moved to slap her fingers across the phone and leave them until the emergency operator inquired as to her status.

Emory grabbed her wrist and yanked her arm around behind her back.

"AAAAAA— mmmm" Campbell pressed a hand against her mouth.

"We are sorry," Emory whispered. Like the chief's boys whispered to him, though never apologizing. He held her like the chief's boys held him. "We really only need you to make a call."

"I'm going to bring the bracelet up," Campbell said, "and take my hand from your mouth, OK? If you scream, this event will become something different. Blink twice for OK."

The woman shivered. Emory could feel it through her body.

Campbell took his hand from the woman's mouth. She made a warbling sound. It reminded Emory of his little girl, when she was just about done crying.

"Call Lillian Leveski," Emory said.

"C-C-Call Lillian Leveski," the woman barely got out.

Emory placed his ear on the woman's. She made one, tiny whine. She smelled clean, like fresh vegetables, in a garden, with hints of tropical flowers.

"No Lillian Leveski local, India Group."

Emory said, softly. "Ambyr Consolidated, 93 Calumet, Buffalo Catchment."

The woman repeated the information. Campbell watched the area, a hawk on a pole. Emory heard the ring in the woman's ear.

"This is Lillian?" came the answer. Emory gulped a ball of air.

"Ask her where she is?"

"Where are you?" the woman asked.

"Who is this?"

"I'm calling for Emory," Emory said. The woman repeated it.

"Oh God, what's wrong?"

"You're in trouble," Emory said. The woman said nothing.

Campbell said, "Someone's coming."

"Tell her she's in trouble," Emory hissed.

"You're in trouble," the woman said.

"What's this about?" Lillian demanded. "Where's Emory?"

"Tell her to get Lizzie and run."

"A man," Campbell tried to whisper, watching the sidewalk behind Emory and his captive.

"Run? This is crazy?"

"To the place in John's picture. That last one he sent me," Emory's voice shook and bubbled. "Tell her to run to the place in the picture."

The woman complied, fast, mumbled, Emory wasn't even sure if Lillian understood.

"Time's up," Campbell said.

They let go of the professional woman in the now wrinkly blue skirt and jacket, and ran, full out, away from the entrance. She stood and screamed. They heard it all the way down the street.

❧ · ❧

Sylvia couldn't move. She sat in the hotel room chair, upright, horizontal positions were out of the question, face down, on your back or sideways, it all hurt. It all forced an acidy fire out of her squished stomach and into everything else. She hated sleep. She hated food. She hated anything other than the baby and his or her imminent departure.

The baby must come out. The baby can't come out.

She volleyed the phrases in her head, a thoughtless mantra that can come to replace sleep. She'd heard that people who didn't sleep went insane. Always figuring she was more than three-quarters of the way there already, this current dream drought would finish the job. She'd go nuts, trying to sleep upright, because the baby got in the way.

Never in the way. She'd promised herself. She promised her bosses in a silent, they'll-never-know kind of way. Movie and baby. The show must go on. The baby must come out and baby can't come out.

The hollow knock of a hotel room door. Flesh rapped on glue and dust pressed and printed to resemble wood. No resonance. No firmness. No cheery 'Company's here!'

"Yes," Sylvia said as she lifted herself out of the chair. It took all of her upper body strength. She waddled to the door, flicked up the handle and waddled back without looking to see who she'd let in.

"You're looking well," Samjahnee said.

"As are you," Sylvia said. "Did you have your eyes done? A little lift and tuck under the chin?"

"Not until I get my bonus for this gig," he said. "If I get a bonus."

Sylvia lowered herself back into the chair, careful not to get the creature within active again. He was obviously filming some kind of martial arts film in her womb. The apple wasn't going to fall far from the tree. If it ever fell.

The baby must come out. The baby can't come out.

"Your concern warms my cockles," Sylvia said.

"Can you do it?" Samjahnee asked.

"Have to," she answered. "They want a Sylvia Cho movie. That means Sylvia Cho snagging the Milkman."

"I can do this. We can edit you in later."

"Inauthentic. Not what they signed up for. I don't know who these people are. I do know what they want. They want what every financier in the movie business wants: the same thing only different. They want my last movie, changed enough to make even more money. They don't want new, fresh, artistic, clever or anything other that what worked before. They want Tobacco Road about milk. They want me finding this nut bag and getting his face to pop in surprise. A fucking jack-in-the-box. That's all anybody ever wants. The fucking jack-in-the-box. A nice, safe surprise. Set to music."

Samjahnee crossed his arms. "You're lovely."

"I'm never buying my kid a jack-in-the-box. Maybe he won't imprint on it and want the same thing his whole damn life."

"Absolutely lovely." He held his hand out.

Sylvie took it and yelped. The pain. If you set electricity on fire and drank it. That was the pain.

She said, without wanting to, "Pain."

"*Is the wind that blows us,*" Samjahnee sang.

"Yeah, see," Sylvia said, standing. "Things are always easier with a sound track."

The baby can't come out.

— Chapter Twenty-Five —

"HE'S SUSPICIOUS," Snyder said. They walked on the outer path, near the river. The temperature felt 10 degrees cooler, just a few hundred yards down from the ramparts. "Just like me."

"It's understandable," McCallum returned.

"We thank you for your understanding." Snyder walked a step ahead of McCallum, partly due to the thinness of the path, partly because she led. She seemed to have a destination.

"I've come a long way." Snyder continued down the path. A small, stone shed sat at the end, with a black iron gate blocking an arched doorway.

"How long?" McCallum fished in his pockets.

"Hard to say, the way I travel. A little by train, a little by car, a little on foot. I begged rides all the way up here."

"You must really like old forts." He found his brush case and dug his fingers down.

"No, I really hated the place I left."

"I take it this wasn't an official transfer." McCallum found his gray, gooey gum erasure.

They reached the iron gate. Snyder took out a key and opened the shiny new lock hung on the antiquated bars.

"No." She swung open the gate and entered. "I left my employer without notice."

"That's uncommon," McCallum followed her, brushing by the gate. "What is this?"

"We pump our water from here. I check on it every day to make sure of no leaks. I am a very cautious woman." Snyder ducked around McCallum. She grabbed the gate and whipped herself out, using her momentum to ram the bars closed. McCallum caught the gate as it clicked.

Snyder smiled. "Who are you Eddie McCallum?"

"The name's not enough?"

"John thinks you're Ambyr Systems Security."

"What do you think?" McCallum rattled the gate, banging the cross bar in its slot.

"I think you're here for me."

"Like I tracked you from wherever you're from?"

"Eh. Maybe not. I know you didn't come here to paint."

"I'm not a blank canvas you draw your fears on."

"Some time down here will help you remember." Snyder held the lock and brought out the key. McCallum jabbed his hand through, knocked the lock off and slid the bar back. He pushed the gate open.

Snyder bent down and picked up the lock. She pinched the gum eraser stuck over the keyhole. "Who is paranoid?"

McCallum took the gum back. Then he took Snyder's hand and kissed the back of it. "I couldn't hurt you even if that was my job. Which it's not."

Their hands dropped. He didn't let go.

"So you're not here for me?"

"Trick question. It's not how I started out, though." He smiled. She didn't smile back.

McCallum gently tugged Snyder back up the path, along the outside of the fort and the narrow walk between the walls and the river. The wet air and bright sun and the feel of the supple hand ensconced in his own, made him smile all the way, over the murders, the fear, the fact that he'd been made and nearly locked up. He realized he did not fully agree with John Raston's view of the world. The company didn't trap everything in its closed economy, wrapped so tight you can't find a seam. They had yet to fully monetized fun, laughter, love, trust.

Trust. His first drawing teacher told him not to fight his hand, but to trust it. Let it lead lines in space. His hand. In Snyder's, as if that could possibly be her real name. As if he had any right to know. He had been no more honest with her.

"John's right," McCallum said. "I came here to arrest him for murder."

❧ · ❧

The train stopped at the butt of the city, where the river and creek met. That would be the easiest place to hop on board and stow away. They could ride, hidden, through the city, the suburbs and up into the Niagara Catchment. That's why Systems Security watched the station so closely. Cameras, sensors, even real live ops patrolling the rails. With two fugitives from a chain gang at large, they were probably paying attention. Emory knew something about the local trains. They were part of his system. What used to be his system. Back when he made sponges. He sat at his computer and watched the delivery of raw materials, the creation of cakes and their return to Ambyr's transportation web, always looking for ways to make things just a little bit better. He knew the train slowed before making the wide turn at the river and following it north. Slow meant 15 miles an hour.

Emory and Campbell sat inside a bush with too few leaves to cover them. The temperature dropped by the water. They hid in a restricted area. The voices of passing vehicles carried, burying any useful sounds, like those an approaching posse of ops might make.

"This is the only way," Emory said.

"Yep." Campbell stared at the tracks as if watching his house burn.

"The trains are smooth," Emory explained. "Very aerodynamic. There's only a couple of gaps, not much bigger than us."

"Yep."

"You've got to run and jump. If you miss…"

"Pizza cutters. Those wheels are like pizza cutters with 200 tons on top."

"Pretty much."

They saw the lights of the engine through the branches. Red, white and green, brilliant even on a brilliant day.

Emory put his hand on Campbell's shoulder. "You don't need to do this."

"Yep."

"You don't need to go north. In fact, it would be better if we split up. You go back to the yards, near the mills. I bet ollies hop rails there all the time."

Campbell watched the train approach. "We don't know when there will be another. This is the one."

Emory squeezed his shoulder. He looked at the side of the man's head, half-shaven, tiny plots of earth still stuck randomly around his face, over his cheeks and forehead, the sides of his nose. He bent like a reed, his head having taken on too much extra weight. All the running and hiding and twitching at every sound. Emory had nothing left in his body; only Lilly and Lizzie pulled him along. He didn't know what propelled Campbell.

The engine passed, with a rush of air and the eerie whine of steel on steel. A long, dull silver snake, with small breaks in the skin, at the links between cars. Emory couldn't see the end. He wasn't going to wait and try.

"Go," he said.

He ran, eyes locked on the gap between the third and fourth boxcars. He couldn't run as fast as the train. He could only run to meet that space. The soft ground grabbed at his feet, slowing him. Uneven, rocky, with a slight incline leading up to the track bed. There were no cameras here, no engineers watching out for hobos, because this was impossible. The train grew huge, towering, slippery, loud and slow. It slowed. Or, for Emory, time itself slowed.

He couldn't look behind him. He couldn't take his eyes from the gap, or change his momentum. This would be milliseconds. His legs cocked and released, hands clawing, just as the hand bars passed.

He screamed through the air. He hadn't planned to. He'd never been the screaming type. The silver and black. The noise. He swore he could feel the gravity of the huge vehicle lifting and tugging. He smashed into the edge of the boxcar, his feet only inches off the gravel and rails. Pain exploded in his wrist. More followed from his chin and knees. Nothing overtook the fire in his right wrist. He clung to the handrail, unfurling his legs into the gap, onto the dirty steel platform on the front of car four.

He glanced back as Campbell leapt for the next gap. He struck the side, arms extended. He pivoted, turning on an invisible pin that stabbed through his middle and into the ground. For a moment, Emory thought he'd be tossed free. He'd drop and roll to the side. Safe. He knew, later, when he replayed the memory in his head for the 50th, 100th, 150th time, that it should have happened that way. He shouldn't have curved back under the car, landing on the tracks to be sliced across the hips.

━ Chapter Twenty-Six ━

MCCALLUM CHOPPED ONIONS for the soup. They didn't make him cry.

"Irreverent clown," the woman next to him said. Fiftyish, hair like silver cotton candy, limbs thin enough to snap between your fingers. She spouted something every five or six minutes, but nodding constantly. She nodded at sounds— hers, Synder's, McCallum's, the birds.

Snyder said, "Make that hearty soup tonight."

The woman started pulling groceries from the larder. "Asshole cheese."

"Still probably better than limburger," McCallum said.

The woman nodded.

John Raston walked in, making a track for the coffee machine. He took a mug and filled it and McCallum continued to French the onions, cutting the orbs into small, shallow canoes. He liked to see the onions in his soup. John sat down across from him, elbows on the stainless steel table.

"You taking me away before or after dinner?" he asked.

"Don't know. I think I'm going to want to taste this."

"Donna does a pretty good job."

Donna, he thought. They should've been properly introduced. "John, you kill Geri Vasquez?"

"I don't know who that is," John said, "but I've never killed anyone, so I'm confident in saying no."

"Yeah," McCallum said. "Of all the people I've ever asked about an insubordination, not one as ever said 'Yep. You got me.'"

"Yet you keep on asking."

"You know the girl I'm talking about. Back in the fall. The night before you came here, I'm betting. Young, pretty."

"Geri was her name, huh?" John took his huge glasses from his face. His head shrank, got pin-shaped. He pinched his hand across his eyes, squeezing the vision out of them.

"Grade 15. Marketing. Designed her own clothes on the side."

"She was pretty. Even in that stupid coat."

McCallum put his knife down, and placed his palms on the tabletop. Donna dumped hard potatoes into a kettle of water. He didn't have a good way to make her stop.

John's hands dropped. He gazed out through the window to his right. "She caught my eye as she walked. I was sitting in my truck. She was the kind of girl you watched walk, even if you're not into girls. She passed in front of my car in that jelly coat and this guy comes out of nowhere. I mean nowhere. I'd been sitting there for a good quarter hour and had never seen him and he appears on the sidewalk, grabs her by the arm and stabs her right in the back. I couldn't believe it. It... I couldn't believe what I was seeing. He pounded away on her, holding her up, then letting her drop and giving her one or two more for the road. Then he was gone. I'm getting out of my truck now. The shock's wearing off and he's gone."

McCallum let him stare for a while, hold his coffee mug, suck some of the warmth out and stare.

"God damn blood leech," Donna said.

"You know the stabber?" McCallum asked.

"Never seen him before."

"Could you describe him?"

"Thin, about your age. Short, brown hair. Nothing special. He was no pro, I could tell that. He'd never stabbed something before in his life. He couldn't get the knife out. He couldn't decide whether to hold onto the poor girl or let her go. The whole thing was sloppy. Except his clothes. All black. He planned that part, what he was going to wear. He wanted to hide in the shadows. He got that part right."

"Why didn't you tell us this?" McCallum asked. "Why didn't you stick around and help?"

John closed his eyes slowly, moving them while they hid under their lids, opening them to match McCallum's gaze.

"Can't say."

McCallum leaned in, forearms flat on the steel. "What were you doing there?"

"Meeting a friend?"

"At an India Group bar?"

"It would seem."

"What's your friends name?"

"Can't recall."

"That's the kind of thing guilty people say. You remember what coat Geri Vasquez was wearing and you can't remember the name of the friend you were meeting?"

John slid his glasses back into place. "I've got lots of friends."

"No you don't," McCallum said. "I've run your cuff. You've got nobody. And you haven't called cross company in years. You've been paring down your life since Roger died."

"You leave Roger out of this."

"Killing off your old life, getting ready to hide out here. Then a girl's murdered and you run. You put your plan in action. Why, John? What were you doing there?"

"Just meeting a friend."

"You've got no friends. After Roger there's no one. Nothing for you."

"I had acquaintances."

"Roger's friends? They fade away with him? He was the fun one, right. You were the engineer. The sensible one. Work friends? They stay at work, don't they? No job, no husband— what were you doing in that parking lot? Besides watching a girl get knifed to death."

John made fists and skated them around the smooth stainless steel. McCallum pushed his kitchen knife farther right. John looked into his coffee, steam rising up into his face. He stood straight, hands spread and loose.

"Flying fudge," Donna said, tossing a chunk of butter into a skillet.

"No freaking way," Snyder's voice rang down the hall.

"Way," came another voice. Feminine. Sharp.

McCallum didn't take his eyes off John. John didn't lift his face from the coffee.

"You think because you're pregnant I won't take you down?" Snyder's anger brought out her accent. Her threat sounded like a little song. McCallum didn't give in to it and look.

"That's exactly what I think. I've been waiting nine months to come here because I knew my baby would get me through."

John looked up and over. McCallum risked the glance. A black-haired woman stomped through the kitchen, white sweater, white pants, white boots, white glasses. Snyder followed her closely. Another figure trailed them both, holding two orbs high, one in each hand. The disturbance fixated John, so McCallum took another glance. Cameras, he determined. That guy in the back had two video cameras.

The woman in white approached like a train. She walked with an odd gait, McCallum thought. She didn't appear pregnant... until you caught her from the side. Big. Just about ready to go.

Snyder ducked around a table and zipped up the side, reaching McCallum and John first. Donna dragged McCallum's cutting board from in front of him.

"Go, John," Sndyder said looking at McCallum. "You've been sweet. Go now and I'll take care of this."

McCallum saw the determination in her hard, narrow face. Her dark eyes glowing. Her long thin lips pressed hard together, neck stretched out. A dare. A front.

The man with the cameras stopped behind Snyder. Dark skinned, dark hair, muscular but in the roundest of shape. Arms up, with one lens aimed at John, the other at the woman in white.

"Are you John Raston?" she asked him.

"Who wants to know?"

"Sylvia Cho. I'm making a film about the Milkman."

"Fuck you," he said.

"Fuck 'em all," Donna shouted, tossing onions into the skillet. Sizzle.

❦ · ❦

Emory walked well off to the side of the highway. He needed more cover, more undergrowth. The trees and bushes hadn't filled in yet so he had to cut through the thick of it to feel safe. Safer, he corrected himself. He hadn't felt safe in months. Walking this way took longer. The brush tore at his clothes. The ground offered all kinds of rocks and downed branches and the odd hole to trip him up. He walked mostly with his head bowed, to keep from breaking an ankle. That meant the occasional whip across the forehead. It would get worse as the darkness came. He couldn't drift too far from the road, though. He'd never find the fort without the road.

The cold would come, too. Walking briskly helped keep him limber. With the sun dropping, he could already feel the temperature going with it. No more solar warming, not enough energy in the air and ground to maintain a decent degree in its absence. He'd need a fire. They'd have a fire. John stood in the fort right now, fire roaring, a side of beef turning over it, dripping fat onto fresh bread.

Car. He crouched and let it pass. From that distance, if they saw him at all, they'd think he was a garbage bag tossed from the road. Unless they were specifically looking for someone in yellow chain-gang coveralls, they'd have little trouble picking him out of the brush. They were too dirty now, he wondered if even an op or the chief's crew would spot him. He had to risk it regardless. He couldn't last in this chill without a bit more protection.

Jugs of water. Not too cold. John Raston would have those, too, by the fire, and he'd pour them into his mouth and over his face. He'd dry himself near the flames as his hugged his Lillie and Lizzie.

Car. He crouched down again. He'd have to move farther into the woods. He'd never progress stopping every two minutes. A Civet. His heart buzzed. A silver Mahindra Civet, with a woman's head up in the front window and a little head behind, in a car seat. His car. His girls. Lillian was so smart. She'd figured it all out from his stuttering, pitiful message, through a woman he'd almost frightened to death. Before Campbell died.

They would make it. They were only minutes from the fort now, traveling by car. They would be fine. John was there and he was so smart. He knew everything. Emory's heart danced around. A fountain of energy — a reserve he couldn't believe he had — opened and shot through him. He inched closer to the road. He needed more open ground. If he hurried he'd be only 20 minutes behind them. He could be kissing his girls in 20 minutes.

Car. He dropped. A pick-up truck, four-door utility style. White. Dirty and banged up on every surface. Two male heads bobbing inside, two more in back.

"No," Emory said into his hands.

The sticker on the door said Ambyr Works. Four men from the chain-gang followed his girls. He knew those men. From 100 meters, looking at only silhouettes, he knew the special detail the chief had sent out to retrieve him. He knew them intimately.

▪ CHAPTER TWENTY-SEVEN ▪

"ARE YOU THE Milkman?" Sylvia asked again.

John turned his attention to McCallum. "It would seem you're going to get your answers."

"No one's more surprised than me," McCallum said. He addressed Sylvia. "I don't imagine I can get you a cup of coffee. Snyder, do we have tea? The kind with no caffeine?"

"Water, coffee, wine and milk," Synder said with a sneer. McCallum grinned. Mad, nasty and she was still hospitable.

"I'm fine," Sylvia answered.

"And you, sir?" McCallum asked Samjahnee, who opened his mouth and paused. He looked to McCallum like a kid who got found playing hide'n seek. He never thought he'd be noticed.

"Nothing for me, thank-you," Samjahnee managed after recovering.

"Well I'm ready." McCallum went to the coffee machine and went about serving himself with careful deliberation. *Milkman? Movie?* McCallum began to sketch the picture in his head. The lines were fuzzy. The meaning began to take shape regardless.

"What else you involved in, John?"

Synder came along McCallum's side. She made the motions like she wanted coffee too. He caught the questions in her eyes, though. She was a rabbit with two holes and thinking seriously about using one right now.

"Film everyone," Sylvia said to Samjahnee out the side of her mouth. "We'll fill in names and shit latter."

Samjahnee panned the camera in his left. Snyder swung the round, glass coffee pot and doused the orb in a scalding back sheet. Samjahnee screamed and dropped the camera. Snyder set the pot down on the table — she didn't want it to break — and ran.

"Whoa, Snyder," McCallum jerked in her direction, and stopped. "You all right?" he asked Samjahnee. He saw Snyder disappear through the back and knelt next to Samjahnee, who yanked his dripping, steaming sleeve back from his gleaming red hand.

"I'll get some ice." John jogged off to the right.

"Asshole cheese," Donna said, stirring the soup.

Sylvia remained focused on the far end of the kitchen. She touched her glasses and moved her attention to her cameraman. Who, McCallum realized, wasn't the only one with a camera. He'd used glasses like that, putting them on people inside a skimming operation or sex-for-work scam. She'd taken video of Snyder, who it seemed really, really didn't want her image posted around the big wide world.

"I didn't expect her to be so camera shy," Sylvia said.

"Thank you," Samjahnee said, "These second degree burns will be fine, boss."

"Of course they will. Everyone gets coffee spilled on them from time to time. How's the camera."

"I've rolled them through fires."

"Excellent. This stuff is seething. I love it."

McCallum stood. He glanced back at the back end of the kitchen. Snyder wasn't coming back. He thought about chasing her down, then thought some more. Best to get to the root of a problem.

He picked up the orb, bounced it in his hand twice, and said, "Donna, stand back a ways."

The woman backed up without acknowledging him. McCallum tossed the camera into the soup. A thick splash rose and fell

"Filthy butternut," Donna growled.

"HEY!" Samjahnee sat and reached for the other camera. McCallum got there first.

"Excuse me," Sylvia said. "I wouldn't do that."

McCallum tossed the second orb into the soup. "Couldn't see why you would." He stepped around the rising Samjahnee and grabbed Sylvia's arm.

"I don't think so," she spat.

"I do apologize." He ripped the glasses from her face and threw them into the pot as well. "Donna, could you be a dear and wipe that up for me."

The woman picked up a towel and started sopping up the liquid on the side of the pot and around the stove. "Messed up mother."

"Bullies never come across well on camera," Sylvia said.

"I don't intend to be on camera," McCallum said. "Didn't I just make that clear?"

Samjahnee took two steps, intended to retrieve his equipment, McCallum figured, so he said, "Take five, pal."

"I appreciate the enthusiasm," Sylvia said, "but I'll direct."

McCallum fought the urge to squeeze Sylvia's arm more tightly. She didn't struggle. People usually did. And the lack of physical fight fascinated him.

John returned with a towel, hanging like a hobo sack. "Here you go," he said to Samjahnee. "Hold this on your hand for as long as you can stand it."

"After you get the cameras," Sylvia added.

McCallum let go of Sylvia and passed in front of her. He leaned back on the counter, next to the stove with the big pot of soup and crossed his arms.

"Cameraman, ice your burns." McCallum said. "Director, stop making sounds or I will lodge a carrot in your throat to assist you with that. John, you can talk. In fact, I insist."

"I need—" Sylvia started. McCallum grabbed a carrot off the counter, flipped it in his hand and pointed it at her like a sword.

"I'm not the Milkman," John said. "That would be Emory Leveski."

"Him?" McCallum said. "I put him on work deferral."

"You're an op?" Sylvia popped.

"Amber Systems Security."

"Shit," Samjahnee added.

Sylvia laughed. "Too awesome. You've got to let me get a camera. This is like skipping a grade. Like skipping a fucking grade, my new best friend."

"This Milkman business," McCallum said, "It's not exactly company business is it?"

"The policy is unclear," John said.

"But you and Leveski didn't want anything to do with an investigation."

"So you are involved," Sylvia stated, moving towards the stove.

"Was," John said. "Past tense."

McCallum walked towards the back of the kitchen.

"Where are you going?" Sylvia asked.

"I'm running after the girl," he said. "I don't do that nearly enough."

■ Chapter Twenty-Eight ■

AT THE FRONT gate, a woman held a baby. McCallum watched her from the window in Snyder's room. Snyder wasn't there and he wanted to search for her but that woman and the baby— they looked like acrylic cutouts in an oil painting. Clean, fresh, and out of place. She turned, back and forth, at the hips, like she was in a train station, looking for her ride.

He walked down the steps, out through the doors and onto the parade grounds. Dusk was about to give way to night. The sun wasn't helping the air anymore. The chill grew. Most everyone drifted to the left where John Raston and Donna set up a table to serve soup and bread. His stomach gurgled as he walked, straight ahead, towards the main gates. He focused on the newcomer. If Synder had made it all the way here from the equator, she'd certainly survive another couple of minutes without him. He didn't want it to be that way. As he thought it, he came under a powerful urge to tell her she wouldn't have to scurry around alone any more. She could settle. He'd see to it.

After he took care of this.

McCallum knew the woman with the baby. He'd talked to her, just a few months ago. She'd been stressed, worried, beaten down like nearly everyone he met on the job. Special, though. Not a person of interest, not a victim. She'd been something else.

She focused on him. As he approached, she must have realized he aimed at her. He knew he had an air of authority around him, an inescapable aura, like the fumes clouding a skunk. Her mouth opened as he closed in. Addled surprise, he called it. A sudden, sad realization he so frequently delivered.

"You," she said. "Shit."

"Mrs. Leveski." McCallum's mouth remembered a step before the rest of him.

Her eyes welled up. Her lips moved without making a sound. A chant, it seemed, to ward off evil. She bounced the quiet little girl on her hip.

"What are you doing here?" he asked.

"I…" She turned back towards the gate. She wanted to bolt. "Don't know, really. I really don't know."

The gates flew wide. Four men swaggered through, dirty, ranging in age from late 20s to an early fifty, McCallum thought. Work pants, loose shirts and jackets. They moved as a gang, taking in the whole scene, fully expecting to be the new center of attention.

All of McCallum's hairs stood — neck, arms, legs. The kid on the far left, 175 pounds, mid-twenties, carried a chain over his shoulder. Medium gauge, so that it was neither slow nor pointless. He'd been in fights before. Taking him was going to hurt. Next man in went 220 easy. He walked with his arms back and gut out. Thirty something, bushy hair. No discipline, no martial training, he probably relied on his muscle pack. The kid on the far right might have made thirty. Tough to tell under all that hair and dirt. Maybe he weighed 150, if wet and fully dressed. He carried a pipe low. Ten-pounder, two-feet long, McCallum guessed.

That left the oldest guy, in the middle, the one fixated on Lillian Leveski. You'd think he just fond his Easter basket the way he grinned. He had a lot of true muscle, the kind made from years of hard labor, and moved with the confidence of someone who'd won about a thousand yard fights.

They all had matching clunky, white ceramic bangles on their left wrists. Industrial cuffs. The mark of an alternative work detail. These men moved like a gang because they were. A chain-gang.

McCallum touched his wrist, forgetting the cuff sat on his kitchen table, 25 miles south. He couldn't signal he was an op, open a live channel so control could monitor his situation, dispatch backup and an ambulance to save his life.

Lillian clutched her baby more tightly. McCallum moved in next to her.

"Where is he?" the man demanded.

"What are you talking about?"

The man walked up to her. He looked so happy, McCallum thought. A big, yellow-toothed smile, hands on his hips, about to burst into laughter. "We were hoping this would be hard."

The other men spread into a circle. McCallum tensed, bent his knees, moved his arms out a few degrees from his body. This had become the kind of scenario they instruct rookies to avoid at all costs.

"There a problem here?" McCallum asked.

The man didn't look at him. "No one's talking to you, asshole."

"You need to be using that kind of language around a child?"

The man looked at McCallum. Not the face. The arms and legs. He assessed, McCallum figured, trying to decide how much a scuffle might cost him.

"You got a cock in this fight?" the man asked. "Or you just trying to be all shining armor and shit?"

These guys wanted to fight. It was just a matter of when. McCallum needed the baby out of the way. A little surprise wasn't bad either. He rammed an open hand into the 50-year-old's windpipe, drew his hand back, closed it and punched him hard on the end of his nose. The man fell back, gasping.

"Run," McCallum said to Lillian.

The kid with the pipe actually stepped back. What a moron. McCallum had all the room he wanted. He ran, jumped and spun, kicking the boy across the face. He landed, punched him in the center of the stomach and grabbed the pipe. He cranked it out of the kid's hand and turned. The 50-year-old clutched his throat. The other two men had to move around him, giving McCallum an extra second. He crouched and snapped the pipe against the hairy kid's right kneecap. The kid screamed and collapsed as McCallum stood.

Lillian turned and the older guy took a fist full of her sweater. McCallum raised the pipe. The other two men rushed him. As he figured, the big guy had no technique. He swung a big ugly punch. McCallum smacked it away with the pipe. The younger one whipped his chain, catching McCallum on the lower leg. He hadn't expected that. The dumb ones always went high. He pivoted and stomped the chain with his free foot, almost ripping the links from the kid's hands. Bad position. For both. McCallum needed to—

The big guy bear-hugged him from behind. Immobile. Tight on air. McCallum flicked his wrist and conked the man on the head with the pipe. The bear hug loosened and McCallum shoulder-rolled the man onto the ground. He skipped left. He'd smash the young guy holding the chain and—

"Give her back!" Lillian screamed. McCallum heard others come running. He couldn't decide if that was good or bad. The oldest man held the baby over his head. She hung by her clothes. McCallum only knew she could breathe by her crying.

The man looked at McCallum, who stood frozen, panting, slowly realizing he'd lost. "Tie him up before you beat him dead." The man's voice sounded weak and sandy.

The big guy wrapped McCallum's legs in his arms and flopped him on the ground. McCallum lost the pipe. He curled as some-one from behind kicked him in the kidneys.

"Where is he?" The 50-year-old tossed the crying child under his arm, carrying her like a log. McCallum could tell it hurt him to speak.

"Give her back." Lillian clutched at the air.

"Put the baby down," McCallum said. Someone jumped foot-first onto his head.

He knew a bunch of the ollies had gathered. The show had been loud. He couldn't see or hear anything specific. Sudden pain in the thigh. More pain in the head. Fuzzy lights in what would've been his field of vision could he open his eyes.

"What kind of man doesn't come running to protect his child?" the older man asked.

Lillian's lips trembled through a wet, sloppy, "Just, please, give her back."

"Maybe the kind that ain't here yet. Maybe we made better time. Could be." He coughed.

A kick to the knee. A kick to the arms McCallum held over his face.

"I said tie him up. We'll do him after we got the runner. He might be here right now watching or he might still be making his way. So secure this asshole and then start looking around."

McCallum heard one of the female ollies yell, heard some-thing crash and felt himself dragged and rolled. He didn't fight as they tied his wrists. He concentrated on his breathing: Sharp pain in, dull pain out.

The big man dragged him, turned him over and propped him against the wall. They'd used the nylon cord that had held an ollie's shack together.

"Gem," the man ordered, "close the gates. Conner, Teddy, take the prisoner. We'll stick over at the fire. See if Emory shows up for his kid."

Gem was the big guy, McCallum said to himself. *Conner and Teddy the two younger guys, with weapons.*

"Lady," the man handed Lillian her baby. "Keep this thing from getting noisy. Or I will."

He walked through the makeshift village in the direction of the operative's quarters. Lillian followed, eyes locked on her daughter.

Conner and Teddy lifted him by the arms and pushed him down the muddy path. Gem stepped to block him. He drilled a finger into McCallum's chest.

"You gonna die tonight," Gem said. "I'm gonna watch the life come right out you eyes."

❦ · ❦

Sylvia recovered her glasses and put them on, even though they smelled like trash. She wanted to puke, though she pretty much always wanted to puke. The baby pressed on her stomach. Not her figurative stomach — not that middle area everyone calls their tummy even though it's really a mass of intestines, pancreas and liver — she meant the actual stomach, the small, rubbery cavern you sent your chewed food. The baby used it as a kick bag. He or she needed to get out and hit the gym.

She walked out to the circle that had collected around the fire. Rough, haggard people sat on a log, eating soup from mismatched bowls. The air was cold, but she liked it. Cold air fought the pukies.

"Gets dark fast here?" she said.

Samjahnee walked two paces behind her, his cameras in a backpack. "This light's no good."

"We'll fix it post."

"I need the gear to get anything."

"We best wait on that."

A cluster of maybe a dozen ollies and four men she hadn't noticed before sat around the fire, eating. The op had his arms behind his back, seemingly tied up. John Raston sat next to him like the log was 200 degrees. He couldn't keep his ass steady. It went a long way towards explaining what all the yelping might have been about. But not all the why.

"What did I miss?" she asked.

"Look at that?" one of the younger, new guys said.

"This place just gets weirder," another of the men said. She knew he was the leader, though not from any due loyalty or rank. He'd slit your gut for a beer. Sylvia knew that by sight. She'd seen it before, on Tobacco Road. She decided to make a headcount of low-functioning high grades. She panned, caught sight of a woman with a baby and stopped.

"Hi," Sylvia waved. "She's adorable."

"Thank you," the woman said.

"You two don't look like no ollies," the leader said. His voice had a grit-in-the-vacuum cleaner quality.

"Aren't you clever." She turned to John Raston. "Is the Milkman here?"

"No," John grumbled.

They were straying from her script. Her subject was absent and the op had been arrested, she presumed by the thugs. Served him right, the big bully. Making her glasses smell like garlic. If she wanted to finish her film, she'd have to sit here with these nut-structures and men so bold as to tie up a Systems Security operative. Who did that? Who risked that kind of break in policy?

Samjahnee put his hand on her shoulder and his mouth near her ear. He said, "we should go" with next to no air.

"No," the leader said, "seriously, I can't figure out what the likes of you two are doing here."

"Just passing through," Samjahnee said in full voice.

"Why don't you have some soup? It's not half as shitty as I expected."

"Thank you," Samjahnee said, gently pulling Sylvia backward. "But we had our fill inside."

"Aren't you looking for someone? Didn't you say milkman?"

Sylvia touched her glasses. "Do you know the Milkman?"

"I don't. What's funny, though, is I'm looking for someone and you're looking for someone. You think maybe they're the same person?"

"I can't imagine us having any mutual interests."

"You're a lippy one. Gem, give the lady your seat. I like talking with her."

The man that rose looked like a barrel with arms and legs and a head stuck on top. His pants, shirt and jacket had sat at the bottom of a tool chest too long. His gaze had calluses.

"Can you take him?" Sylvia asked Samjahnee.

"Out to dinner."

"I hate to see a good piece of log going to waste." She crossed the circle and fell onto the space Gem had left. The baby made sitting down so inelegant. She hated it. Wobbling diminished her authority.

The leader man looked like pale driftwood. He kept still, but his eyes darted around, always passing the op on their trips into the darkness that was quickly encroaching on the party.

Gem stood next to Samjahnee, bigger in every way. The op sat between John Raston and a young man with a chain over his shoulder. Most of the other people in this group were ollies, in her estimation. The battered, holey, unmatched layers of clothes. Excessive, matted hair. The way they mumbled or stared or twitched. She'd thought often of doing an ollie film. She assumed a good deal of comic drama ran through the tiny enclaves like this one. She had also assumed she'd hate the setting. The stench, the grime, the drool and the danger. Everyone had cautionary tales about an ollie camp. Usually a friend of a friend. Now she had a story first hand. And hoped it didn't turn into one of those profoundly icky tales.

"Who the flaming fuck is the Milkman?" the leader asked.

"Oddly enough, that's what I'm here to learn."

"You're big, lady," he said, "just not big on answers." He laughed. Two of the others laughed. The man with the chain, and another, to the far right. "I should be doin' stand up. Really. In fact, I should stand up." The man stood and stepped forward. "Ha. Ha. You get that." He raised his voice, though it seemed to pain him. "Emory Leveski. I got your wife and your kid and there's no way you should be comfortable with that."

"How far away do think this man is?" Sylvia asked. "You're not projecting."

"You got a mouth on you. Why don't you give it a try."

Sylvia stood and made a megaphone with her hands. "Emory Leveski. Come out, come out wherever you are."

The guy could surface, she figured. All she had to capture it all were her glasses. For the tiny, concealed cameras, the light was pitiful, even with the campfire, and she needed to get close to collect any decent sound. She couldn't tell Samjahnee to break out the spheres. The shit-bags would spin out. Still, she could salvage something from this. So long as nobody killed anyone. That would taint the film. If she could just get some ghostly image of the Milkman, in the early nightfall. That could be very, very effective.

Sylvia watched the man at the far right, the one wearing hair for three. He had a pipe across his lap. The four were some kind of group, but were smattered through the crowd like concert security. Only they weren't exactly making things more secure. At least not for her.

That woman and baby didn't belong here. She was all put together in a catchment style. She belonged on a sidewalk, passing homes with shutters and porches. Sylvia wanted to plop down next to her and ask about breastfeeding and when you start cereal and how long before that little doll started sleeping through the night.

"He's not coming," she said to the leader.

"Oh, he'll be here," he snarled. "That's why his woman drove out. Why else would she bring a baby to this pile of crap? Really? Would you bring your baby to this pile of crap unless you thought your husband's life depended on it?"

The woman with the baby might snap her own bones if she didn't loosen up. Raston wasn't much better. The op had pulled his brow so far down she wondered if he saw anything. She knew the look. She had it herself, when a shoot's gone wrong. When you still had to get the scene even though everything's gone to shit. As in right now.

The leader rounded the fire and stopped in front of the mom.

"No," she said.

"Don't touch them," the op added.

"Forgot you were still alive," the leader said. "Why's this guy still alive?"

"Because I can help you."

"Yeah." He pushed an open hand into the mom's face and ripped the baby free with the other. "You get back to me on that."

The baby squealed. The crowd grumbled. The leader stood and held the girl high over his head.

Sylvia skipped next to him, arms out. "What are you doing?"

"I ain't got all night." He turned to the baby dangling high over the fire.

"Oh my God." Sylvia said. No one heard her over the chorus of screams."Put her down, man. Put her down.'

"Em-or-ee!" he shouted. "EEMM-OOOR-EEE!"

This was nuts. She walked over to Samjahnee, put her arms around him and leaned in to speak directly in his ear. "This guy's a psychopath. I don't want him in my movie." She lifted a multi-tool out of the side pocket of the backpack. She moved it to her coat pocket as she walked back to the fire.

"EEMM-OOOR-EEE! EEMM-OOOR-EEE!"

Sylvia dropped the tool at Raston's feet. He watched it hit the ground, too stunned to realize what happened.

A rumbling noise started behind Sylvia. It reminded her of vehicles in old movies. She turned as headlights came on, glaring their way into the circle. It was an old vehicle. The lights burned her eyes. She refused to look away. She needed the glasses to take it all in.

A man-shape stepped into the beam of the driver's side headlight. "Set her down, Clark. Now!"

"Or what?" The leader laughed.

Sylvia didn't think the man heard him over the engine and the fire and the crying toddler roasting above it. He certainly hadn't noticed Raston cutting the op loose. She shouted, "He said, 'or what?'"

"Set her down!" he screamed. "It's me you want. So come and get me."

"He's right about that," he said to his men. "Go fetch him. We'll do him so his woman can watch, then get back to the city. Hate to miss bed check."

Two high grades rose, the one with the chain and the one with the pipe. They walked through the circle picking up the big man at the edge. They marched three abreast into the twin blasts of light and the black cutout Sylvia took to be The Milkman.

"Samjahnee," she chirped. "Light up the eyes."

"Roger that, boss." He dropped to a knee and threw his backpack to the ground. Sylvia turned slowly — her eyes velcroed to the Milkman and the thugs — back to the leader, still holding that baby high, her own camera recording.

"Hey, op." She angled her mouth to her left, not averting her eyes from the child. "I've got that baby if I have to fucking stand in the middle of that mother fucking fire, I've got that baby."

"All right then."

The op stood.

❦ · ❦

Emory stood. He saw Lizzie, dangling from the hand of a monster. The other three approached with no sense of urgency. He wanted them closer, faster, now. They couldn't see him too well, he knew that. Counted on that. He put his heel on the front bumper of the Jeep. He grasped the edge of the hood. They walked at the same pace. Conner on the left, taking a chain down from his shoulder. Teddy on the right, held a bar in both hands. Gem stomped up the middle, cocky as ever. They always sent fear surging through his body, the sight of any one of them, any time. Until today. No fear today. That gland dried up, he thought. No fear to pump. Get Lizzie, get Lilly, get out.

Timing, balance, the way things work. Everything had an optimal setting, a right moment. This system required velocity greater than reaction time. Force came from velocity. There was a moment at which the speed of cars and brains signaling muscles met.

Now.

He used his heel to vault onto the hood. He grabbed the edge as tight as he could. The Jeep lurched forward. It raced at the three men. Emory loved their faces, wide and dumb. They paused for a moment, completely confused. Emory let the momentum push him back. He cocked up his legs. Conner dove left, Teddy right. Gem couldn't decide. He jerked one way, then the other, and the Jeep plowed into him. It didn't have much speed, but the mass hit him sideways, mid dive. The truck ran over him, its left front wheel snapping his back, bringing out a horrific wail. The bump shook Emory's grip loose. The back left wheel silenced the man. The force of the Jeep coming down from the bump rolled Emory off the passenger side of the hood. He hit the soft ground hard.

❧ · ❧

"What the…" Clark brought the baby down. He fit her under his arm, preparing to walk off.

"I'll take her." Lillian lunged for the girl. He swung her back out of the way. Waiting behind him, Sylvia plucked the baby from his hands, spinning to put her back between the man and the child.

"I don't think so." Clark half-laughed.

McCallum dropped and whirled his right leg around, sweeping Clark's legs off the ground. Clark fell backward into the fire. Lillian ran around it. She and Sylvia disappeared into the darkness outside the circle. All of the ollies stood and backed away and Clark howled and rolled and rolled, smashing out the flames clinging to his back.

"Stay down!" McCallum hollered.

Clark bounced up, flung his arms out like a smoking bird and screamed.

McCallum stared at him as the sadness set in. The guy had gone over. A wild beast now, a demon of pain and rage. He regretted not bringing a stunner or a dart pen or one of the other non-lethal arms they'd invented to prevent this, the total liquidation of an asset. He'd come here to punish a killer, not to be one.

Clark charged him, arms out for a grapple. McCallum took Clark's left arm, spun and flipped the man over his shoulder. Flat on his back, he torqued the arm, as if attempting to unscrew it from its shoulder. McCallum placed his foot between Clark's chin and collarbone and applied all his weight. The man gurgled and twitched and slapped at his ankle. McCallum brought his foot up and down fast and ended him.

"That baby OK?" he asked out into the dark.

Lillian came closer, pulling the baby into her chest like she wanted to melt the child right back into her. The lady director came up from behind, holding her glasses in one hand, wiping her eyes with the back of the other.

Emory Leveski brushed past him, adding himself to the spire of wife and baby. McCallum moved in the direction Emory had come from. Two figures in the light of the Jeep crept forward. McCallum took three more steps and stopped.

They stood facing each other across a couple of yards of darkness and mist. The sounds of the fire and baby and chattering ollies diminished in McCallum's ears. He focused everything outward, at the tense, uneasy young men. At the drooping chain and the dull pipe, spotted orange and black in the firelight. The big one was missing. He thought maybe the Jeep got him. Couldn't be sure. Couldn't let this go on.

"What were you thinking?" he said. "You need to avenge the death of a piece of garbage? He tried to cook a baby. You gonna risk it all for someone like that?"

The silhouettes didn't move. McCallum saw the chain and the pipe jitter.

"'Cuz let me tell you, he will not be appreciating the effort."

They stood for a while. Longer than McCallum might have guessed, had he thought about guessing, had he not been thinking, do I have it in me? Is that big guy dead or recovering? Do they know they've got the advantage from the blinding lights? And youth. *Man, there is no second wind in my sails.*

The Jeep engine revved up. The figures ran right, in the direction of the front gate. The Jeep's lights faded and the engine coughed to silence. The Jeep squeaked and another figure approached. McCallum waited. This one had half the profile of the other two and moved like a cat.

"Thought you'd left," McCallum said.

"Ran into one of John's old friends," Snyder replied. "He has a story more pathetic than mine."

CHAPTER TWENTY-NINE

THERE COULD BE no better wine. No better drink, Emory thought. In all of existence, no one had ever enjoyed a beverage as much as he loved this white, fruity, sugary vino. He wanted to pour the wine into his eyes and ears and throat. He'd have a headache tomorrow. He'd be all contorted from the lack of food and water, from the way he treated all his muscles, like meat in a grinder, and from the come-down. The withdrawal from the chemicals his brain had made to get him from point A as in asshole to point B as in bliss.

He sat by the campfire. Lillian took the baby up to a warm room in the castle, as they called it. Snyder's room, he understood. Kindness from a stranger. He found it a tough concept to remember. Kindness of any kind cowered pretty far back in his head. The fact that he used to be kind to strangers himself hadn't even occurred to him until he told the security operative about being the Milkman. How once upon a time he had a team of people that tested local dairy products for safety and published their findings in anonymous posts. He helped people he didn't — wouldn't ever — know.

"That's a severe breach of policy," McCallum said, slugging back his own mug of wine.

"The company looked the other way," he explained. "They have kids, too, you know? Everyone wants milk that's free of dysentery, even if the company doesn't want to make the investment to ensure it."

"Not everyone, it would appear." McCallum poured more wine. "Who'd you tick off so bad they framed you for murder?"

"No one," John Raston jumped in. "We never reported much. A couple of tanks of overdue, a few dirty lines. The farms keep their stuff cleaned, mostly."

"Somebody hated you two."

"Then why not kill the site?" Emory asked. "That's the part that never made any sense."

"Maybe they couldn't," John said. "We took precautions."

Emory shrugged. "Then why not get rid of me instead of that poor girl?"

McCallum shook his head. All the elements floating in his brain had no form or shape. He had a mobile with no center rod bringing the parts into orbit, into a pattern that made art out of junk. Unification. Theme.

"How'd you do it," Sylvia asked Emory. "How'd you keep the site from being shut down?"

"It's a rolling site," John answered. "We set it up to move periodically. To find it you had to search key terms any time you wanted to visit."

"So even if it got shut down, it would simply pop up some-place else."

"You catch on quick."

McCallum said, partly to himself, "the best way to kill the site was from the source."

"They should've killed me," Emory said.

All art was the same, McCallum always thought. Sculpture, painting, video, dance, even mime. Emotion, edification, nar-rative, held in balance. Insubordination was an art. Not a nice art, not a worthy art, but a blend of craft and desire, forethought and abandon, the wish to perform, achieve and touch a state of contentment, regardless of how fleeting. It was all the same.

"Why the girl?" Emory mumbled, slumping on the log. McCallum saw the wine taking effect.

Every policy breach he'd ever investigated hung like a mobile in which one couldn't see the wires. His job, at its core, was to see those wires binding the seemingly separate parts together. Most of the time it proved fairly easy. Greed, sex, anger and the feeling — he couldn't believe there wasn't a word for it, being so common and so critical to the human condition — the sense that someone was getting the best of you. Those were the cables drawing most people from the clean to the dirty column. Once you ferreted out which tied your suspect, victims, opportunities and rewards together, it usually made sense. It usually turned out to make common sense. Most indiscretions were, in the end, trite.

"We're all insubordinate," Emory said into the fire. "Everybody trades a rake for a shovel or has a buddy cover for you while you nap, because you were up all night playing the guitar in some pub. Or... or... uses the company equipment to see if their milk's clean. Everybody breaks policy, it's just a matter of degree."

"You're OK, Emory." McCallum took the man's mug. "You were smart back there. That thing with the Jeep was very smart."

"It wasn't original." He put his face in his hands. "Saw something similar today. Shit. Was that today? Twelve years ago? Did it happen?"

McCallum motioned for Snyder. She padded over the ground and helped Emory up.

"Come on," she said softly.

"Good night, Em," John said.

McCallum watched Snyder lead Emory, his wife and his little girl up to her room and he felt a pain in his eyes. In his temples. A happy, brutal, piercing relief. It had a temperature. The feeling had heat. A thin, buttery emotion churning through his head and heart. He took another sip of wine. Tonight he'd sleep in his tent, with Snyder pulled up so close no inch of his skin would be out of contact with hers.

"So John," Sylvia said. "How difficult is it to start a site rolling?"

"Depends who you ask."

"I'm asking you."

"The Milkman site took me a couple of days."

"Now tell me if you're in the market for any new friends."

"I, uh, hadn't thought—"

"Smashing. I think we could be the best of friends. Don't you think so, Samjahnee?"

He addressed John. "It works best if she's your only friend."

"Sylvia," McCallum interrupted. "You started this documentary in October? Around the time of the murder?"

"Yes," she huffed. "I imagine I caused it. Not that I could've known."

McCallum dropped his head, peering at her from under a fat, furrowed brow.

"The Milkman is an embarrassment to somebody, I don't know who." Sylvia said. "Somebody else wanted to exploit the embarrassment. I don't know the identity of this person, either. I am coming to terms with the fact that I never will. They're grade fours, each vying for a chance to be a three. Can you name a grade four? A five? I didn't think so. At that level they become invisible. Sitting in high towers, mixing up clouds, throwing down lighting. We are the stones they stand on, or throw at each other, whatever it takes to get a step higher."

McCallum didn't care for this picture, but it worked. The form, the composition. Bleak, strangling, maddening, provocative it portrayed a sketchy truth. The paper notes, the op he fought in his apartment, the money to fund a movie all took resources beyond the average low grades he wrote up everyday.

"Why didn't they kill Emory?" McCallum asked.

"Aren't you the investigator?"

"Yeah," McCallum said. "That's what investigators do. Ask questions. I'm thinking our jobs aren't that far apart."

Sylvia titled her head and dropped the corners of her mouth. "If it were me, I'd tell one of my people to take care of the Milkman problem without making a big splash. You don't want a problem brighter than the one you're trying to snuff, get me? When I'm running the show, I make sure the right person is doing the right job. My $70 an hour guys are doing $70 an hour jobs. My $20 an hour guys are doing $20 an hour jobs. I don't know if that helps, but somebody picked the least valuable person to kill in order to put an end to project Milkman. Does that help?"

"Every little bit does," McCallum said.

"I caused all of this and I'm quite sorry." Sylvia stood. "I'm also quite pregnant and quite tired. Samjahnee, do you think you can get us back to the hotel?"

"Nothing will stop me," he proclaimed.

"Which hotel?" McCallum asked.

Sylvia started walking away from the fire, into the darkness.

"What?" she called back. "Are you going to tell me not to leave the catchment? That's delicious."

He smirked. She would be the easiest person to find on the planet.

❧ · ❧

Sylvia walked through the quaint alley of shacks and tents and leaning pieces of corrugated plastic. Samjahnee followed close behind. Most of the ollies were already asleep. Her eyes had become accustomed to the firelight, making the walk to the front gate overwhelmingly black. And cold.

"Samjahnee," she said over her shoulder. "Do you have a torch?"

"We're almost—"

Snyder stepped into the their path, arms across her chest.

Sylvia caught a tiny yelp in her throat. Actually gasping like a teenager in a horror movie would have been mortifying.

"There is a man looking for me," Snyder said.

"I'm betting you don't mean that op back there." Sylvia smoothed back her hair.

"He runs Managua for the India Group."

"Managua? Is that made with cilantro?"

"I can't be in that movie. Do you understand?"

"Never having heard of Managua, I'm betting it's more than a day's drive."

"It's over 2,200 miles." Samjahnee gazed into his cuff.

"It wouldn't matter if I was on the moon," Synder said.

"You have a high opinion of yourself. Nobody gets over your body, huh. Now I'm wishing I had more footage of you."

Snyder pushed in, nearly touching Sylvia's protruding belly.

"It's a matter of pride with this man. No one defies him."

"But you did."

"I was a… plaything. I got sick of it."

Sylvia leaned in, her face close enough for a kiss.

"No one interferes with my art." She looked up and to the right. "No one who's not paying the bills, anyway." She ducked around Snyder, continuing to the gate. Samjahnee stood still. He lowered his eyes, his lips thinned out. Then he walked, trailing behind his boss.

"Of course," Sylvia said without turning. "You can always talk to John Raston. Perhaps you could tell him to be my new friend for what did he say? Three days?"

The squeaks of the hinges cracked the night as they pushed through the tall wooden gates and left the fort.

CHAPTER THIRTY

MCCALLUM STOOD ON the wall, facing out at the lake. The morning wind stung his cheeks. The deep waters stayed cold long. The wind spread that cold around, even as the sun called it spring. He ached at every joint. Each breath pricked his right lung. None of it bothered him more than something that movie director had said. 'Somebody picked the least valuable person to kill.' That Vasquez girl hadn't had the chance to build her value. She could've been on her way to do something great and wonderful, who knew? Who freaking knew everyone's worth and threw them on a scale and decided the young marketing major had to go?

He touched his wrist. Having the whole of human knowledge between your thumb and forefinger had been convenient. Two days with the ollies and he already felt the jitters of detachment. Although he wondered if they'd be so pronounced if he didn't want to end this investigation. If he wasn't still sketching out a mystery, could he live without the cuff? Without the doctors and steady food supply and a car that put you anywhere you wanted in 20 minutes?

Anywhere you wanted. That presumed you wanted to be somewhere else. Ever.

McCallum watched Emory stroll the parade grounds with his wife and daughter. The image smeared, as if he'd rendered them with pastels and rubbed the bristol board, blending the three separate bodies into a single declaration. He wanted to grab his pad and pencils and preserve the state.

No. He needed to preserve not the image, but the actual, real live state. That was his job.

❧ · ❧

For Emory the world stayed in continuous flux. Energy flowed, taking everything with it. He managed flow, directing, re-directing, speeding up or, in that moment, making it run as slowly as the laws of the universe would allow. His girls. So pretty. So safe. He wanted to gobble them up. Keep them, just like this, secure inside him.

The op approached. He'd chosen the most direct path between them. He moved with a stiff sway. He must have rammed the back-on-duty bar down his spine. Emory looked away from him. Back at the girls. He'd pretend the man didn't exist.

"I need to make a call," McCallum said to Lillian.

"Oh," she said. "I'm not even sure. You know. I've never been asked that before."

"I've never asked, either," the op said. "Can you act as my interpreter? Would that work?"

"Certainly."

"Call Wayne Clement, City of Buffalo, economist, Systems Security."

Emory continued not to look as his wife repeated the information and introduced herself in a polished, professional tone. He loved her just a little bit more for being so keen in such an awkward position. Calling an ASS economist blindly, from an ollie camp, while standing next to your fugitive husband? She should've asked Detective McCallum a lot more questions before getting started. She would have a year ago. Even six months back. Before the op saved their daughter, and maybe him. Not that he would've answered. The guy talked as if he ran everything he was going to say through his head three times before letting it out his mouth. The process produced less information than Emory wanted.

McCallum said, "Ask him who's looked into cost-earnings for Emory, John and Geri Vasquez. Someone out there weighed their lives."

Lillian repeated the message and they waited.

"No one," Lillian conveyed. "No one out of the ordinary looked into their records."

"Maybe they hid their search," Emory said.

McCallum nodded. They both knew if this went up to the fourth grade, anything was possible.

"Who's ordinary?" Lillian asked on her own. A pause. "Human Assets?" she said out loud to Emory and McCallum. "Any commonality in the HA queries?"

McCallum looked at Emory, eyebrows high.

"She's a researcher," he addressed the look, without acknowledging the man making it.

"Walter Whelen," Lillian said. "Walter Whelen, HA Director, City of Buffalo, personally looked at all three. He's a grade 9. In the single digits. He's..."

"...got people for that kind of thing." Emory finished her sentence.

"Tell Wayne thanks," McCallum said. "You've got to go." He waited until she ended the call. "Lillian, time to file for divorce."

Now Emory looked at him.

━ CHAPTER THIRTY-ONE ━

EMORY HATED WEARING the coveralls again. The big, yellow jumpsuit, with the zipper up the front, fought you as you walked, protested with loud rubbing sounds and signaled to everyone that you were a degenerate. Wearing it here, in a gleaming silver office building amplified the humiliation.

Conner and Teddy made it even worse. They slithered behind him, side-by-side. They wore their yellows, too, looking like stains on this long, steel and glass counter. He no longer feared them. Things might have tipped to the opposite, he thought. They might actually be a little leery of him. He hated them, though. Real, permanent hatred. Coal dust in the lungs. The body would never find a means of digesting it. He'd have to learn to live with his new, diminished capacity for compassion, peace, believing in the worth of every man.

A woman rose from a smoke-tinted glass desk and stood in front of the office door at the end of the hall. Tall, sleek, dressed to show those features off, she made him hesitate. Not McCallum. He touched his cuff without breaking stride. Two steps later, the woman looked at her own, dangling, beaded bracelet, up at the entourage, and backed as far from the door as the hall would allow.

McCallum opened the door and entered.

"Hey," came from deep inside. "You ever heard of knocking."

"Yep," McCallum replied. "Do it often. Sometimes doors, other times heads."

A corner office. How special. Big enough to house an eight foot desk, and a small conference table, Emory rated it as the biggest he'd ever personally visited. The tones were all blues and grays, giving the space a frigid quality. The furniture was chrome and glass, not opulent, like you glimpsed sometimes in the movies imagining the really low grades, nor was it standard. None of this stuff could be ordered from a supply catalogue.

The man standing behind the desk could not have been 40. Short, but athletic. Hard, tight brown hair, flawless skin, a dimpled chin. He'd been sewn into his navy blue suit. He put his hands on his hips and got ready to bellow. McCallum held up his wrist, wiggling his cuff. The man didn't take the hint.

"Wait outside," McCallum said to Conner and Teddy. Emory closed the door behind him. The guy behind the desk finally got the idea to see what his cuff buzzed about.

"Detective McCallum?" he read with a puzzled, almost disgusted little sneer.

"Walter Whelen?" McCallum asked back.

"Do we have an appointment?"

"Not necessary." McCallum sat down in one of the two steel and blue tweed chairs facing the desk, and, beyond that, the cityscape.

"I might beg to differ," Whelen said.

"The way this conversation is about to go, I think you're going to be begging for more than that."

Emory sat down. Whelen watched, through half-open eyes. He made his patience appear to be a massive struggle.

"You know Emory Leveski, here," McCallum motioned to Emory.

"I can't recall."

"That wasn't a question. He's the Milkman. You set him up for murder. He's been on a chain gang since the fall of last year."

"You can go now," Whelen said, smiling.

"I'll be leaving shortly. Just a few stray strokes to clean up. I can understand why you wanted to the stop the Milkman. Once I put you in center focus, everything resolved. I found the logs, with the calls from a grade four. You must have been flapping around this office getting a call from a low grade like that. What did he offer you, a step up? Two steps up? Is that what a young woman's life is worth these days? I don't know, because you haven't gotten your reward yet. That movie is still out there, isn't it?"

Whelen sat down, still forcing out a smile. He clicked his cuff on the table and it lit up with applications and files and photos. Upside down, at the wrong angle, Emory couldn't see exactly what Whelen started to manipulate.

"I can't imagine you got to be detective by being stupid," Whelen said. "But I'm going to check."

"What I can't understand is Geri Vasquez. Why her? She had nothing to do with milk or the movie. No part of this."

"It says here you are an exemplary operative. Four commendations."

"You just pick her at random? Find the lowest paid person you could actually overpower?"

Whelen tapped the desktop. "And gone. Zero commendations."

"Not man enough to take on anyone your size or weight. You had to pick a little girl."

Whelen tapped the desktop again. "Aw. Says here you have skipped your medical visits for the last two years. You're out of compliance."

"Why not go even younger? Make it easy on yourself and kill a 12-year-old girl?"

Face hard, Whelen looked up from his desk. "Is that what this is about? You get a little post-mortem crush on that marketing kitten? Fine. Let me close this up for you. It was a dusting, detective. Somebody else with more juice than her boss wanted to put his person in her job. She wouldn't willingly transfer. I didn't have anyplace I could force her to. Funny, how sometimes people just aren't dying fast enough. There were no openings, so I made one. A dusting. It's a procedure of last resort, but this time..." He smiled. He looked proud. "This time, I could kill a couple of birds with one stone."

McCallum nodded. "Free up the girl's position and take out the Milkman."

"Elegant," Whelen said. "Feel better now? Are you through or do I need to alter your records some more."

"That's kind of why we're here. You can change people's lives. In fact, you can EX-change people's lives." McCallum reached into his jacket and pulled out a hatchet. Heavy-headed steel, a black fiberglass handle, a nubby grip. It clinked as he laid it on the glass desk. "I want you to bring up your file. And Emory's."

Emory stared at the hatchet. He didn't know what it meant. McCallum had said he was going to fix things and he only needed one tool from his box. Seems it was a small ax. Sharp and nasty.

"You're threatening me? With violence?" Whelen's face tightened. Emory thought he might be trying to keep up the sarcastic smile, though his nerves were getting the better of him.

"I brought along a tool I might need."

"You're crazy. I'm calling your superior right now."

"Won't matter. No other op is getting through that door until I'm through with you. Bring up the files." McCallum paused. He looked out the window, down at the hatchet, then right into Whelen's eyes. "Then switch the biologics."

Emory's head jerked around. Whelen's mouth opened, stuck in a silent scream. His right hand shot for the hatchet. McCallum had been waiting for the move. He yanked the tool away with his right hand, grabbed Whelen's wrist with his left and brought the small ax down, stopping right above the hand.

"Aaagh!" Whelen attempted to pull free.

"You understand now?" McCallum said.

"You can't do this? It'll never take. I know thousands of people."

"I'm betting not two of them care." McCallum released Whelen's arm, but kept the hatchet in his hand.

Emory asked, "What are you doing?"

"Putting things right. For you, anyway. Too late to help the girl," he said. He aimed his voice at Whelen. "Make the switch."

Whelen sat, arms on the desk, hands clawed like a vulture, his face trying to tear itself down the middle. Emory couldn't tell if his eyes saw anything in the room. He seemed to be sorting files in his head. His life, Emory guessed, for the past year. The call, the chance at advancement, the excitement and planning and the kill. Maybe he saw his most likely future, on a chain gang, devoid of chrome and tweed and opportunity. Those stories collided, conveyor belts misaligned, crashing the hopes and memories, breaking his visions on the floor. Whelen started to cry. Pathetic. The tears cutting two rivulets down his cheeks. His hands shook so hard he couldn't move any of the images around his desktop.

"I know people," Whelen blubbered.

McCallum said nothing.

"You think he can just walk into my life and take over? It'll fail in seconds and it will all get traced back to you, detective."

McCallum got up and circled the desk. Emory's head swirled. Switch? Take over his life? McCallum stood behind the Human Assets Executive as he tapped and swiped his fingers across the desktop.

❦ · ❦

Sylvia Cho cinched her white robe as she glided to the front door. Gavin Stoll stood on her porch, arms behind his back, rocking on his feet. She unbolted the lock, turned the handle and zipped back the way she came.

"Come on in, Gavin," she hollered.

In the sunroom, she scooped the infant out of bassinet. The baby made gurgling noises. Her flawless, chubby arms pumped slowly at nothing. Sylvia sat back in a rocking chair, nuzzling the child to her chest.

Gavin leaned on the room's door jam, crossing his arms and legs. "She's beautiful."

"Thanks. You sound very close to sincere."

"No one's more surprised than I. Didn't know I was a baby person."

"You can't have her," Sylvia said, not sure it was a joke.

"So you said. Your message was provocative."

Sylvia pointed to the large monitor on the far side of the adjacent room. Large white letters on a black background read The Milkman. "The rough cut's done."

"Can I have it?"

"No." Sylvia ran her hand down the baby's back. "I've posted it."

"What!"

The baby jumped.

"Shush," Sylvia shot. "You don't want to wake her. Trust me on that."

"It wasn't yours to post."

"Tell your backer it's on a rolling site. Just like the Milkman's posts. I'll give you the search terms and you can find it, use it for leverage, bargaining, whatever. But you can never have it. It's mine and I can release it to as many or as few people as I want, any time I want. Or make it disappear."

"That was not our deal."

"Yeah, well, I'm dealing for two, now."

❦ · ❦

McCallum read everything on the desktop. Whelen could plant all kinds of bombs and traps in his system if not watched. So McCallum watched. He was no computer guru, but he'd spent enough time in personnel databases to know what went where.

Whelen whimpered as he moved the stats, photos and biometric information. It only took a few minutes. His photos, retina scans and prints all pointed to Emory Leveski. Emory's new name was

Walter Whelen, Ambyr Human Assets, Grade 9. McCallum took Whelen's hand and pressed the 'enter' key.

McCallum looked at Emory. "You just got a raise."

He took a white ceramic cuff out of his pocket. The industrial type, you only saw on employees serving on alternative work details.

"Take off your cuff," McCallum said.

"No no no no no" Whelen shook his head.

"I will chop off your hand and slip it free. That's what this tool is for."

Whelen cried more quietly as he snapped open his cuff and pulled if from his wrist. He tossed it on the desk. McCallum nodded at it, like he was moving the bracelet towards Emory with his nose.

Emory picked up the cuff and snapped it on. He stood and unzipped his yellow coveralls. Underneath, he wore a gray suit, with a pressed white shirt.

"This is why you wanted me to wear my Sunday best, huh?"

"Sorry I couldn't fill you in," McCallum returned. "Didn't know if you could swim, so throwing you in seemed best. Give him the coveralls."

"I'll be back in hour," Whelen spat. "I'll kill you first, Milkman. Then your dog."

"I don't have any pets," Emory replied. "Or do I? Do I have any pets now, Emory?"

"I think he was referring to me." McCallum clamped the ceramic cuff on Whelen's wrist. "Emory Leveski you are hereby transferred to alternative work detail indefinitely."

"You think this is a valid plan? You honestly think you can just swap people? Like parts?!" Spittle sprayed from Whelen's mouth.

McCallum motioned for him to don the yellows. "This is what I think. I think the Milkman's a nice guy. I'm betting you're such an asshole anyone who knows you is going to be thrilled with your replacement."

Whelen stepped into the coverall and zipped it up. He pressed his lips together so hard it looked to McCallum like he'd squeezed the color out, forcing it into the rest of his wet face. McCallum rounded the desk and opened the door. Conner and Eddy stood in front of the woman's desk. She sat, doing her best to ignore their leering.

"Gentlemen," he said. "Mr. Leveski is ready to return to the detail." He waved Whelen out of his office and put his hand on his shoulder. "You remember Emory, right? Here he is." He pushed Whelen forward.

Conner and Teddy exchanged glances, shrugged their shoulders and led the man down the hall.

"Sherri!" he yelled. "Tell upstairs what's happening. I've—"

Teddy knocked him in the small of the back, pushing him farther down the corridor.

"Sherri," Emory said. "That man is confused. I'm Walter Whelend."

She ran her eyes over Emory, then McCallum. She bit her lip. She glanced down the hall, briefly, then back to Emory.

This was, McCallum knew, the moment. He wasn't about to muscle anyone else into his scam. Not this young lady, not the people 'upstairs', not anyone back on the chain gang. He'd put his hatchet away for the day.

He believed what he'd told Whelen. He knew corrupt, self-centered, arrogant man-shaped shits capable of killing a girl because it might advance their careers. He knew it wasn't one thing, with them. It was everything. They didn't make friends, they made accomplices, some willing, some not. The difference being, friends stayed with you. Accomplices might just as well accompany somebody else.

"Whelen," the young woman said. "There's no 'D'."

Emory smiled. "We're going to get along famously." He turned to McCallum. "After I throw up."

"You'll be fine."

"Emory was right," Emory said. "You are crazy. I can't do this job."

"Ask Sherri here how it's done. It's got to be easier than digging sewers, right?"

Emory blew a ball of air out his mouth. "I don't know…"

"No one ever does. I do know Lillian Leveski separated from her husband. You should ask her out."

"I will. I will… this will never work."

McCallum said, "It will work as well as most things."

EPILOGUE

MCCALLUM GAVE THE bartender a small print by Richard Copley. It depicted a thick group of men each carrying a sign that read "I am a man." The man scanned it with his cuff, waited a moment for his service to tell him what the item's current value was, and then held up four fingers. The photo was irreproducible. It should've bought six, but he wasn't going to drink that many anyway. He nodded once and turned on his stool to watch the guitar player in the back of the room.

Pain is the kin that knows us
Pain is the wind that blows us
Down from the mountains, in from the sea
All ye, all ye out come free
Out from the allies, up from your knees
All ye, all ye out come free
Come out, come out wherever you be
All ye, all ye out come free

"He's got a solid voice," Rosalie slid in next to him, bending an elbow to the bar.

"That why you picked this place?" McCallum half-turned and wagged two fingers at the bartender.

"Just knew it to be noisy, is all."

"A loud pub in which neither of us can buy a drink."

The bartender brought over two long neck brown bottles. McCallum didn't know the brand or style, but accepted them just the same.

"You seem to be doing all right." Rosalie smiled in a tight, thoughtful line. The majority of the patrons started singing along. They leaned closer.

"Should the hairs on my neck be standing up?"

"Tell 'em to stand down. We're fine." Rosalie took a sip from her beer. "It's your friend."

McCallum watched Rosalie's face. He knew her well enough, deep enough, to see the slight changes in muscles around her eyes, and nose. Inside, she softened and didn't like it to show.

"Pretty girl, Ed."

"You think?"

"That footage was loopy. Did it come from some kind of ollie camp?"

"Some kind."

"I don't blame you for the two word answers. You may want to get it down to one where this lady's concerned. I got a hit on her. Then I got hit."

Now McCallum's facial muscles let his inner workings out. He knew he wasn't hiding his concern. Maybe from a trained interrogator, but not from Rosalie.

"She's one of ours. A tier 12 out of Ecuador City. Off line for the last 22 months. I don't know all the details for reasons I'll get to in a moment. It's looking like she bit some old low-rider's dick almost clean off and transferred herself elsewhere. I dipped into the story when I noticed a trace on my search. I shut down and the next morning I get called upstairs to meet with some suit I've never seen before. He wants to know where I might have seen your friend and when and what I had for breakfast and how many times I pee per day."

"I'm sorry," McCallum said. "I didn't mean to—"

"No." She patted his forearm. "Goes with the job."

"What did you tell them?"

Rosalie smiled again, thin and long. "I told them it was an error. The image-rec nonsense gave me a false positive. Whether they bought it or not is unknown at this time."

"That's kind of you."

"I'm a sweetheart. You know that."

"Did you catch her real name?"

"She's gone," Roslie said. "I'll bet you anything she's even farther up north now. She must think the colder the clime, the safer she is."

"Under a blanket of snow," McCallum said over Roslie's shoulder, out through the pub window, into the night.

"What an artsy thing to say. You should let that side of you out more often."

"Or not at all," he replied. "Can't seem to find a proper balance."

"There isn't one." Rosalie put her arm around McCallum. "There's just swaying. Back and forth."

They moved side-to-side to the music.